SURPRISE PARTY

I had my carbine in my hand as I scrambled up the slope. When I got to the top I collapsed behind a bramble of greasewood and peered out. I could see the riders now. There appeared to be about thirty or forty of them. A voice to my left said, quietly, "*Federales* and *rurales.*"

I looked over. Señor Elizandro was lying just to my left with a rifle laid out before him. "They have good horses," he said. "They will come straight on. They are not very intelligent. They will have expected us to do what they would do—keep running. They would not have considered the ambush."

I said, "Then they got a hell of a shock coming."

Books by Giles Tippette

Jailbreak

GILES TIPPETTE

JOVE BOOKS, NEW YORK

JAILBREAK

A Jove Book / published by arrangement with
the author

PRINTING HISTORY
Jove edition / June 1991

ISBN: 0-515-10595-3

Jove Books are published by The Berkley Publishing Group,
200 Madison Avenue, New York, New York 10016.
The name ''JOVE'' and the ''J'' logo
are trademarks belonging to Jove Publications, Inc.

PRINTED IN THE UNITED STATES OF AMERICA

10 9 8 7 6 5 4 3 2 1

*The best book
that I've written so far,
to the best wife,
Betsy Anne,
I've had so far.*

1

At supper Norris, my middle brother, said, "I think we got some trouble on that five thousand acres down on the border near Laredo."

He said it serious, which is the way Norris generally says everything. I quit wrestling with the steak Buttercup, our cook, had turned into rawhide and said, "What are you talking about? How could we have trouble on land lying idle?"

He said, "I got word from town this afternoon that a telegram had come in from a friend of ours down there. He says we got some kind of squatters taking up residence on the place."

My youngest brother, Ben, put his fork down and said, incredulously, "*That* five thousand acres? Hell, it ain't nothing but rocks and cactus and sand. Why in hell would anyone want to squat on that worthless piece of nothing?"

Norris just shook his head. "I don't know. But that's what the telegram said. Came from Jack Cole. And if

anyone ought to know what's going on down there it would
be him.''

I thought about it and it didn't make a bit of sense. I
was Justa Williams, and my family, my two brothers and
myself and our father, Howard, occupied a considerable
ranch called the Half-Moon down along the Gulf of Mexico in Matagorda County, Texas. It was some of the best
grazing land in the state and we had one of the best herds
of purebred and crossbred cattle in that part of the country. In short we were pretty well-to-do.

But that didn't make us any the less ready to be stolen
from, if indeed that was the case. The five thousand acres
Norris had been talking about had come to us through a
trade our father had made some years before. We'd never
made any use of the land, mainly because, as Ben had
said, it was pretty worthless and because it was a good
two hundred miles from our ranch headquarters. On a few
occasions we'd bought cattle in Mexico and then used the
acreage to hold small groups on while we made up a herd.
But other than that, it lay mainly forgotten.

I frowned. ''Norris, this doesn't make a damn bit of
sense. Right after supper send a man into Blessing with a
return wire for Jack asking him if he's certain. What the
hell kind of squatting could anybody be doing on that
land?''

Ben said, ''Maybe they're raisin' watermelons.'' He
laughed.

I said, ''They could raise melons, but there damn sure
wouldn't be no water in them.''

Norris said, ''Well, it bears looking into.'' He got up,
throwing his napkin on the table. ''I'll go write out that
telegram.''

I watched him go, dressed, as always, in his town
clothes. Norris was the businessman in the family. He'd
been sent down to the University at Austin and had got

considerable learning about the ins and outs of banking and land deals and all the other parts of our business that didn't directly involve the ranch. At the age of twenty-nine I'd been the boss of the operation a good deal longer than I cared to think about. It had been thrust upon me by our father when I wasn't much more than twenty. He'd said he wanted me to take over while he was still strong enough to help me out of my mistakes and I reckoned that was partly true. But it had just seemed that after our mother had died the life had sort of gone out of him. He'd been one of the earliest settlers, taking up the land not long after Texas had become a republic in 1845. I figured all the years of fighting Indians and then Yankees and scala-wags and carpetbaggers and cattle thieves had taken their toll on him. Then a few years back he'd been nicked in the lungs by a bullet that should never have been allowed to head his way and it had thrown an extra strain on his heart. He was pushing seventy and he still had plenty of head on his shoulders, but mostly all he did now was sit around in his rocking chair and stare out over the cattle and land business he'd built. Not to say that I didn't go to him for advice when the occasion demanded. I did, and mostly I took it.

Buttercup came in just then and sat down at the end of the table with a cup of coffee. He was near as old as Dad and almost completely worthless. But he'd been one of the first hands that Dad had hired and he'd been kept on even after he couldn't sit a horse anymore. The problem was he'd elected himself cook, and that was the sorriest day our family had ever seen. There were two Mexican women hired to cook for the twelve riders we kept full time, but Buttercup insisted on cooking for the family.

Mainly, I think, because he thought he was one of the family. A notion we could never completely dissuade him from.

So he sat there, about two days of stubble on his face, looking as scrawny as a pecked-out rooster, sweat running down his face, his apron a mess. He said, wiping his forearm across his forehead, "Boy, it shore be hot in there. You boys shore better be glad you ain't got no business takes you in that kitchen."

Ben said, in a loud mutter, "I wish you didn't either."

Ben, at twenty-five, was easily the best man with a horse or a gun that I had ever seen. His only drawback was that he was hotheaded and he tended to act first and think later. That ain't a real good combination for someone that could go on the prod as fast as Ben. When I had argued with Dad about taking over as boss, suggesting instead that Norris, with his education, was a much better choice, Dad had simply said, "Yes, in some ways. But he can't handle Ben. You can. You can handle Norris, too. But none of them can handle you."

Well, that hadn't been exactly true. If Dad had wished it I would have taken orders from Norris even though he was two years younger than me. But the logic in Dad's line of thinking had been that the Half-Moon and our cattle business was the lodestone of all our businesses and only I could run that. He had been right. In the past I'd imported purebred Whiteface and Hereford cattle from up North, bred them to our native Longhorns and produced cattle that would bring twice as much at market as the horse-killing, all-bone, all-wild Longhorns. My neighbors had laughed at me at first, claiming those square little purebreds would never make it in our Texas heat. But they'd been wrong and, one by one, they'd followed the example of the Half-Moon.

Buttercup was setting up to take off on another one of his long-winded harangues about how it had been in the "old days" so I quickly got up, excusing myself, and went into the big office we used for sitting around in as well as a place of business. Norris was at the desk composing his telegram so I poured myself out a whiskey and sat down. I didn't want to hear about any trouble over some worthless five thousand acres of borderland. In fact I didn't want to hear about any troubles of any kind. I was just two weeks short of getting married, married to a lady I'd been courting off and on for five years, and I was mighty anxious that nothing come up to interfere with our plans. Her name was Nora Parker and her daddy owned and run the general mercantile in our nearest town, Blessing. I'd almost lost her once before to a Kansas City drummer. She'd finally gotten tired of waiting on me, waiting until the ranch didn't occupy all my time, and almost run off with a smooth-talking Kansas City drummer that called on her daddy in the harness trade. But she'd come to her senses in time and got off the train in Texarkana and returned home.

But even then it had been a close thing. I, along with my men and brothers and help from some of our neighbors, had been involved with stopping a huge herd of illegal cattle being driven up from Mexico from crossing our range and infecting our cattle with tick fever which could have wiped us all out. I tell you it had been a bloody business. We'd lost four good men and had to kill at least a half dozen on the other side. Fact of the business was I'd come about as close as I ever had to getting killed myself, and that was going some for the sort of rough-and-tumble life I'd led.

Nora had almost quit me over it, saying she just couldn't take the uncertainty. But in the end, she'd stuck by me. That had been the year before, 1896, and I'd convinced her that civilized law was coming to the country, but until it did, we that had been there before might have to take things into our own hands from time to time.

She'd seen that and had understood. I loved her and she

loved me and that was enough to overcome any of the troubles we were still likely to encounter from day to day.

So I was giving Norris a pretty sour look as he finished his telegram and sent for a hired hand to ride it into Blessing, seven miles away. I said, ''Norris, let's don't make a big fuss about this. That land ain't even crossed my mind in at least a couple of years. Likely we got a few Mexican families squatting down there and trying to scratch out a few acres of corn.''

Norris gave me his businessman's look. He said, ''It's our land, Justa. And if we allow anyone to squat on it for long enough or put up a fence they can lay claim. That's the law. My job is to see that we protect what we have, not give it away.''

I sipped at my whiskey and studied Norris. In his town clothes he didn't look very impressive. He'd inherited more from our mother than from Dad so he was not as wide-shouldered and slim-hipped as Ben and me. But I knew him to be a good, strong, dependable man in any kind of fight. Of course he wasn't that good with a gun, but then Ben and I weren't all that good with books like he was. But I said, just to jolly him a bit, ''Norris, I do believe you are running to suet. I may have to put you out with Ben working the horse herd and work a little of that fat off you.''

Naturally it got his goat. Norris had always envied Ben and me a little. I was just over six foot and weighed right around a hundred and ninety. I had inherited my daddy's big hands and big shoulders. Ben was almost a copy of me except he was about a size smaller. Norris said, ''I weigh the same as I have for the last five years. If it's any of your business.''

I said, as if I was being serious, ''Must be them sack suits you wear. What they do, pad them around the middle?''

He said, "Why don't you just go to hell."

After he'd stomped out of the room I got the bottle of whiskey and an extra glass and went down to Dad's room. It had been one of his bad days and he'd taken to bed right after lunch. Strictly speaking he wasn't supposed to have no whiskey, but I watered him down a shot every now and then and it didn't seem to do him no harm.

He was sitting up when I came in the room. I took a moment to fix him a little drink, using some water out of his pitcher, then handed him the glass and sat down in the easy chair by the bed. I told him what Norris had reported and asked what he thought.

He took a sip of his drink and shook his head. "Beats all I ever heard," he said. "I took that land in trade for a bad debt some fifteen, twenty years ago. I reckon I'd of been money ahead if I'd of hung on to the bad debt. That land won't even raise weeds, well as I remember, and Noah was in on the last rain that fell on the place."

We had considerable amounts of land spotted around the state as a result of this kind of trade or that. It was Norris's business to keep up with their management. I was just bringing this to Dad's attention more out of boredom and impatience for my wedding day to arrive than anything else.

I said, "Well, it's a mystery to me. How you feeling?"

He half smiled. "Old." Then he looked into his glass. "And I never liked watered whiskey. Pour me a dollop of the straight stuff in here."

I said, "Now, Howard. You know—"

He cut me off. "If I wanted somebody to argue with I'd send for Buttercup. Now do like I told you."

I did, but I felt guilty about it. He took the slug of whiskey down in one pull. Then he leaned his head back on the pillow and said, "Aaaaah. I don't give a damn what that horse doctor says, ain't nothing makes a man feel as good inside as a shot of the best.''

I felt sorry for him laying there. He'd always led just the kind of life he wanted—going where he wanted, doing what he wanted, having what he set out to get. And now he was reduced to being a semi-invalid. But one thing that showed the strength that was still in him was that you *never* heard him complain. He said, "How's the cattle?"

I said, "They're doing all right, but I tell you we could do with a little of Noah's flood right now. All this heat and no rain is curing the grass off way ahead of time. If it doesn't let up we'll be feeding hay by late September, early October. And that will play hell on our supply. Could be we won't have enough to last through the winter. Norris thinks we ought to sell off five hundred head or so, but the market is doing poorly right now. I'd rather chance the weather than take a sure beating by selling off.''

He sort of shrugged and closed his eyes. The whiskey was relaxing him. He said, "You're the boss.''

"Yeah," I said. "Damn my luck.''

I wandered out of the back of the house. Even though it was nearing seven o'clock of the evening it was still good and hot. Off in the distance, about a half a mile away, I could see the outline of the house I was building for Nora and myself. It was going to be a close thing to get it finished by our wedding day. Not having any riders to spare for the project, I'd imported a building contractor from Galveston, sixty miles away. He'd arrived with a half a dozen Mexican laborers and a few skilled masons and they'd set up a little tent city around the place. The contractor had gone back to Galveston to fetch more materials, leaving his Mexicans behind. I walked along idly, hoping he wouldn't forget that the job wasn't done. He had some of my money, but not near what he'd get when he finished the job.

Just then Ray Hays came hurrying across the back lot toward me. Ray was kind of a special case for me. The only problem with that was that he knew it and wasn't a bit above taking advantage of the situation. Once, a few years past, he'd saved my life by going against an evil man that he was working for at the time, an evil man who meant to have my life. In gratitude I'd given Ray a good job at the Half-Moon, letting him work directly under Ben, who was responsible for the horse herd. He was a good, steady man and a good man with a gun. He was also fair company. When he wasn't talking.

He came churning up to me, mopping his brow. He said, "Lordy, boss, it is—"

I said, "Hays, if you say it's hot I'm going to knock you down."

He gave me a look that was a mixture of astonishment and hurt. He said, "Why, whatever for?"

I said, "*Everybody* knows it's hot. Does every son of a bitch you run into have to make mention of the fact?"

His brow furrowed. "Well, I never thought of it that way. I 'spect you are right. Goin' down to look at yore house?"

I shook my head. "No. It makes me nervous to see how far they've got to go. I can't see any way it'll be ready on time."

He said, "Miss Nora ain't gonna like that."

I gave him a look. "I guess you felt forced to say that."

He looked down. "Well, maybe she won't mind."

I said, grimly, "The hell she won't. She'll think I did it a-purpose."

"Aw, she wouldn't."

"Naturally you know so much about it, Hays. Why don't you tell me a few other things about her."

"I was jest tryin' to lift yore spirits, boss."

I said, "You keep trying to lift my spirits and I'll put you on the haying crew."

He looked horrified. No real cowhand wanted any work he couldn't do from the back of his horse. Haying was a hot, hard, sweaty job done either afoot or from a wagon seat. We generally brought in contract Mexican labor to handle ours. But I'd been known in the past to discipline a cowhand by giving him a few days on the hay gang. Hays said, "Boss, now I never meant nothin'. I swear. You know me, my mouth gets to runnin' sometimes. I swear I'm gonna watch it."

I smiled. Hays always made me smile. He was so easily buffaloed. He had it soft at the Half-Moon and he knew it and didn't want to take any chances on losing a good thing.

I lit up a cigarillo and watched the dusk settle in over the coastal plains. It wasn't but three miles to Matagorda Bay and it was quiet enough I felt like I could almost hear the waves breaking on the shore. Somewhere in the distance a mama cow bawled for her calf. The spring crop were near about weaned by now, but there were still a few mamas that wouldn't cut the apron strings. I stood there reflecting on how peaceful things had been of late. It suited me just fine. All I wanted was to get my house finished, marry Nora and never handle another gun so long as I lived.

The peace and quiet were short-lived. Within twenty-four hours we'd had a return telegram from Jack Cole. It said:

YOUR LAND OCCUPIED BY TEN TO TWELVE MEN STOP CAN'T BE SURE WHAT THEY'RE DOING BECAUSE THEY RUN STRANGERS OFF STOP APPEAR TO HAVE A GOOD MANY CATTLE GATHERED STOP APPEAR TO BE FENCING STOP ALL I KNOW STOP

I read the telegram twice and then I said, "Why this is crazy as hell! That land wouldn't support fifty head of cattle."

We were all gathered in the big office. Even Dad was there, sitting in his rocking chair. I looked up at him. "What do you make of this, Howard?"

He shook his big, old head of white hair. "Beats the hell out of me, Justa. I can't figure it."

Ben said, "Well, I don't see where it has to be figured. I'll take five men and go down there and run them off. I don't care what they're doing. They ain't got no business on our land."

I said, "Take it easy, Ben. Aside from the fact you don't need to be getting into any more fights this year, I can't spare you or five men. The way this grass is drying up we've got to keep drifting those cattle."

Norris said, "No, Ben is right. We can't have such affairs going on with our property. But we'll handle it within the law. I'll simply take the train down there, hire a good lawyer and have the matter settled by the sheriff. Shouldn't take but a few days."

Well, there wasn't much I could say to that. We couldn't very well let people take advantage of us, but I still hated to be without Norris's services even for a few days. On matters other than the ranch he was the expert, and it didn't seem like there was a day went by that some financial question didn't come up that only he could answer. I said, "Are you sure you can spare yourself for a few days?"

He thought for a moment and then nodded. "I don't see why not. I've just moved most of our available cash into short-term municipal bonds in Galveston. The market is looking all right and everything appears fine at the bank. I can't think of anything that might come up."

I said, "All right. But you just keep this in mind. You are not a gun hand. You are not a fighter. I do not want you going anywhere near those people, whoever they are. You do it legal and let the sheriff handle the eviction. Is that understood?"

He kind of swelled up, resenting the implication that he couldn't handle himself. The biggest trouble I'd had through the years when trouble had come up had been keeping Norris out of it. Why he couldn't just be content to be a wagon load of brains was more than I could understand. He said, "Didn't you just hear me say I intended to go through a lawyer and the sheriff? Didn't I just say that?"

I said, "I wanted to be sure you heard yourself."

He said, "Nothing wrong with my hearing. Nor my approach to this matter. You seem to constantly be taken with the idea that I'm always looking for a fight. I think you've got the wrong brother. I use logic."

"Yeah?" I said. "You remember when that guy kicked you in the balls when they were holding guns on us? And then we chased them twenty miles and finally caught them?"

He looked away. "That has nothing to do with this."

"Yeah?" I said, enjoying myself. "And here's this guy, shot all to hell. And what was it you insisted on doing?"

Ben laughed, but Norris wouldn't say anything.

I said, "Didn't you insist on us standing him up so you could kick him in the balls? Didn't you?"

He sort of growled, "Oh, go to hell."

I said, "I just want to know where the logic was in that."

He said, "Right is right. I was simply paying him back in kind. It was the only thing his kind could understand."

I said, "That's my point. You just don't go down there

and go to paying back a bunch of rough hombres in kind. Or any other currency for that matter."

That made him look over at Dad. He said, "Dad, will you make him quit treating me like I was ten years old? He does it on purpose."

But he'd appealed to the wrong man. Dad just threw his hands in the air and said, "Don't come to me with your troubles. I'm just a boarder around here. You get your orders from Justa. You know that."

Of course he didn't like that. Norris had always been a strong hand for the right and wrong of a matter. In fact, he may have been one of the most stubborn men I'd ever met. But he didn't say anything, just gave me a look and muttered something about hoping a mess came up at the bank while he was gone and then see how much boss I was.

But he didn't mean nothing by it. Like most families, we fought amongst ourselves and, like most families, God help the outsider who tried to interfere with one of us.

Norris got away on the noon train the next day. I took him in myself as a good excuse to go by and see Nora. The last thing I told him was not to spend much time or money on the matter. I'd said, "Just put it in the hands of a good lawyer and then get on back here. Your time is too valuable to waste fooling around with that worthless land."

He'd said, "I'll wire you my plans."

I'd said, "You just wire me what train to meet in the next couple or three days."

I'd come into town in the buckboard because I intended on bringing home a few supplies. So before I went to hunt up Miss Nora I took the wagon and team over to the livery stable to see to their watering and feeding. Besides, it was the noon hour and I didn't want to just drop in at the Parkers' unannounced.

For lack of something better to do I went into Crooks
Saloon & Café and had a beer and a bowl of stew. I never
passed up a chance to eat in town when I could. It meant
just one less meal I'd have to endure at Buttercup's hands.

Lew Vara, the sheriff, was at the bar. When he seen I'd
finished my stew he ambled over. Lew and I were pretty
near the same age. Before he'd got to be sheriff he and I
had had just about the roughest fistfight I'd ever been
involved in. I'd finally won it, but I'd done so unfairly.
He'd had me nearly finished and I'd grabbed a revolver off
the floor and split his head open with it. It had been understood that he was going to come for me when he got
able, but that hadn't been the case. Instead of holding what
I'd done against me, he said he reckoned he'd of done the
same himself if he could have reached anything. Then,
after that, he'd been a big help to us in some trouble we
were having at the time. The upshot had been that we'd
stood him for sheriff against the then sheriff, a man we
felt had gone wrong. He'd won and it had been the making
of him.

Lew had a good bit of Mexican in him, but you'd have
never known it to look at him. We weighed about the
same, but he was a couple of inches shorter than I was,
with heavy shoulders and big, muscled-up arms. The man
could hit like the kick of a mule.

We talked a while about nothing and I sent for another
round of beer. After a time, I told him about the business
down along the border and he was as surprised as I was.
He said, "Hell, I know that country like the back of my
hand. They ain't nothing worth stealing down there if you
threw in Laredo and Nuevo Laredo in the bargain."

I told him I knew but that we had to look into it. I said,
"I just put Norris on the train there."

He raised his eyebrows. "Norris? Padnuh, that's pretty

rough country down there. Bunch of bad hombres. You sure you should have sent Norris?''

I told him how we were going to play it. I said, "I can't see how he could get into any trouble that way."

But he shook his head. "I don't know about that. Laredo is one town you can get into trouble just being on the wrong side of the street. Maybe you should have sent Ben with him."

I said, "Huh! Now *that* would have been looking for trouble. Naw, it'll be all right. Norris will get a lawyer and the sheriff will run the squatters off. It won't come to nothing."

When it was good after one o'clock I went and got the buckboard and stopped it in front of Parker's Mercantile. The interior was cool and dark and felt mighty pleasant after the heat of the day. Lonnie Parker, Nora's dad, was behind the main counter. His face lit up when I came in. "Why dog my cats," he said. "Here's the bridegroom."

"Unless Nora's come to her senses."

"I wouldn't count on that," he said. "You never saw such a power of sewing as has been going on at the house in all your life. How come ever' time a woman goes to get married they got to take to needle and thread? I tell you, a man is lucky to get a meal around my place these days."

I told him he looked to be holding his own and gave him my list of supplies. He let out a yell—"Harvey! You, Harvey!"—and about a seventeen-year-old rawboned kid came skidding out of the back and reported for duty at the counter. Lonnie gave him the list and told him to load it in my buckboard.

I said, "Reckon Nora's home?"

"Yeah, but you'll play hell finding her amidst all the material and cloth goods and thread."

I said I thought I'd stroll down and make a short visit

while Harvey was getting my order up. Lonnie said he'd send the kid down with the wagon and have him park it under the shade tree. He gave me a wink and said, "You might be surprised how short yore visit is. Right now you is the least part of this wedding. Women set a great deal of store by weddings and they don't much take to men gettin' in the way."

Lonnie hadn't exaggerated over much. Both Nora and her mother were rushing around like chickens with their heads cut off. Nora answered the door with a oh-it's-just-you look on her face, but she bade me come in. "But stay out of the way," she said.

So I went in and watched them, taking a seat on the divan. They had a huge cedar chest in the middle of the room and they were busy filling it up and then taking sheets and pillow cases and comforters and I don't know what all out and then putting them back in again. And when they weren't doing that they were having hurried conversations about swatches of cloth and hemlines and other things I didn't know a great deal about.

I just sat there watching Nora. As hot as it was and as hurried as she was she still looked as cool and collected as a cold beer. Her light brown hair bore a deep sheen, like she'd just finished brushing it, and the square-cut opening in the top of her bodice was big enough to reveal a span of clear, cool, cream-colored skin. Just below that bodice was the swell of her breasts against the thin gingham of her dress. I'd touched those breasts bare in the moonlight one night when we'd both got carried away. I'd even kissed one. But that had been as far as it went. But just the thought, just looking at her and remembering, made my neck get thick like a rutting bull and put the taste of copper in my mouth. I could only guess at what the silken feel of the inside of her thighs would do to me. Just thinking about it was doing enough and I forced myself to wrench my mind around in another direction before it became obvious what I was thinking about.

After about a half an hour of watching two women scurrying and scattering I figured I'd been ignored long enough. I got up and said, "Well, I reckon I'll be getting on back. Y'all appear to be pretty busy."

Nora turned around and looked at me like I was a truant trying to slip out of the schoolroom. She said, "Justa Williams, you sit right back down there. I want to talk to you."

I said, "When?"

She had several pins in her mouth so it come out kind of mumbled, but she said, "Here in a minute. Besides, you ought to stay for supper."

Of course the idea of eating hers or her mother's cooking was always bribe enough for me. But I couldn't see when they were going to have time to fix it. I said, doubtfully, "Y'all are plannin' on cooking, are you?"

"Well, of course," she said. "Did you think we couldn't hem up a few sheets and cook too? Now you go on down to Crooks and drink a beer. But don't you dare drink too many. You come back in about an hour."

So I went down to Crooks and had a beer. Since she'd told me not to have too many I didn't. But since she hadn't said nothing about whiskey I did have several tumblers of that. I also played a little poker and managed to win about forty dollars. I arrived back at the house at about five, just in time for supper, and got a good eye-scolding from Nora.

Later, when it had cooled down a little, we sat in the swing on the front porch. I was feeling pretty mellow after a supper of fried chicken and mashed potatoes and gravy. Or at least I was until Nora wanted to know when the furniture was going to arrive. We'd picked it out in Galveston better than a month before and some of it had to come from New Orleans and other points. I said, a little uncomfortably, "It'll be here right about the time the house is finished."

She asked, "And when will that be? You keep saying we'll go see it when it's finished. And I keep expecting you every day."

I said, reluctantly, "Well, there's been a small delay."

"Oh, no," she said, and put her hand to her cheek.

"Now, don't worry," I said hastily. "It'll be all right. Fact is we run short of those red Mexican roof tiles you wanted. Said they went with the house. Well, the contractor has gone back to Galveston to get more. Said a boat ought to be in from Vera Cruz right away with another shipment."

She genuinely looked distressed. She said, "Oh, Justa, don't tell me it's not going to be ready in time."

I said, "I'm not telling you it's not going to be ready in time. Did I say it wouldn't? Listen, if I have to I'll stand over that building crew with a whip in my hand."

She said, "Justa, it just has to be. The invitations have gone out. Mother and I are working ourself to death to finish my trousseau."

Well, I didn't know what that was, but I figured it had something to do with all the sewing and flaying around. I said, "Hell, Nora, even if it's not finished on the exact date we can always stay in the big house until it's done."

I might as well have slapped her across the face the way she jumped back. She said, with plenty of gumption, "Justa Williams, I am not going to be staying in someone else's house. I'll stay in my own house or I won't get married at all."

I said, "But we're going on a honeymoon. That's two weeks."

"I want it ready before we leave. And that's that."

There wasn't a hell of a lot I could say to that. I just stood up and put on my hat and said I'd better be getting back to the ranch. She gave me her cheek to kiss, which was not a good sign. As I left I said I'd have the house ready if I had to go to Mexico myself and fetch the tiles back single-handedly. It didn't warm her up over much.

2

Next afternoon, late, I was sitting on the ranch house front porch worrying about Nora and the house when a rider from town came tearing up with a telegram. We had an arrangement with the telegraph office that they'd send out anything marked important soon as they got it. Of course such a service cost a deal extra, but, some of our dealings being fairly important, it was worth it.

I opened the telegram with dread. I was sure it was from the contractor in Galveston with bad news and words of other delays.

But it was from Norris, sent from Laredo. It said:

SQUATTERS CONFIRMED STOP SITUATION VERY COM-
PLICATED STOP INVOLVES SPANISH LAND GRANT STOP
LOCAL AUTHORITIES IN LAREDO USELESS STOP MUST
GO TO MONTERREY TO STRAIGHTEN OUT TROUBLE STOP
TAKING JACK COLE WITH ME STOP WILL WIRE SOONEST
FROM MONTERREY STOP

Well, that left me a good deal troubled. Nearly all the land in Texas could be traced back to Spanish land grants when Texas was part of Mexico and Spain owned all of it. Spanish land grants were large parcels of land that were given or sold to colonizers who, in turn, would break up the grant and parcel it out to smaller colonists. It was all a pretty tricky business and more than one family in Texas had lost valuable land because of some sloppy paperwork a hundred or so years in the past.

But we weren't talking about valuable land. I couldn't for the life of me figure why Norris hadn't just left the matter in the hands of a lawyer and hied himself home. Plus I didn't much like Norris messing around in Mexico and certainly not the border. Mexico, if you don't understand it, is bad enough. You can get in trouble there without half trying. And Norris didn't understand Mexico.

Much more, he sure as hell didn't understand the border, a strip of land some forty or fifty miles wide on either side of the Rio Grande. You might as well call it a separate country unto itself. It's got its own ways and, if you can call them that, its own laws. It's full of every brigand and thief and swindler and murderer that can squeeze in.

Norris hadn't any business trying to operate in that part of the country. I got up, cussing out loud, and went in and showed the telegram to Dad. I said, "Now look what he's gone and done. That damn land isn't worth a sack of dried beans yet Norris is spending time and effort and money making a fight over it. Back here he can make us more money in one day with one deal than that whole five thousand acres is worth. What has come over him?"

But Dad wasn't going to be drawn in. He said, "Well, you gave him his orders. It appears he hasn't followed them. Reckon you'll have to decide what to do about it when he gits back.''

"Yeah, but what would possess him to go off on such a wild-goose chase?"

Dad shrugged. "Reckon he thought he was doing what he thought was right."

"What he's doing," I said grimly, "is acting like a damn stubborn fool. He's got his back up about that patch of sand and nothing is going to do until he gets to the bottom of it. And hang the cost. Goddammit, he makes me so angry I feel like knocking his head off."

Dad gave a slight smile. He said, "Guess you never affected me that way. Listen, what say you and I have a whiskey and forget about all this. Norris will be back in a couple of days. You need to be thinking about your wedding."

I went and got the whiskey and poured us both out a healthy measure. I said, as I handed him his glass, "You blindsided me on this drink, old man. If I hadn't been on the prod about Norris you wouldn't have slicked me as easy as you did."

He drank off half his whiskey and said, "Aaaaah. In that case I've got Norris to thank. Maybe you can get mad at Ben and give me another one?"

I said, "I've heard you got the money to start this ranch by being a horse thief. I'm damned if I don't half believe it."

"Wasn't horses," he said. "Was cattle."

I was glad to see him having a good day for a change.

We got a break that evening for supper. Buttercup had drunk himself senseless and was sprawled out on his bunk just off the kitchen snoring like a bawling calf. As a consequence the Mexican women served us a good meal of roast beef and gravy and pinto beans and sliced tomatoes. Even as irritated as I was at Norris, I was able to enjoy it.

Ben said, "Oh, Justa, you are always worrying. You reckon if you're not leading the whole bunch of us around by the hand we're liable to fall over dead. My Gawd, you are worse than a mother hen."

Dad had felt well enough to join us at table. He said, "Now, now, Ben. Your brother has got considerable on his mind, what with the wedding and all. I fear he reckons his bossing days are coming to an end and he wants to get his licks in while he can."

"Very funny, Howard," I said. But I was glad to see him teasing. It showed his strength was rallying. Though how anyone could have had much strength in the heat wave we were having was beyond me. I said, "Oh, I'm not really worried about Norris. I'm just mad he didn't follow orders. But, other than getting robbed, I can't see how he can get in much trouble in Mexico."

"Whosh in trubble in Mesico?"

It was Buttercup. He'd woke up and come staggering into the dining room carrying a cup of what was supposed to be coffee, but what I suspected was about half whiskey. I said, "Buttercup, get the hell out of here and go sleep it off."

He said, "You tell me whosh in trubble in Mesico. By Gawd, Ah'll take my Sharps 'n' go down 'ere an fis they wagon."

Ben said, "Hell, old man, you can't even talk. How you going to fix anyone's wagon?"

Buttercup wagged a finger at Ben. "You jus' watch you mouth, young feller. An' quit 'at Buttercup stuff."

His real name was Butterfield, Charlie Butterfield, but we'd started calling him Buttercup as soon as we'd found out it irritated him. He had taught every one of us to shoot and he was, without a doubt, the best long-distance shot I'd ever seen. He had an old .50 caliber buffalo gun that, as he said, "killed at both ends." It would kill whatever you hit with it, be it a cat or a railroad locomotive. It

would also make you think you'd been hit in the shoulder
by a stump. The few times I'd fired it I'd brushed my teeth
left-handed the next morning. How an old, dried-up,
scrawny scarecrow like Charlie could still shoot it and
make shots of up to four hundred yards was a mystery
none of us could solve.

Dad said, "Charlie, why don't you go on back to bed.
Get a little rest."

Buttercup got up, but he said, "Naw, nearly supper-
time. I got to go cook for you boys."

Then he lurched out of the dining room and into the
kitchen.

I got up quickly. I said, "I'm getting the hell out of here
before he does manage to cook something."

Dad said, "Somebody ought to go in the kitchen and
get him to bed. That stove would still be hot and he could
burn himself."

I said, "Ben, you do that."

I left the room before he could say a word.

That evening I sat on the porch in the cool of the night.
I was drinking a little whiskey and smoking a cigarillo.
Far off in the distance I could hear the nine o'clock pas-
senger train blowing for the crossing outside of Blessing.
Between the whiskey and the cool night air I was feeling
more than a little bit peaceful. If I could just get those
damn roof tiles and get that damn contractor back to work
I wouldn't have a care in the world.

Two days later I got another telegram. Only this one
was from Jack Cole. It said:

BETTER COME QUICK STOP NORRIS IN JAIL IN MONTER-
REY STOP FIND ME IN LAREDO STOP

I looked at it a long time and then I started cussing.
Norris had managed to get himself in jail in Mexico. About

the worse place to get put in jail in the world. What he'd done or how he'd done it I had no idea. But there it was. I went in and told Dad what had happened. He said, "What are you going to do about it?"

"Go down and get him out," I said bitterly. "And my wedding less than two weeks off. It's got to be done fast."

Dad said, "Better take plenty of money. From what I know of Mexican jails you might have to buy him out."

"Oh, I've already figured on that," I said. "What I haven't figured out is who is going to stay after that building contractor while I'm gone." Boy, was I angry.

Dad said, "Ben can do that."

I said, "I'm taking Ben with me."

"You expecting trouble?"

I said, "I don't know what I'm expecting. How am I supposed to figure from here what damn mess Norris has got hisself in?"

Dad said, "Well, maybe I can oversee that contractor for you."

"Don't worry about it, Dad," I said. "I'll put Harley to it."

Harley was our foreman, a steady, dependable man that had been with us for eighteen years.

I said, "My biggest worry right now is who is going to oversee Nora. She's gonna be mad as hell and I don't blame her."

"Then why don't you just send Ben down with Ray Hays?"

I said, "Because it's my job. Look, I got to get moving."

I went out on the porch and called up Ben and Ray Hays. Ben started laughing when I told him about the telegram, but he shut up mighty quick when he seen the look on my face. Ray said, "Lord, boss, this is trouble."

"Yeah," I said. "Look, we got to get that southbound train at four o'clock and that don't leave us no hell of a lot of time. Pick your best horse and figure to be gone at least a week. Don't waste no time. I want to be gone from here inside of an hour. Ray, have somebody saddle me that new bay gelding I've been riding lately. And send Harley to me right away. I'll be in my room packing."

Harley found me just about the time I finished shoving some clothes in a roomy pair of saddlebags and checking my .40 caliber saddle gun. It was an odd caliber for a carbine, but it matched my revolver so I only had to carry one caliber of ammunition. My handgun was a .42/.40, a revolver chambered to fire a .40 caliber cartridge but set on a .42 caliber frame. It was my belief that a .40 caliber bullet carried enough wallop to stop nearly anything, and what you lost in hitting power to, say, a .44 caliber or a .45 you more than made up in better accuracy. And of course I liked the .42 frame because it was heavier and made for better balance in the hand.

Anyway, I told Harley as briefly as I could what had happened and what I had to do. As I said, Harley was a rock-solid, dependable foreman, but he wasn't all that imaginative when it come to overseeing house building. So I said, "Now, Harley, when that contractor gets back with those roof tiles I want you to send into town and fetch Miss Nora back to the ranch. Then I want you or some other good man to stand over that contractor and make sure he does everything Miss Nora wants done. You understand?"

He was chewing tobacco and he shifted it around a second before he said, "Wahl, I reckon."

I said, "And if that contractor ain't back here within three days I want you to send two men into Galveston to drag him back. That house has got to get built."

Now he really did look uncertain. He said, slowly,

"Boss, you kind of throwin' me in a bind. You takin' Ben an' Hays an' that'll right off make me shorthanded, not countin' yo'self. Now you talkin' 'bout another man fer that house. Boss, you know we got to keep workin' them cattle from water to fresh grass."

I said, "Harley, don't give me no trouble. I got enough as it is."

But he said, doggedly, "An' then they is the matter of the hayin'. The way thet grass is curin' off we might need to git it in at anytime."

He was right of course. Normally we wouldn't have even been thinking about hay for another month, month and a half. But between the heat and the drought the grass was drying up fast. If you let it go too far it would burn up and be worthless. But I said, with heat, "Goddammit, Harley, don't you reckon I know that? Look, I got enough on my plate without you mentioning that damn hay. Now you just do the best you can and let me do the worrying."

"Well, yessir—" he said.

He sounded like to me he was about to throw a "but" in there right after the "yessir" so I cut him off. Shouldering my saddlebags and picking up my rifle, I said, "Just do it, Harley."

I left him standing there looking worried. Hell, how did he think I felt? I still had Nora to talk to. And Norris to get out of a Mexican jail.

We made good time into town, arriving there just about three o'clock. I sent Ben to the bank to get two thousand dollars in cash and a letter of credit for five thousand more and I sent Hays down to the railroad station to make arrangements to have a car added to the passenger train to carry our horses. Then I started down to the Parker house. Jogging along, I was about halfway hoping that Nora would be out, that I could just leave a message with her mother and take off.

But that didn't turn out to be the case. She come to the screen door almost as soon as I'd knocked. She said, "Justa! Whatever in the world are you doing back in town so soon?"

I held the screen door open and said, "C'mon out here a minute. I got to talk to you."

Her face got all troubled but she came along and took a seat in the swing. I sat down beside her. Lord, she looked pretty. She was wearing a lemon-colored frock, a color that had always looked the best on her. She said, "What's the matter, Justa? Something's wrong, isn't it? Is it about the wedding?"

"No," I said, "it's not about the wedding. Just promise me you won't start getting all upset because everything is going to work out fine." I was as nervous as if I'd been facing a court trial.

She said, steadily, "Just tell me. Without the buildup."

So I did. I finished by saying, "You see, it ain't going to affect the wedding. All it means is that I might not be here for a week while the house is being worked on."

I had truly expected her to be loving and understanding. But I hadn't considered the number of times I'd disappointed her and the gathering effect it had had. She got a pout on her face and said, "I don't see why you've got to go. Norris is supposed to be so damn smart. Why can't he get himself out of jail?"

I said, "Now, Nora honey, it ain't all that easy to get out of a Mexican jail when you're on the inside. You need somebody working for you on the outside."

"Then send him a lawyer."

I was squirming. It was going much harder than I'd reckoned. I said, "Well, thing is, there's some delicate matters that a lawyer can't exactly handle as well as a member of the family."

"You mean like bribes?"

"Money talks in Mexico," I admitted. "But first off I don't know what they got him in jail for. I got to get on the scene so I can figure out how best to act."

"Can't Ben do that? He's not getting married in nine days."

"Nora, be reasonable. Ben's good at a lot of things, but delicacy ain't one of them. And this is likely to be a delicate situation."

"Or a shooting situation," she said with a pretty good trace of hardness in her voice.

I said, "Now don't go to thinking that. That is the last thing I expect."

"Then how come you're taking Ben? And Hays?"

Damn the woman. She read me too easy. I said, "Well, for backup. I'm going into a situation where I don't know what to expect. I'm trying to cover all the gates. Besides, I'm mainly taking Ben for learning. It'll be a good education for him. After we're married I want him to take over more and more of the running of the ranch. So I won't be so busy."

I thought the last would mollify her a little, making it sound like I'd have more time for she and me. But she just said, "Oh, Justa, you're such a liar. You're taking your two best gun hands. You must think I'm awful silly."

What was awful about that was that I wasn't really expecting any shooting. I was taking Ben for the experience and to make sure I had a member of the family for a backup. And I was taking Hays because he was handy at doing a lot of things and had had considerable experience along the border. For once I was telling nearly the straight truth and getting called a liar in the bargain.

I got up. I stood there and said, a little stiffly, "Well, you can believe me or not. But I'm doing what I think has to be done. For everybody's benefit. I can't let my brother stay in jail. And if I was to send Ben down there, more than likely he'd try some hotheaded kind of play and get hisself jugged. Then I'd have two brothers in jail and then I would have to go. And then there shore as hell wouldn't be time enough for me to get back here for the wedding.''

She stood up and put both her hands flat on my chest and looked up in my face. She said, ''Oh, Justa, I'm sorry. I know you have to go. It's just that I've had so many disappointments and I've just been waiting for something like this to come up. Sick cattle. Cattle rustlers. Floods, famine.'' She laughed without any humor in it. ''Something. Anything.''

I leaned down and kissed her lightly on the lips. ''I'm sorry, Nora. I wouldn't have had it happen for the world. And believe me, if I get Norris out of that jail, he's liable to wish he was back in by the time I get through with him.''

She said, ''Well, you go along now. You can't miss that train.''

She walked me to my horse. I said, ''Now you understand what I told Harley. They'll send for you soon's that building contractor gets back. Harley has strict orders to make sure he does things the way you want them.''

''All right,'' she said. ''I'll manage. But I'll still wish it was you there giving the orders.''

''Nora, it's going to be all right. I promise you. Your dad can check on the furniture and I'll be back before you know it.''

''How long do you think?''

That was kind of a hard question to answer, not having any idea what Norris was charged with. But I lied and said, ''Four days. No more.''

''Starting tomorrow?''

''Starting tomorrow.''

I kissed her hard then and swung aboard my horse.

Shading her eyes against the sun, she said, "You had better be careful."

"I'm always careful."

"Justa, I mean it. Don't you make no grass widow out of me. You watch out for yourself."

"I will. Now quit fretting and get on out of this sun. I'll see you quick's I can."

Then I turned my horse and spurred for the railroad depot. In the distance I could hear the sound of the incoming train.

It was a long, wearisome trip, but we finally got into Laredo about ten that night. I figured it was too late to look for Jack Cole so we got our horses dismounted from the train and rode over to the Hamilton Hotel. It was a big, elegant old place that I always made my headquarters when bad luck caused me to be in Laredo. A boy took our horses to the stable and we clumped in to the lobby, our spurs going *chink-chink-chink* on the marble floor. I wanted us all together so I took a big suite with plenty of beds and we went up and got settled in. Even though it was late, the kitchen managed to fix us a good supper of enchiladas and rice and beans. We'd gotten a couple of bottles of whiskey from the bar and were pretty well set for the night.

After we'd eaten and got a couple of drinks down, Ben wanted to go out looking for Jack Cole. I shook my head. "It's too late. We'd have to look in every saloon and all we'd find would be a bunch of drunks looking for a fight. No, we'll get some rest tonight. We might be on our way to Monterrey in the morning."

But no sooner had I said it then there came a knock at our door. Hays answered it. It was Jack Cole, or Black Jack Cole as he was called. Jack was a small, middle-aged man who'd been a friend of our family for years. Word was he'd rode the owl-hoot trail, but, so far as I knew, he'd never done no serious jail time. Now it was my understanding that he made his living smuggling Mexican gold into the States. I don't reckon it paid much, but them as didn't need much were said to be content with it.

I got up and we shook hands all around and then got Jack seated and a drink in his hand. He was called Black Jack because he was so swarthy. On the border he could easy pass for a Mexican, but his coloring didn't come from any Spanish blood, but Cherokee Indian.

When he'd got his drink down and Hays had poured him another I said, "Well, Jack . . . what's it all about?"

He had a pleasant face and creased and crinkled skin around his eyes. He gave a half laugh and said, "Well, I don't know if I can explain it or not. It started out purty simple, but it jest kep' a-goin' and a-goin'. Best I can say is you know Norris and how he can git."

"Yes," I said dryly. "Only too well. Tell me what you can."

He said, "Wahl, we went out and taken a look at that land and, shore enough, he finds they is a rough bunch of hombres staked out there. See, the Rio Grande had done took a shift here a while back where it kind of throwed your land downhill from the river. Well, some smart *compesinos* figured it out and they dug 'em a drainage ditch right down the middle of that patch of land and damned if they didn't get some grass growin'. So they've turned a bunch of scrawny Mexican cattle in there and is fattenin' 'em up at a right smart rate."

Ben said, "I bet that set right good with Norris."

Jack laughed. "Oh, he got a little hot about it. 'Fore I talked him out of it he was all for ridin' in thar and clearin' out the bunch of 'em. We finally went into the courthouse in Laredo. He'd seen the sheriff, but they discovered the deed was clouded by something that had happened a hunnert years ago. I never really got the straight of it. But

they told him he'd have to go over to Mexico, on account
of it being a Spanish land grant. You know how them
goes. So we went over there an' he got another lawyer, a
Mex lawyer. Upshot was he didn't git no satisfaction from
the authorities in Nuevo Laredo. They told him he'd have
to go to the capital, to Monterrey, where they had com-
plete records."

Ben said, "Oh, shit."

Jack looked at him and smiled a little. "Yeah, that's
about the size of it. By then ol' Norris was gettin' his back
up higher'n his head. So we goes down there to Monterrey, only this time he ain't gonna git no lawyer. Says he's
tired of payin' out to clear his own land. 'Course I went
along as kind of an interpreter since ol' Norris don't speak
that much Spanish." He stopped and shook his head and
looked at me. He said, "Justa, the whole damn matter
could have been cleared up for a hunnert dollar bill. But—"

I nodded. "But Norris had his back up."

Jack said, "Yeah. We taken this here official out to git
a drink to some cantina and the ol' boy just let it slide that
a little fee of a hunnert dollars would get Norris a clear
title. A title he could have taken back down to Laredo and
had the sheriff run them hombres off the land with maybe.
But then Norris got stiff-necked. He said he happened to
know for a fact that a title search didn't cost but ten pesos
and he was damned if he was going to pay ninety-nine
dollars for something that was already his. Got right angry
about it, too. Right there in that cantina."

"I can see it," Ben said.

"Then what?" I asked.

"Wahl, Norris announced to that official that he was
gonna report him for askin' for a bribe, which me and you
know is about as good as pissin' in the alley down here.
But what it done was make that official damn mad. So he

ups and tells the police that Norris has done threatened his life."

"Oh, shit!" I said. It was looking worse and worse.

Jack said, "It might have still been all right. They sent a captain of police and a couple of *federales* around to the hotel. I happened to be in the room when they come in and I tried to grease the captain on the sly, but Norris wasn't having any of it. He said he was a United States citizen trying to protect his property from a bunch of god-dam thieves and he was damned if he'd be arrested for something he hadn't done."

"I bet that impressed the hell out of them," I said.

Jack smiled. "Naw, they got impressed when the captain laid hands on Norris. Norris busted him square in the mouth. Knocked the shit out of him."

Ben laughed, but Hays and I sort of groaned. I said, "What's the rest of it?"

Jack shook his head. "I dunno. When I left Monterrey they hadn't made no formal charges, but last I seen of him, he was still giving them trouble. Justa, I'm sorry, wadn't a damn thing I could do."

"I know," I said.

"Fact of the business was, it cost me fifty dollars not to git arrested myself. I figured the best thing I could do was get on back to Laredo and git off a wire and wait for help."

"You done right," I said. "And you won't be the loser for it. What's the earliest train we can get out on in the morning?"

"Eight."

"What you reckon it's going to cost to square matters?"

Jack shook his head. "I ain't got no idea, Justa. Them Mexican police don't take too kindly to havin' no gringo punch 'em. I ain't even sure it can be squared with money."

"You'll go with us? I'll make it worth your while."

"Oh, sure. An' you ain't got to pay me. Yore family has done me more than one favor I ain't forgot."

I got up. "It's past midnight. I reckon we ought to all get some rest. Jack, we'll be taking our horses. How about you?"

That sort of raised his eyebrows. But he said, "Well, long's you is gonna go ahead and pay fer a horse box, I might as well take my old nag along."

I said, "We'll see you at the depot a little after seven. And I'm much obliged to you."

He shrugged. "Nothin' you wouldn't have done fer me."

Before we went to bed, Ben took occasion to lift my spirits by saying, "I reckon you're pretty relieved Nora don't know how much trouble you got on your hands or how long it's going to take to fix it."

I looked at him. I said, "Ben, one of these days that mouth of yours is going to get filled up. With my fist."

He laughed. "Big brother is worried. Listen, I'll protect you from Nora."

"Oh, shut up. We got work ahead."

We loaded up on the Texas side of the river. The train wasn't too crowded until we got into the station in Nuevo Laredo. Then it got swarmed on and over and in by so many peons carrying crates of chickens and leading goats that we all elected to go back and ride in the horse car we'd paid for.

It was about a hundred miles to Monterrey, but because we would stop at every village along the way, the trip would take at least four hours. The train was so overloaded that they had to put sand on the rails so the locomotive wheels could take a grip. Sitting, waiting, it seemed to be even hotter than it had been back in our part of the country. But once the train got moving, the breeze blowing

through the opened side doors was a welcome relief. I'd
got the hotel kitchen to put us up some roast beef and
cheese and bread, and about midmorning we brought out
the grub and had a feed. Jack had a bottle of tequila and
we had the remains of the two bottles we'd bought the
night before.

Jack finally said, "Justa, how come you're bringing
horses? You figuring you might need to leave in a hurry?"

I said, chewing on some beef, "Jack, I ain't figuring on
anything. I'm just trying not to leave anything I might
need later."

He hesitated and then said, "Only reason I'm pryin' is
that I figure I ought to tell you I ain't much of a gun hand
anymore. That is if it comes down to it."

I looked at him in some surprise. I said, "Jack, I'd
never involve you in our scraps. But I'm kind of took up
to hear you lost your touch. You always impressed me as
a man could handle himself."

He said, "The spirit's still there. But—" He held out
his right hand. It was visibly shaking.

I said, "What the hell, Jack?"

He shrugged. "I don't know. Age, I reckon. I'm near
fifty. Too damn much whiskey. Too many scares. Started
about a year ago when a bunch of *rurales* caught me brang-
in' some gold up from the interior. Fer a joke they acted
like they was gonna hang me. 'Cept they didn't let me in
on the joke until my heart had nearly stopped beatin'.
Ain't really been the same since."

Rurales were Mexican rural police. Or at least that was
what they were supposed to be. They was also supposed
to suppress the outlaw bands that roamed the countryside.
But from what I'd heard, most folks would rather fall in
amongst the outlaws than the *rurales*. I said, "Yeah, them
boys got a hell of a sense of humor."

Jack said, "They cut the rope three quarters of the way

through figuring it would break before my neck did. It didn't break and neither did my neck. I was pretty blue in the face before they finally figured to cut me down.''

I shook my head. "How you stay over here, Jack?''

He started to say something, then just shrugged. Finally he said, "I really ain't got that much selection, Justa.''

I didn't ask him anymore.

Outside the countryside rolled by, becoming even more desolate with every passing mile. The country was mostly flat, but here and there it was marked by little humps of rock and sand and slashed by severe ravines and deep canyons. Far off in the distance you could see the beginnings of the Sierras, the several lines of high mountain ranges that cut Mexico up like fenced-off pastures. About every twenty miles or so the train would come to a grinding, jolting halt and dozens of peons dressed in white britches tied at the ankles and white shirts and wide straw sombreros would stream off, their women and children following behind. There would be no apparent village, just a marker by the track, but the Mexicans would go off across the hot, flat plain, walking with that patient stride that could take them miles. Somewhere out there would be a tiny *pueblo*, adobe and straw huts built around the only water in the district. To live they raised corn and beans and peppers and skinny cattle. Looking at it, it was hard to understand how anyone could make a living on such land. But the peons did, and had for centuries.

As we got closer to Monterrey the land became more hilly and a little greener. But it was never going to get very green because Coahuila was about as poor a state as there was in Mexico.

Monterrey was a pretty big city. Where our hometown, Blessing, didn't have quite a thousand souls, Jack said Monterrey had a population of near forty thousand. That was big for a city in that part of Mexico.

We come steaming into the depot about two in the afternoon. Some railroad workers brought up a ramp and we led our mounts down and then swung aboard. We rode for the center of town. Even though Monterrey was a big city it wasn't much to look at. The streets were all dust and there were no boardwalks in front of the buildings. Most of the houses we saw were poor shanties. We finally pulled up in front of what looked to be the best hotel in town, the Mirador. Some boys came out to tend to our horses so we unslung our saddlebags and went into the lobby. It was a big, cool place with a high-beamed ceiling and a lot of that heavy Mexican furniture sitting around. I took two rooms. Hays would bunk in with me, and Ben and Jack would share a room.

We got upstairs and got settled on the second floor. Hays and I had drawn a big room with big casement windows and a big table with a couple of washbasins. The desk clerk had booked me for a bath at the end of the hall. But first we crowded into our room, sat in chairs and on the beds and talked over what we should do. I was for going straight on over to the jail and looking into matters, but Jack thought it would be better to hire a lawyer who had some pull and let him front for us. I said, "Just how are we supposed to know which lawyer has got the pull around here? I bet this town has got a hundred lawyers in it."

He got up out of his chair. "Why don't you get that bath and slick up a little while I go have a look around. I think I know a couple of hombres here and I figure I can find out what we need."

I said, "My plans for today are for me and you to do the scouting around. I'm going to leave Ben and Hays here."

He half smiled. "Just in case you and I get throwed in jail?"

"Something like that," I said.

While he was gone I dug some clean clothes out of my saddlebags and then went on down the hall to the bath and had a shave and then a bath in cold water. When I was dressed in clean clothes I felt a deal better though I knew I'd be sweating five minutes after I left the hotel.

Jack got back a few minutes after I returned to the room. He said, "I think I found our man. Name of Julio Obregon. He's crooked, but then they all are. But it sounds like he stands in with the *politicos*, which means he's automatically in with the *jefes* in the courts and the police. His office ain't but a couple of blocks from here."

I said, "Well, you go get cleaned up and we'll go."

I got a couple of hundred dollars off Ben, who was carrying our bankroll. I figured I'd need at least that much for a retainer. As near as I could figure, Norris was in some serious trouble. I'd been mad as hell at him back in Matagorda when I'd first got Jack's telegram. Now I was plenty worried. You just didn't go around punching police captains in Mexico. It was just like Norris. He thought I solved everything with my fists or a gun. He never realized how much more thinking I did. And for a man as smart as him to use his fists was just plain foolish. He was going to come to a bad end someday if he kept on trying to prove he was as tough as Ben and me.

But that could wait. Right then I had to figure out a way to get him home before he could get into any more trouble.

Señor Obregon was a short, fat little man of some thirty years with a thick, black mustache and sleek, black, oily hair. He had just returned from siesta when we arrived, and one could see he'd changed into a clean white shirt. He was just hanging up his coat when his clerk showed us into his office. We made our howdies and then sat down. I said, "Señor Obregon, my family, the Williamses, are ranchers down in Matagorda County, Texas. That's about three hundred miles north of here. We're considered well-to-do business people and have some little influence in the Texas state government. Through a misunderstanding my younger brother, Norris Williams, has run afoul of your local police and is now in jail. I've come to you for your assistance in getting his release to get out of this trouble.'' I looked at Jack.

Jack started to translate, but Obregon held up his hand. ''Pleese,'' he said. ''Ah heeve some Anglish. An' I know of choo brudder. Et es a very deffecult matter. He es in *mucho* trouble. The *policía* are, how choo say, very angry.''

I glanced at Jack and he shrugged as if to say, ''I told you so.''

Señor Obregon said, ''Choo brudder hes been telling meny, meny peoples that he es a *muy importante hombre* in *Estados Unidos*. He make meny threats to meeny peoples. He make *el jefe de policía muy* angry.''

I cussed silently under my breath. Damn Norris didn't know when to keep his mouth shut.

Señor Obregon leaned toward me. He said, ''Choo *comprende*, Señor Williams, *muy importante* in *Estados Unidos* es no the same as *muy importante* in Mexico.''

''Yes,'' I said. ''I understand. Sometimes my brother *tiene caliente de cabeza.*''

Señor Obregon looked puzzled. He said, ''What means thees hot of head?''

Jack said, dryly, ''Justa, I reckon you better let me handle the Mex talk.'' In rapid-fire Spanish he told Señor Obregon that Norris was a man with a strong belief in right and wrong and when he felt he'd been wronged he tended to get stubborn. Also angry.

I said, ''Tell him Norris doesn't speak any Spanish and that he might have punched the captain through a misunderstanding.''

Jack whipped off a round of Mex. Obregon answered him back. Jack looked around at me, that usual half smile on his face, and said, "He wants to know if it would be all right for a Mexican to punch a sheriff in Texas just because he didn't speak English."

I said, "Just ask him if he can help us."

Jack talked and then Obregon talked and then Jack talked again. Finally, Obregon leaned back in his chair, intertwined his fingers over his ample belly and pursed out his lips. After a moment he said something to Jack. Jack answered back. Señor Obregon shook his head and said something firmly to Jack.

"What?" I said.

Jack turned to me. "He says he'll look into it to see how serious it is but that it will cost you a hunnert dollars U.S. I told him we already knowed it was serious an' couldn't he do a little more for that kind of money. Justa, it ain't worth it. He knows you got money an' he's jus' tryin' to bleed you."

"Let's get him started," I said. "I expect this to cost a great deal. All of which I'm going to take out of Norris's hide." I dug in my pocket and came out with five twenty-dollar bills. I laid them on the desk and looked at Señor Obregon. "Okay?"

He picked up the money with his fat fingers. "Hokay," he said.

I said to Jack, "Ask him if we can see Norris."

That brought on another exchange of that rapid-fire Spanish. Jack said to me, "He thinks that will perhaps cost another forty dollars. To use his words. Take careful not to count on it over much."

"All right," I said. I leafed out two more twenties. Señor Obregon picked them up. I said, "When?"

He looked at Jack and Jack said it in Spanish. Señor Obregon shrugged and said something to Jack. Jack got up. He said, "We're to come back in the morning. He ought to know something by then." He gave me a slight grimace. "He wants you to understand he can't promise anything and that these matters take time."

"Tell him I understand," I said. "And tell him in your most flowery Spanish how much we appreciate such an upstanding gentleman as himself coming to our aid and that we are in his debt."

Jack raised his eyebrows, but he did it. From the length of the speech, I figured he was setting Señor Obregon up to run for Congress.

We shook hands and then Jack and I left, leaving Señor Obregon to count his money and figure out just how much I was good for.

Walking back to the hotel I said, "Well, I got a problem."

"You mean Norris has got a problem."

"Yeah, him too. But time is something I ain't got a whole hell of a lot of."

Jack said, "You ain't forgot where we are."

"No, I understand time is something they got a surplus of down here. But they is a date on the calendar when I got to be on my way back to Blessing. Norris just might have to do a little jail time."

Jack looked at me in surprise. "You wouldn't do that to your own brother."

"Listen," I said, looking sideways at him, "I didn't get Norris in this mess. And if he'd followed orders he wouldn't be in it. One of us in a mess is enough. I'm not going to lose the most valuable thing in my life to keep him from having a couple of rough weeks."

Jack said, "What most valuable thang?"

"Never mind," I said.

3

I guess what really startled the hell out of the bunch of us was just how different Mexican law was from the United States. I'd known it was some peculiar from what I was used to, but until we'd talked to Obregon I hadn't had no idea how severe it was. Seemed it was based on the Napoleonic Code, held over back from the days when the French operated Mexico. For instance, Norris hadn't even been charged with anything and didn't have to be charged for a hundred and eighty days. They could hold him that long just for the hell of it before any formal proceedings had to commence. Worse, there was no bail and no trial by jury. If ever there was an opportunity for a corrupt judicial system, Mexico was all set up and ready to operate.

When I told Ben and Hays they naturally got mad as hell. Of course getting mad wasn't going to do us a damn bit of good so I just told them to shut up and let me think.

Jack didn't have much to say. He'd known in advance what a fix Norris was in.

We went out and ate supper about seven o'clock. After that we went into a couple of cantinas and Jack asked about the general conditions in the particular jail. It wasn't too heartening. Seems they didn't believe in wasting a whole lot of money on feeding and caring for their prisoners. They more or less took the position that it was their job to keep the prisoner confined, and if he wanted to eat or drink, why, it was up to him. I figured Norris had had plenty of money on him to see to his wants, but Jack said they more than likely had confiscated it.

"Generally they do," he said. "And it's hell to get it back. They figure a prisoner's family or friends will see to him. What money he's got on him they take as a reward for his capture. Least that's the way they look at it."

When we got back to the hotel room Ben said he was mad as hell. He said, "I'm going over and have a look at that jail in the morning. By God, I ain't gonna stand for this."

"Then you better sit down," I said. "You'll stand for what you have to. Ain't nobody, including me, going anywhere near that jail house until we get a handle on this matter. I don't want them to be able to recognize a one of us."

Hays said, "You thankin' about breakin' him out, boss?"

I said, "I ain't thinking about anything right now, Hays. I'm waiting to get a better feel for the lay of the land. And I don't want anybody getting a wild hair up their ass and doing something that might cut me off from any plans I need to make. The two of you got that?"

I glared at them hard until Ben finally nodded. Hays followed suit. I said to Hays, "Ray, you are responsible for Ben. Jack and I will be with that lawyer tomorrow morning and if you let him go anywhere near that jail, or do any other dumb thing, I'm gonna fire you on the spot."

Hays said, "Aw, hell, boss."

And Ben said, "That ain't hardly fair, Justa. Hays works for me. He can't give me orders."

"Yeah, and you both work for me. I can't fire you, Ben, because you're family. But I'll damn fire your good buddy if you go to messing around where I've told you to stay out of."

"Shit!" Ben said. "That is pretty poor."

I said, grimly, "Well, consider you ain't the easiest in the flock to handle. And you have gone off on your own before. This time I can't take the chance."

I'd actually pulled the same stunt before. Ben could get awful hardheaded sometimes, but he and Hays were tight and he knew I'd fire Hays if he screwed up.

After that we had a few more drinks and then everybody went to bed. I reckon we was all a little disgusted.

Next morning Señor Obregon kept us cooling our heels for a solid hour before he saw us. He looked grave when we got shown in his office. We sat down and, without much fanfare, he said, "Es *mucho* trouble. Es *malo*. Es bad."

Jack whispered, "He's settin' you up for another bite."

"Talk to him," I said. "Get the story. Let's see what we're up against." In anticipation of what I'd felt was sure to come I'd taken another five hundred dollars from Ben. We'd also gone around to the Banco Nacional de México and made sure our letter of credit from our bank in Blessing would be honored. They'd said they'd wire on the matter. We'd represented ourselves as cattle buyers, not wanting to arouse curiosity as to why we were packing around such a healthy sum of money. At least we didn't want the wrong parties getting curious.

Jack pitched in at Señor Obregon. The lawyer started

shaking his head right away. He said to me, in that fumbling English of his, "Theees matter es veery grave. *El Capitán* Davilla es *mucho* angry. He feels hes honor has, how choo say, been broken."

I figured it would save time and effort all around if we just ran everything through Jack. It was a strain on Señor Obregon to get the words out and it was a strain on me waiting for them to arrive.

I said to Jack, "You and him do the talking. Ask him how bad this Captain Davilla's honor is broke and how much he figures it will take to fix it."

Jack said to me, "Don't sound like no hundred-and-forty-dollar report to me. I could have tol' you for a shot of whiskey and change that ol' *Capitán* Davilla's honor was gonna been hurt."

I said, "Jack, keep it going. I know what that hundred and forty went for. Just talk to the good señor."

They conversed for about five minutes with me looking back and forth from one to the other to try and get some sign. While they were talking, Obregon's clerk brought us in coffee. It was already mixed with sugar and it was strong and black and sweet as hell. Jack took his down like he was used to it, but I just sipped as politely as I could.

Occasionally, in the midst of the exchange, Señor Obregon would hold out his hands, palms upward, as if to say there was nothing else he could do.

Finally Jack turned to me. He said, wearily, "They figure they got some big fish on the line and they gonna play you for all you worth. Right now your shyster buddy here is trying to let me try to talk him into acting as go-between."

Jack was leaning toward me, half whispering and speaking very fast. I said, "Can't you get some idea out of him what it's going to take to square this Davilla?"

He shook his head. "We ain't that far along yit. All's

we got done is to decide that our lawyer here might be talked into approaching Davilla for another hunnert dollars. But you can figure on more down the line when the negotiating over Davilla's honor comes on the auction block. I reckon he's gonna set a mighty heavy store by his honor. Most of 'em do if they figure they is any money to be made.''

"All right," I said. I got out another hundred dollars and pushed it across the desk to the lawyer. He took it with the same delicate touch that seemed rigged into his fat little fingers where money was concerned. "Okay?" I said.

"Hokay," he said, and nodded. Hell, I probably looked like the best thing he'd seen since he'd robbed his first widow.

I said to Jack, "Now ask him when we get to see Norris. And ask him what we can take him."

Jack said, "You can take him just about anything you want to—*if* they'll let us see him." He commenced on Obregon again and they had at it for two or three minutes. Finally Jack said, "Our buddy is going over to the *calabozo* right away and make a special effort. He says he'll get word to us as early this afternoon as he can."

I said, "Better tell him what hotel we're at."

Jack just smiled slightly. "Oh, he knows what hotel you're at. And I reckon he knows a good deal more by now, too."

We done a polite good-bye and then got up and left, leaving Señor Obregon looking mighty pleased with himself. Well, he might need to get a feather to tickle himself with if I didn't get some action pretty soon. I was one well that might go dry a little sooner than he expected.

Walking back, Jack said, "I wonder how wise we was to show that letter of credit at that bank. Mexican banks ain't like U.S. banks. These bankers here will talk. Obregon might likely already know about that five thousand dollars. If he does he's gonna try and bleed you fer every bit.''

I said, ''Jack, I had no choice. I had to get it wired on before I needed it. Time's important right now.''

We found Hays and Ben restless as hell. They'd been out walking around, but they both swore they hadn't been anywhere near the jail.

To kill time we all went downstairs and ate lunch in the hotel café. It was pretty poor going, but the beer was good. Apparently they were an up-to-date concern with an ice plant somewhere in town because the beer was cold. It come in bottles, too, something we didn't see much of in Blessing. I said, ''If we get to see him we ought to take Norris an iced-down bucket of a bunch of bottles of this beer.''

Ben bristled up. He said, ''What you mean, *if* we get to see him? By God, I'm about to get tired of this bullshit. Something don't happen pretty damn soon I'm likely to do a little negotiating on my own.''

I just looked at him and didn't say anything. That was Ben; you had to let him blow off some steam ever so often or risk a major explosion.

It was around two o'clock when Obregon's clerk came hurrying over to tell us that we could see Norris, but that we had to come quickly. I protested that I wanted time to get some stuff together for Norris's comfort, but the clerk insisted that we had to come immediately. I finally said, ''Well, all right. We'll come now.'' Then I detailed Ben and Hays to gather up what they could in the way of food and drink and to hurry over with it. ''We'll stall as long as we can. Just hurry.''

One look at that big block of a jail told me it wouldn't be any easy proposition to break somebody out of. It was two stories high and built out of granite rock. The only windows to speak of were at the very front. The rest, including those on the second floor, were just slits.

There were a good many police around. They weren't hard to spot. They all wore kind of green uniforms and those military caps that got a bill on them. You could tell the officers from the regular police because the officers just carried a side gun in a military holster while the common troops had to lug around a carbine.

Once we got in through the front door we were in a big kind of anteroom with a bunch of policemen sitting around and a big desk with some kind of *jefe* behind it. Obregon's clerk went up and spoke to the *jefe*. Jack listened while they jabbered.

I said, "How's it going?"

"All right," he said. "Except they ain't going to let him out of his cell. We'll have to go back there and visit him through the bars of his cell."

I said, "Tell them we got some food and drink coming over for Norris. I want to make sure it gets through."

That took a few more minutes. Then Jack took a five-dollar bill out of his pocket and passed it to the officer at the desk.

"What the hell's that?"

"That's so Norris can git his food and drink. I just thought I'd save you the trouble of going in yore pocket. Mine was closer. They callin' a jailer now to take us back."

"Thanks," I said. While we waited I looked around the place. It looked mighty formidable. I didn't see any way to jailbreak a man out of the place. I figured the stone walls were at least three feet thick, too thick to blast a hole in. And there were way too many soldiers and police around for the four of us to overwhelm. It didn't look good at all.

Pretty soon a guard with a big bunch of keys in his hand

came for us. He passed us through a door and then down
a long corridor that must have held a lot of offices. I seen
one door that was marked for the chief of police, but I
didn't see any for this Davilla. We came to another door
and the guard passed us through that. That put us into a
block of cells. They looked to be about five along each
side, open bars facing open bars. Jack whispered to me,
"Better slip this monkey a ten-dollar bill to make sure he
gits Norris good treatment and lets us stay a bit longer."

Then we came to the very end cell built against the
outside wall of the building. There, slumped on a broken-
down-looking cot, sat Norris. He was still in his sack suit,
but it looked some the worse for wear. It was rumpled and
dirty and his tie was gone. He looked up as we neared the
bars. I thought he'd make some kind of smile, but he just
said, "These people will regret this to their dying day. If
I have to take it to the Supreme Court of the United
States."

I said, "Well, Norris, I don't think that will work in
Mexico."

"You know what I mean," he said.

I hadn't exactly expected to find him in good spirits, but
I had thought he might have been a little sorry for the
trouble he'd caused. But he apparently wasn't of that turn
of mind. I said, "How are you?"

"I am angry," he said. "My rights have been violated
and I will see justice done before it is over. Do you know
why I'm incarcerated? Do you have any idea?"

"Yeah," I said. "You punched a policeman in the face.
Wasn't too smart, Norris."

He got up from the cot and came to the bars. "Punched
him nothing! That's not why I'm here. I'm here because I
refused to pay a petty official a bribe of one hundred dollars for something that was rightfully mine. Then I'm in
here because I refused to give a corrupt policeman twenty

dollars to forget the whole thing. And finally I'm in here for defending myself when they went to lay hands on me because I refused to pay yet another bribe!''

Boy, he was wound up and no mistake. I said, ''Yeah, that's a lot of money. Nearly a fourth of what I've already laid out trying to get you out of there.''

He jerked back. ''You better not be trying to buy me out of this. I'll have my day in court, you can bet on that.''

I said, ''You keep forgetting you're under Mexican law. You ain't got no rights.''

That made him look at the floor. He muttered, ''Damn their uncivilized ways.''

He didn't look like they'd roughed him up over much, but I could see the remains of a bruise on one of his cheeks and one of his lips looked like it had been split. I said, grimly, ''Now, look Norris, I've listened to you blow off and that's all I'm going to listen to. You didn't follow orders and consequently you've got yourself and us in a mess. If you weren't so damn valuable to the family, brother or not, I'd leave you here to rot. But I'm going to be doing what I can to get you out and I want you to cooperate. With your big mouth you've already let them know we've got money, so they are going to work me for everything they can. I swear, if you'd drawed yourself up a blueprint to see how bad you could fuck up you couldn't have done no better. So while I'm busy on the outside you sit in here and behave yourself and keep your damn mouth shut! You got that?''

He was drawing himself up to come back at me when the door to the cell block opened and another guard brought Ben and Hays in with him. Ben was carrying a big bucket of iced beer and Hays had a tow sack full of what I figured was grub.

Ben and Hays came up and shook hands with Norris. He seemed glad, at least, to see them. Of course I under-

stood why he hadn't exactly hugged my neck. He'd
screwed up and he and I both knew it. My very presence
must have made him feel guilty.

The two guards made a big show of going through the
goods that Ben and Hays had brought, even digging down
into the ice. When they finished I gave each of them a ten-
dollar bill and Jack told them we'd be grateful if Norris
received special treatment.

While Ben and Hays were visiting I looked around the
double line of cells. There were five on each side and they
were smaller than the Texas variety, being only about six
foot wide and eight foot long. On Norris's side the first
two cells were occupied by two Mexicans each. Both of
them appeared to be peons. They were asleep, it being
proper siesta time. The cell across from Norris was va-
cant, but the other four on that side were filled, two with
two prisoners and two with one prisoner each. The men
in the individual cells were much better dressed and looked
much more genteel than any of the hombres enjoying double occupancy. I figured you had to pay to get a room to
yourself. I looked at the two *caballeros*, one of whom was
standing at his cell front watching us, wondering what
they were in for. They looked well born and well dressed
enough that they ought to have been able to buy themselves out.

About that time one of the guards was unlocking the
cell door and passing the goods into the cell to Norris.
Ben said, "Goddammit, if I had a gun right now we'd
have you out of there before these two *jefes* knew what
happened."

Of course we'd left our gun belts back at the hotel,
knowing full well we'd of just had to surrender them as
soon as we'd got to the jail. Better safe back at the hotel
than lost somewhere in some policeman's pocket.

Pretty soon the guards said we had to leave. Norris

shook with Ben and Hays and thanked Jack for getting word out about his predicament. But when it came my turn he just looked at me defiantly and said, "Well, why don't you go on and do what you think is right. Give in to these bastards. Pay 'em off. See if I care."

I said, disgustedly, "You sound about ten years old, Norris. I'll do what I have to to get you out, but when I get you home you're gonna work about twenty hours a day because you'd better plan on bringing in two dollars for every dollar I have to spend to make up for your dumb-ass play. And God help you if this interferes with my wedding."

His face suddenly fell and he once again looked like my brother. He groaned. "Oh, hell, Justa, I completely forgot about that. Oh, my God! Listen, you forget about me. Get back to Blessing. How far off is it? A week? Ten days?"

"Eight days," I said grimly. "And my house ain't completed."

"Oh, damn!" he said. He left the bars and went back to his cot and sat down. With his head in his hands he said, "I'll get out of here somehow. Leave Jack here with some money. You go back and tend to your business."

I said, "I ought to. But it does my heart so much good to see you sitting there feeling sorry for yourself that I got to stick around and watch."

He looked up. "Oh, go to blazes."

The guard was tugging at my sleeve. I turned. "I'll see you as quick as I can. Just don't make it any harder on you or me than you feel you righteously have to."

Walking down the line of cells the well-dressed man who'd been watching us said, "Señor."

I stopped. He was wearing well fitting *charro* britches with silver conchos down each side and a leather jacket. He was obviously a well-to-do rancher. I said, "Yeah? I don't speak Spanish."

He said, in good English, "Your brother talk too much. He make trouble with a policeman here."

"Davilla?"

"*Sí. Capitán* Davilla. A very bad man. Your brother should be quiet."

"Thanks," I said. "I told him so already."

He was smoking and he took a second to drop his cigarillo on the floor and grind it out with his boot before he said, casually, "*Mi nombre*—my name is Elizandro. Miguel Elizandro. I have a hacienda some thirty kilometers south of here in the little village of Zapata. I have about ten good men working for me. Very good men." He looked at me.

I studied him in return. He was a well-set-up young man of about my age though not up to my size. But he had the attitude of a gentleman. I said, "And they don't know you're in here."

"*Sí.*" he said. "Not yet."

The guard pulled at my sleeve. "*Pronto!*" he said.

I said, "I'll see what I can do."

Just before we left the cell-block area I looked back. It was an awful somber place to be shut up in—dank and dark and sort of close fitting. About the only thing I could say about it was that the stone walls made it cooler than outside. I glanced back once more toward Norris's cell. I'd have hated to been where he was.

I pulled Jack back as we went through the door into the corridor where all the office doors were. I said, "Ask one of these jailers which office is Davilla's."

He said, "You reckon that's a good idea?"

"Just do it."

He spoke quickly to one of the guards. The jailer just shook his head. He said something back to Jack.

"What?" I said.

Jack said, "This hombre says Davilla ain't here. Ain't

been for a couple of days. Says he don't know anything about no office. Says he generally hangs around the chief."

"Son of a bitch," I said. "If he ain't been here for the last couple of days, who the hell has Obregon been negotiating with?"

Jack said, "That ain't a serious question is it, Justa?"

"I guess not," I said. "We better get back to the hotel and do a little figuring."

But the clerk was waiting for us in the outer office. He said it was urgent that I see Señor Obregon at once. I sent Hays and Ben back to the hotel and Jack and I trotted along behind the clerk, who was about the fastest thing I'd seen so far in Mexico. Going over I couldn't help thinking about the gentleman with the ranch down in Zapata. He'd said he'd had ten men, ten *good* men. I wondered if he meant that the way I'd taken it. *Pistoleros.*

Señor Obregon was not alone. Seated by the side of his desk was an ordinary-looking Mexican in a badly fitting business suit. He introduced the man as *Capitán* Davilla's representative. Making depreciating gestures, he explained, through Jack, that, naturally, Captain Davilla, being an honorable representative of the police couldn't negotiate directly for the price of his honor, that it would have to be done through a representative.

Hell, I was beginning to wonder if this Davilla actually existed. I asked Jack to ask Obregon what the representative's name was, but the lawyer declined on the basis that it was *"inaplicable al caso,"* of no consequence.

Well, it seemed like everything was *inaplicable al caso* except me passing money across the desk. I told Jack to insist on knowing the man's name.

Jack tried, but after a pretty spirited exchange all he could come back with was that the man was willing to be called "José."

"That's just dandy," I said. I was plenty disgusted. I

said, "Tell the lawyer that we heard Davilla wasn't even
in town. Ask him who the hell he's been talking with."

When he'd finished Jack turned back to me and said,
with that natural little smile he wore, "Says the good *capitán* has a ranch outside of town and he's been there resting, healing up from that awful blow yore brother struck
him with."

"Norris? Hurt somebody with a punch?"

Jack pulled a face. "Hell, they goin' to play it for all
it's worth."

I sighed. "Well, when do we start the negotiations?"

Jack spoke to Obregon. The lawyer shook his head and
said something that didn't take long. Jack said to me,
"He says they ain't gonna be no negotiations. Already
been decided. The price is twenty-five hundred dollars.
Flat."

I was startled. I really hadn't expected it to be that
much. It wasn't a great deal of money, but I had the bad
feeling we were being taken and I ain't ever been a big
hand for that.

Jack said, "You realize how much money that is in
Mexico? I don't reckon Davilla makes more than fifty dollars a month. Remember Norris saying he could have
bought himself out of the arrest for a twenty-dollar bill? I
figure our fat friend across the desk is the one looking for
a big payday."

I said, "Tell him it's too much. Tell him we can't pay."

When Jack had finished, Obregon looked at me but
talked to Jack. Jack said, "Our buddy here says it was his
understanding you and your family were *ricos*, rich, very
important businessmen and ranchers in the United States.
He wants to know, if that is true, how such a sum could
be so significant to you when yore brother's life is involved."

I said, "Offer him fifteen hundred. Total. Including his fee."

I didn't have to understand Jack's words. All I had to do was watch the expression on Señor Obregon's face. I don't know whether the outrage was put on or not, but he made a mighty good show of it. You'd of thought we'd insulted him. Kind of made me wonder whose money we were talking about, his or this Captain Davilla. And there was the fact that he was sort of supposed to be my lawyer, although those little finer points didn't seem to count south of the border. But I did find it interesting that, while him and Jack argued back and forth, Obregon never once turned to Davilla's "representative" and asked his opinion. I found that passing strange.

Finally Jack leaned over to me and said, lowly, "I got him down to two thousand. But I think if we stall him a little, couple of days, say, that he'll come down. Maybe to fifteen hundred."

I shook my head. "No, I've got to get Norris out of there before he does or says something to get himself in deeper."

"What shall I tell him?"

It was pushing for five o'clock so I figured the banks would be closed and I'd have to exercise that letter of credit to have the two thousand. I said, "Tell him we'll have the money here tomorrow morning at eleven o'clock."

When Jack had told him the lawyer folded his hands on his desk and looked satisfied. He still hadn't paid any attention to the "representative." I wondered what cantina they'd dug him up out of.

I told Jack to ask when we could expect Norris's release. Obregon looked at me and said, smiling so broadly that for the first time I noticed he had a gold tooth, "Queekly."

I smiled back at him. I said, "Is that a Texas *quickly* or a Mexican *queekly*?"

Apparently he didn't get it for he looked over at Jack and said, *"Cómo?"*

Jack explained what I'd meant, though I reckon he did it a little more polite. Señor Obregon said, "Very queekly. En the *tarde*?"

Jack said, "In the afternoon. That'll be fast if it happens, Justa."

I got up. "Okay," I said. "Tell him we got a deal. We'll be here with the money in the morning."

We shook hands all around, formally, even the "representative," though I was damned if I could see what part he played.

Once outside I asked Jack how much of the two thousand this Captain Davilla would see. "Not a hell of a lot," Jack said. "Obregon will use some of it to grease the local magistrate and some for the chief of police and a little for the guards. The rest will go in his pocket. But that's what you pay his kind for down here. They knows who to grease and how to do it. A gringo can't operate down here like a real Mex. Don't care how long he's lived in the country."

A little wind had blown up and the dust was swirling in the streets. I looked at the horses that were hitched along both sides of the streets. Mostly they were a poor, underfed-looking lot. So were a lot of the people. As we walked to the hotel I could feel eyes following us. Gringos were welcome down there as long as they brought money and left the biggest part of it.

Ben and Hayes received the news in good spirits. They were tired of Mexico and tired of worrying about Norris and just wanted to go home. I felt the same way, but I wasn't going to do any celebrating until I saw Norris safely across the border.

That night I told the other three about the conversation

I'd had with the *caballero*, Señor Elizandro. I asked Jack how far twenty kilometers was.

He said, "Oh, 'bout twelve miles, give or take a little."

I said, "We might ought to do that fellow a good turn and get word back to his ranch that he's in jail."

Ben said, "Let's get Norris out first."

"I'm for that," Hays said.

I said, "I meant after we see to Norris. I could give a peon a few bucks to carry word. Seems like a nice fellow. Told me Norris ought to keep his mouth shut."

Ben laughed. "I want to see that day."

We made an early breakfast and then sat around waiting for the bank to open, which it finally did around ten o'clock. I wasn't too worried about the letter of credit. The night before we'd taken an inventory of what cash we all had and it had come to a little over $2100. So even if they hadn't of cleared our letter of credit we would still have had enough for the payoff.

But it went all right. The only hitch was they didn't have that many dollars on hand and insisted on giving us two thousand of it in pesos. Well, that wasn't too bad although you lost a little on the exchange rate every time you swapped currencies. But considering the money we were already out for nothing it didn't seem like much to worry about.

At eleven o'clock we were all in Señor Obregon's outer office. This time he didn't keep us waiting. To keep things from getting jammed up in the small office, I left Ben and Hays outside. Señor Obregon was at his desk, as was the representative of Captain Davilla. Obregon stood up as soon as we came in, as did the go-between. Obregon said, "Choo have the moneys?"

"I got the moneys," I said. "When do we get my brother?"

"Queekly," he said. "*Primero* the moneys."

I started to hand him a packet of bills, but he drawed back like I was offering a live snake. "No, no," he said. *"Por este hombre."* He pointed at the go-between.

Well, hell, I didn't care if they wanted to have their little game. I handed the money to the representative. Obregon was right over his shoulder, watching as he counted the peso notes. When they were done he looked at me in startlement. He said, *"Es uno sólo."* Only one.

Jack had been told what to say. In Spanish he said, "You get the other one thousand when his brother walks out of that jail."

"Oh, no, no, no, no!" Señor Obregon said. He was shaking his head so violently that a little of his black hair somehow worked its way loose from the plaster of grease he had it held down with and fell around his ears. He was very excited. *"Dos es necesario!"* He held up two fingers. *"Dos. Ahora."*

I said, "No, I'm not going to give you all of it now. One now and one when my brother is out."

Jack didn't even have to translate. Señor Obregon understood well enough. He just kept shaking his head, getting more and more agitated and saying, "No, no, no."

"All right," I said. "I'll just take this back." I reached over and jerked the packet of money out of the hands of the representative, who looked like he needed a drink.

That brought Señor Obregon up short in his tracks. He turned a volley of Spanish loose on Jack. Jack answered him back a time or two and then turned to me. He said, "He spouted a lot of words, but what it comes down to is he feels you be questioning his honor."

I said, "They do set a heap of store about that honor business down here, don't they? No, tell him it has nothing to do with honor. That it's just business. Tell him if I were buying cattle from him I'd do the same—give him half as a binder and the other half on delivery. It's the same.''

That led to another volley between Jack and Obregon. The lawyer just kept looking sourer and sourer, but, finally, he heaved his shoulders and spread his arms out, palms upward. ''Hokay,'' he said.

Jack said, ''He said, 'Hokay.' ''

I just give him a look. Then I passed the money back to the representative. I said to Obregon, ''When?''

''Queekly, queekly,'' he said.

''This afternoon?''

''*Sí,*'' he said. He said something to Jack.

Jack said, ''We're to go back to the hotel and wait. The lawyer here said he'll get word to us when it's time to come collect Norris.''

''All right,'' I said. We done the hand-shaking business again and then gathered up Ben and Hays as we left. Outside, in the street, I turned to study Obregon's office. It was a long, low, whitewashed affair that held a couple more offices besides his. Other lawyers, I reckoned. I looked across the street in the opposite direction. There was a cantina with a bench conveniently placed out front. I said to Hays, ''Ray, go in there in that cantina and get you a cold beer and come set out on that bench and watch the front of Obregon's office. See who comes and goes, especially if he goes. About one o'clock I'll send Ben down here to relieve you.''

We had a lunch of sorts in the hotel café and then went back up to the room to await word about Norris. When two o'clock had come and there was still nothing from Obregon I sent Ben to spell Hays. Ray came in a few minutes later looking hot and sweaty. His shirt was soaked nearly clear through. He said, ''Boy, that beer don't do you no good at all. Might's well not drink the stuff. Goes right through a man's skin and ends up on his shirt.''

I said, "That's fine and dandy. Now tell me what happened."

"Not much of nothin'," he said. "Wasn't but the one transaction. Thet little fat lawyer y'all was jawin' with come out just before Ben come over. But he jest headed down the street."

"He didn't go toward the jail?"

"No sir. Went in the exact opposite direction."

"Nobody went in?"

"Nary a soul. Like I said, wasn't but that one piece of business an' that was the lawyer strollin' away from town."

That left me a good deal troubled. From two until four o'clock was the traditional siesta time. If Obregon was heading home for his nap there wasn't going to be no "queekly" about this business of releasing Norris, not unless he was on his way to see Davilla. I asked Jack what he thought. He shook his head and said, "I've learnt one thang since I commenced doin' business down here in Mexico: believe only one half and doubt the rest."

I said, "But, hell, he's got to deliver Norris. He took my money."

"Did he?" Jack said.

"Hell yes. You were there. You saw it."

He was chewing tobacco and he took a second to spit. He said, "What you reckon my word is worth down here?"

I said, "A man can't just make a deal and not live up to it."

"He can't?" Jack said. "What's to stop him?"

"I am," I said.

Jack spit again. "Then we'd have two of you in the hoosegow."

I studied him. "This is getting serious."

"It always was," Jack said. "These folks ain't got a

whole lot of sand in their craw, but they dearly do love to git a gringo in a tight. They real good at squeezing. Ever notice the folks that carry on the most about honor are generally the ones with the least supply?''

We waited all through that long afternoon, sitting in the room sweating. About five o'clock I sent Hays to spell Ben off. He came in hot and sweaty and angry. He said, ''If that son of a bitch is supposed to be doing something he must be doing it by mail. He come back to his office about four and ain't been a damn thing happen since then. Justa, I'm telling you we got to do something. That fat bastard is taking our money for nothing.''

We had a tub of iced beer sitting in the middle of the room. I took the tin cap off one with a little metal opener that came with it and handed the beer to Ben. I said, ''Sit down and cool off, little brother. We got to let things fall out a little more. Game ain't over. Let's wait and see.''

But by late evening nothing had happened. We had some supper sent up and then, about nine, went wandering around the town. Ever' so often we'd see a policeman slouching against a post, looking like a soldier with his carbine slung over his shoulder. I finally sent Jack over to see if he could find out where Davilla was or where he lived. After a few minutes Jack came back. He shrugged. ''Man says he don't know where Davilla is. Says he's probably out arresting a gringo. Wasn't all that friendly. Says he thinks Davilla has got a ranchero out south of town somewheres.''

We wandered into a few cantinas, but all we got was what we'd got before—suspicious looks and overpriced whiskey. The high-class cantinas were full of businessmen in suits whispering together. The cheaper joints were full of drunk peons and *charros* who looked at us resentfully. I reckoned in the latter it wouldn't have been no trouble at all for a lone Texan to get in a fight. But there was four of us and that kind of balanced out the odds. We saw few Americans, and since they didn't pay us any mind, we replied with the same courtesy.

We got back to the hotel about eleven. I said, "Let's get to bed." I looked around grimly. "Tomorrow we're going to make something happen. I don't know what, but something."

Jack said, "Go slow, Justa. Remember what I said earlier."

"I remember," I said.

4

Obregon's clerk said we'd have to wait, but I wasn't in a waiting mood. We shouldered him out of the way and Jack and I opened the door to the lawyer's office and went in. Obregon was leaning over a mirror on his desk, a pair of scissors in his hand, trimming his mustache. He looked up in astonishment as we came in. *"Perdone ustedes."* That was kind of a strange thing to say considering it was us doing the busting in and, by rights, us who ought to be asking *his* pardon.

But right then I wasn't in any mood to worry about the niceties of the situation. I put my hands on his desk and leaned into his face. I said, "Señor Obregon, where is my brother? He should have been released yesterday."

Wasn't no need for Jack to translate. I reckon the good señor had been expecting us. He said, "Es *complicaciones. Muy malo.*"

I said, "It's gonna get much more than very bad if you

don't produce my brother. You got my money, now keep your word. Tell him, Jack."

I'm sure Jack did it a good deal more diplomatically than I'd stated the case. Señor Obregon just leaned back in his chair and then made a short reply.

Jack said to me, "Would you like some coffee?"

"Hell no! I want my brother." I was having a good deal of trouble keeping my temper in check.

Jack said, "Well, Señor Obregon generally has some 'bout this time. He hopes you'll forgive him if he goes ahead."

Sure enough, about then the clerk came in with a pot of coffee and three of those small cups they drink that stuff out of. I waved him away, but Jack took a cup. I said, "Jack, get after his ass."

He gave me a warning look and said, quietly, "Take it easy, Justa."

I finally sat down and waited for them to finish their coffee and get to talking. Jack said, "Señor Obregon says he's sorry 'bout the hold up, but Davilla is giving him some trouble."

"I'll bet," I said dryly. "What comes next?"

"Wahl," Jack said, "he claims Davilla has done got his honor upset again because we ain't come across with all the money."

"I'll bet on that, too."

"That's what he claims."

"Ask him when he saw Davilla."

When he came back to me he said, "He says him and Davilla had a long talk yesterday afternoon and then again last night at Davilla's place."

"Davilla is supposed to have come here?"

Jack pulled a face. "That's what he claims."

"Then this place must have a back door we don't know nothing about." I looked around the whitewashed walls.

"I don't see a back door, nor a side door. You see one, Jack?"

He was giving me a kind of strained look. He said, "Justa, take it easy. Don't call him no liar. We on a little muddy ground right now. Listen, he says if you fork over another five hunnert he's purty sure he can deliver Norris this afternoon."

"He was sure yesterday. What about that?"

Jack was still talking low, trying to get me not to make any disturbance. He said, "Don't go to challengin' him, Justa. This ain't the time er the place fer it. I'll tell him you'll thank it over."

I shook my head. "No. I'm going to give him the five hundred." I dug in my pocket and handed Jack a wad of peso notes. "Count off the right amount and hand it over to him. You know how to figure it better than I do."

Jack did as he was bade. The lawyer picked up the money and counted it. Then he looked at me and said, "Hokay."

I didn't say anything.

And this time I didn't bother with the hand-shaking. I let Jack handle that chore. I was already out in the street by the time he caught up with me. I said, "Jack, I got a hard job for you. I want you to find out where this Davilla feller lives. Or where he is. I want a look at him."

"You want me to start now?"

"Yeah. Make up some story that ain't got nothing to do with this."

"All right," he said. He veered off and started back toward the police station while I continued on toward the hotel.

The minute I walked into the room Ben said, "Well? What'd the son of a bitch have to say?"

"Shut up," I said. I sat down at the table we had in the middle of the room and poured myself out a shot of whiskey. While I sipped it I let my mind run. An idea was starting to come into my mind, but the first thing I needed was someone who spoke Spanish like a Mex and who looked enough like a Mex to get by except on close inspection. I said to Ben, "I want you to go down to the telegraph office. I reckon it's at the train depot. Get off a wire to Lew Vara. Tell him I need him in Monterrey and I need him right now."

Ben got up. He said, "What good is a Texas sheriff down here?"

I said, "Just do it."

Then I turned to Hays. "Ray, I want you to go find whatever passes for a mercantile store in this place and buy about ten pounds of black powder. I also want you to get about ten feet of primer cord and a hammer and a handful of tenpenny nails."

Ben was standing with his hand on the doorknob. He said, "What the hell are you up to?"

"I don't know," I said. "Maybe I'm taking out a little insurance. Now go on and telegraph Lew."

He said, "What makes you think he can just up and come down here? Leave the town without a sheriff for three or four days."

"Be the same if he got the grippe or a bad cold." I lit a cigarillo. "Now get going. Both of you. I may have some more errands when you get back."

After they'd left I sat and smoked and drank and thought. I wasn't a man who came to anger easy, but when I did I was prone to take a pretty steady stand on it. And I wasn't a man who allowed people to break their promises to me or to play fast and loose with my family's welfare or my family's money. And I was starting to get the idea that I had run into some gentlemen who had that very thought in mind. In fact I was beginning to get the firm impression that I might be dealing with some thieves and scoundrels.

And I didn't like that.

Obregon hadn't kept his word about anything so far and I was already out $1740, not counting expenses and what I'd spent on petty bribes. I figured I'd better go to making some plans that didn't depend so heavily on Señor Obregon.

I didn't know for certain, in detail, what those plans was going to be, but I was sort of beginning to marshal my personnel and ordnance for whatever might come to mind.

Of course I realized that the odds were way against me and that I was operating in a strange country where I didn't know all the rules and style of play and couldn't expect any help, but sometimes you get so fed up you don't pay much attention to the conditions.

I was about at that point.

Of course they might release Norris the next day and then all my planning would have been in vain, but Dad had always said that the brain was just another muscle and needed exercise just like your pecker.

I'd always taken those words to heart.

So even if I didn't need my plan, my brain would have got a good workout just thinking it up.

Hays was back first. He came in carrying the black powder and the other materials like he was lugging a newborn baby. He set it down carefully on the table and said, "Boss, I reckon you know that black powder is dangerous. Especially the older it gits. An' I reckon this is some old. Hell, ain't nobody uses that stuff no more. What the hell you goin' to do with it?"

I just said, "I forgot something. You reckon you can find some kerosene?"

He looked at me slack-mouthed. "Coal oil? Hell, boss, we got some of that in the lamps. They gettin' low? Hotel supposed to handle that."

I said, "I figure to need about a gallon."

"A gallon of coal oil?"

"Yeah. Now."

He went out the door shaking his head. The last I heard him say was, "Well, if that don't beat all."

Ray was a man who needed things explained to him in some detail. I didn't feel like it right then.

Ben got back a little bit later. He lounged in a chair, eyeing the stuff on the table. Finally he took a look in the cloth sack holding the black powder. But that wasn't enough to satisfy his curiosity. He had a to get a dab out with his fingers and smell it and taste it. He said, "You planning on loading up a cannon and putting a ball through the walls of that jail?"

"Maybe," I said.

He poured himself out a drink of whiskey. "Well," he said, "let's do something. Even if it's wrong. This sittin' around waitin' on some fucking crooked lawyer to do something is making me jumpy."

I said, "We'll see what happens this afternoon. We'll go that far. When Hays and Jack Cole get back we'll go eat."

Hays came back not long afterwards carrying a gallon can of kerosene. He set it against the wall and said to Ben, "You know what thet is?"

Ben put his nose up in the air. "Well, judgin' from the smell of it I'd say kerosene."

"Coal oil. Lamp oil. Yore brother sent me fer it. Now what do you make of that?"

Ben shrugged. "I reckon," he said, "he was afraid we'd run short."

"Short?" Hays looked at him. "Heve you both lost yore minds? I never heered of fetchin' in yore own coal oil."

Ben said, "You supposed to in Mexico."

Hays looked at him hard for a moment. Then he said, "Aw, you joshin' me." But he looked back and forth from me and Ben, unsure. That was the problem with Hays; he was too easy to kid. He said, "Bet you it's got somethin' to do with that black powder, ain't it, boss?"

"No," I said. Then, "I wonder where the hell Jack is?"

We waited another hour, but there was no sign of Jack. Neither did any word come from Obregon. The latter didn't surprise me because I'd already made my mind up that Señor Obregon had his own plans. But I was getting considerably worried about Jack. Finding out about Davilla shouldn't have taken him as many hours as he'd been gone.

We passed the afternoon drinking, smoking, pacing, and looking out the window that faced on the main street. If you craned your neck out far enough and looked southeast you could just see the jail sticking up like a rock amidst the adobe and stucco houses and huts that surrounded it. Monterrey was like a rabbit's warren with little streets running every which way. Some of them led to a destination, some of them led nowhere. Seldom was one straight its entire length. Most of them curved around a house or a tree or a wall or just curved for no good reason.

By seven that night nothing had happened—no sign, no signal from Obregon. We went down and ate dinner. Didn't seem like the menu ever changed. You always had beans and you always had peppers and you always had tortillas. About the only choice you had was whether you wanted the tough, stringy beef raw or half-raw. Ben said, "I never thought I'd hear myself say it, but this swill almost makes me homesick for Buttercup's cooking."

Jack came back at about half past eight. He said, "Any word from Obregon?"

I shook my head.

He said, "Wahl, I ain't surprised. I figured this matter

was gonna take a week at the rate of about five hunnert a day. Wonder what his excuse will be in the morning?''

I said, ''What about you? I was getting a little worried.''

He sat down and poured himself out a drink of whiskey. He'd taken in the supplies I'd sent Hays for, but he hadn't said anything. He said, ''Wahl, it took some little doin'. Most folks around here don't like to talk 'bout Davilla. They more or less afeered of him. I finally found me a *charro* who'd worked on his ranchero and got him about half drunk and give him ten dollars and got a little help. Davilla lives on a small place about two miles south of town. Pretty poor-looking place. Seems to keep mostly horses and I don't reckon he's got enough land for cattle. I rode out there with this here *charro*. He was nearly scairt to death. But we got up close enough fer me to peek in the winder. Davilla was there, all right. Jest sittin' in a chair havin' a drink. Had his uniform on.''

''What does he look like?''

''Aw, he's a pretty well set up feller. Couldn't tell how tall he was 'cause he never stood up whilst I was thar an' my *charro* was gettin' mighty anxious. Got a little mustache. Supposed to be plenty mean.''

I smoked for a moment, thinking. Then I said, ''Jack, in the morning I want you and Ben to saddle up and ride down to that little village that Señor Elizandro comes from. Find his ranch and go talk to his men. Tell them he's in jail and wants them to come to me. See how many you can bring back with you. Ben, you look them over carefully. I got the impression from Elizandro that they might be *pistoleros*. Look 'em over carefully. Don't bring no peons back.''

Jack looked around and then said, carefully, ''What are you planning, Justa?''

''I don't know,'' I said, just as carefully. ''But I'm getting tired of this foolishness and I'm getting tired of my brother in jail.''

Jack said, "I wouldn't get too rash. They say it ain't real smart to play against a stacked deck.''

"I got to play what I been dealt, Jack. Look, I ain't asking you to take part in anything you can't handle. We already got an understanding about that. I'm just asking you to go with Ben because you speak the lingo.''

"What about Obregon?''

"Oh, I'm going to see him in the morning.''

"How you going to get along without me?''

"That clerk of his speaks considerable English.''

"Yeah, but you cain't depend on how he might interpet.''

I shook my head. "Doesn't matter. I ain't goin' to Obregon for results. I done found out how much good that does. I'm just going because he'd expect me to show up. I could probably tell you right now what he's going to say. 'There's been complications and give me some more money.' ''

"I would reckon," Jack said. "It'd be the same in any language.''

I didn't sleep good that night. For one thing, I was uncertain if I was doing the right thing. It was my bet that Obregon had gotten on to how much money we had. I could probably settle the whole thing by just turning over to him every cent.

Except that went against my grain. I'd been prepared to buy Norris out, but I hadn't been prepared to be played for a fool. I didn't like that one little bit.

And there was the matter of my marriage, which was getting closer and closer. I was afraid to count the days, scared there might not be enough time. I'd disappointed Nora so many times before I doubted she'd stand for another time. She might not run off with another Kansas City drummer, but she'd run off from me.

And I couldn't have that.

I was in Señor Obregon's office at promptly ten o'clock. Ben and Jack had ridden out early and I'd left Hays with instructions to meet every train coming in from the general direction of Blessing and to find Lew. I didn't really expect him too soon, but there was a chance he might make it by nightfall.

Obregon's clerk, in his heavily accented English, told me I'd have to wait. It was about what I'd expected so I took a chair and studied the clerk behind his little desk. He looked about like a law clerk ought to look. He was thin and nervous, in his early twenties, and wore a shiny suit with a foulard tie. I figured Obregon paid him damn aught little, but he didn't need to worry. He'd make it all up later in what he could learn about deceit and corruption and thievery from his boss.

After about half an hour Obregon opened the door and let me into his office. I had been curious as to how he was going to play it. This day he was contrite and worried and full of solicitude for the worry and trouble and anxiety the whole matter had caused me and my family. Not to mention the money.

I took his apology in the spirit it was given and then explained, as best I could, that Jack had been called away and that it would be necessary for his clerk to interpret for us.

Well, that was just pie for him. Anything he could do to accommodate the Señor Williams was way too little. And would I like coffee?

We talked and it was a sad tale he had to tell me and no mistake. It had all been perfect, it had been arranged down almost to the last detail. At no later than five o'clock the previous evening he, himself, Obregon, the lawyer, had, by his own hands, had my brother, Norris Williams, at the very front door of the jail. Ready to step into the street a free man, ready to be welcomed back into the embrace of his family, ready to forgive and to be forgotten. And then . . .

Señor Obregon had spread his arms expressively.

But what had happened?

"Ah . . ." he'd said. "Ches. Wha' hoppen? Ches."

Turned out that, at the very last second, the chief of police had intervened and demanded that his office be recognized in the arrangement. It was truly a very bad state of affairs, but what could one do?

Naturally, I was as sympathetic as all get-out. I asked what it would cost to satisfy the chief's office and, not too surprisingly, turned out it was another five hundred dollars.

I already had the peso notes counted out in my pocket. I just took them and slid them across to Obregon. But before he could reach out his delicate little fat fingers I asked about seeing my brother.

Well, that took a little more negotiating, but in the end I let loose of my end of the packet of peso notes and Señor Obregon swooped them up. We exchanged "hokays" and then I left, with the understanding that I could see Norris right away. Indeed, Señor Obregon's clerk would accompany me at that very moment. The only thing the señor was curious about was why would I want to see my brother when it was almost a certainty he'd be out that very afternoon, God willing.

I said, wryly, "I just want to be the first to give him the good news."

Getting in went pretty much as it had the time before— stepping around the lounging policemen, giving a five-dollar bill to the officer at the desk, waiting for the jailers to take me back to the cells. The only difference this time was that I was wearing my side gun. I entrusted it to the care of Luís, Obregon's clerk, who would await my return. It amused me to see how nervous it made the young man to accept the gun. He was a serious hombre, this Luís, and he obviously considered a gun on the same par with a live rattlesnake. But he took it and, at my direction, shoved it down in his waistband. I think even that made him nervous for fear it might go off and blow away some of his delicate parts.

I paid particular attention to the search the two jailers gave me before letting me into the cell area. They just sort of carelessly patted me down, the kind of search that might have revealed a shotgun but not much else. They paid no attention to my boots at all.

Once we were inside and the door shut I gave them each a ten-dollar bill. It astonished them. I think they'd expected to get the one bribe and that was to cover my brother's entire stay. To now get another was two Christmases in one year. I reckoned ten dollars was about a month's wages for each of them. But I wanted their goodwill and their carelessness—especially their carelessness.

I had a cigarillo and a lucifer match out as we stepped into the run between the cells. I could see that Señor Elizandro had come to the front of his cell as soon as we'd entered. He was standing close to the bars. I stopped when we got right in front of him. My escorts made no protest.

"Howdy," I said.

"Buenos días, señor," he said. *"Cómo le va?"*

"Very good," I said.

I handed him the cigarillo. While I was lighting it I said, "I've sent word to your ranch where you are."

Puffing at the cigarillo to get it drawing, he said, "Good."

I said, "You say you have good men?"

"Very good. Very loyal."

"How many will come?"

"All," he said, exhaling smoke.

"It will be tomorrow night or the night after."

"Good," he said. "It's better a leetle before six o'clock of the evening."

"Why?"

"They change guards at six. They are tired, careless. *Sabe?*"

"Yes."

One of the jailers nudged me tentatively. I nodded at the *caballero*. He said, *"Mil gracias,"* and held up the *cigarillo* as if that was what he was giving me a thousand thanks for.

Norris at least got off his bunk when I came up to his cell. But he still looked sullen, though his appearance had improved. Either he'd been allowed to shave or someone had shaved him. And it appeared they'd brought him fresh clothes.

But he was still blaming me for getting himself into a mess. More than that, though, I think he blamed me because I'd come to help him out. Norris wasn't one to ever much let on he needed help. Of any kind.

He said, "Well?"

I said, "Get over here to these bars so I don't have to yell."

"Those guards don't speak English."

"Dammit, Norris, move!"

The guards were keeping a respectful distance, demonstrating once again how loud money talked in Mexico.

He finally came grudgingly over to stand in front of me. I said, in a half whisper, "I'm getting you out of here in the next couple of days. Can't say exactly when. Just be ready."

"Buying me out?" He said it with a sneer.

"No, they won't sell. Apparently you're pretty valuable, judging from the way the price keeps going up."

His face took on hope. "Legally?"

"Well, sort of." I wasn't about to tell Norris what I had planned. His convictions being what they were he might feel it his duty to tip off the chief of police.

He said, "What do you mean, sort of?"

I said, "Well, in trying to save some time we might have to cut some corners. You know how this Mexican judicial system is. Could take forever if we just followed the letter of the law."

He slammed his palm up against a bar. "Justa, I want my rights! I want to be heard on this matter! I want the ones that should be in this cell to be occupying it."

I said, "Just simmer down. That's exactly what we're trying to arrange, a prisoner exchange."

"I don't know what you mean."

"You don't have to. I got to go now. You need anything?"

"Yes! An American lawyer."

"Just take it easy, Norris. It will all work out the way you want it to."

"And are you looking into the clear title of our five thousand acres in Laredo?"

I just stared at him. Here he was, rotting away in jail, and he was worrying about a piece of land that wasn't worth half the money I'd already paid out. I said, "You bet, Norris. Got Hays working on it right now."

"Hays? Justa, you can't mean you've put Hays on such a delicate matter. I can't believe that."

I said, mildly, "He can't do no worse than you did, can he?"

I left him staring after me, openmouthed. For once he had nothing to say.

My escorts jabbered at me all the way back and then

opened the door for me and escorted me through with great courtesy. It's very easy to make friends in Mexico. All you got to do is buy them.

Outside, I retrieved my six-gun from Luís, who looked only too happy to be rid of the dangerous thing. As we crossed the street I asked him if it was certain my brother would be released that afternoon.

It made him more nervous than he usually appeared. He said, "Es possible. Es *muy* possible."

"Sure," I said.

I veered off and headed for the hotel. I didn't expect Ben and Jack to be back yet, but, it being noontime, I figured I knew where to find Hays.

He was in the hotel café, eating watermelon and drinking beer. I sat down across from him and eyed his meal. I said, "You'll piss for a week eating like that."

He said, "Too hot for anything else, boss. When in hell we gettin' outta here?"

I signaled for a waiter and then said to Hays, "Pretty quick now. There is one complication, however."

He was busy spitting out watermelon seeds. Finally he said, "Wha's 'at?"

I said, "Well, they're willing to let Norris go, but I've got to leave somebody in his place until the trial. Kind of like a hostage, you know."

He looked up, holding a slice of watermelon halfway to his mouth.

I said, shrugging, "And it has to be a gringo. Of course I can't give orders to Jack Cole, he don't work for me. And Ben's my brother so there ain't no use swapping one brother for another. I'd do it except I'm getting married." I looked up at him. "So . . ."

Like I say, it ain't no fun teasing Hays. He'll bite on anything. If he'd been a fish he'd have swallowed the first hook got dangled in front of his mouth. His eyes got round and his hand started shaking. He swallowed hard. "Boss, now you be funnin' me, ain't you? Tell me you be funnin' me."

I shook my head. "No, you can relax Hays. I tried, but they wouldn't go for it. Said I'd have to throw in two good saddle horses as boot."

"Aw . . ." he said. He tried to act like he'd known all along, but he couldn't keep the relief out of his face. He said, "I knowed you was joshin'. They don't let a feller do that. Trade one fer the other'n."

I said, "Actually, they do. Only reason I didn't do it was because I figured you'd rather be layin' up there in a bunk eating and sleeping and not having any work to do. I know you, Hays."

I ate some tacos and drank some beer and then went out looking for a general mercantile that sold guns. Took me three tries to find what I was after, but I finally found a kind of gun shop. There I bought two .44 caliber derringers. They were used and the rifling in the short little barrels was gone, but they'd serve the purpose. I got them and six cartridges for thirty dollars. It was a touch high, especially when I didn't figure to get but the one use out of them.

I went back to the hotel to wait out the afternoon. It was becoming a familiar routine and I knew it would go as the others had gone—with no Norris and no word.

I just sat there drinking whiskey and smoking cigarettes and wishing that Señor Obregon would prove me wrong just this once. But I knew he wouldn't; I knew what the son of a bitch was up to. Jack had known right from the start. He was going to bleed me as long as he could and then tell me to either get gone or join Norris.

The afternoon passed just like the other two. Hays came in, but he took one look at my face and retired to a chair and stared out the window at the business on the street.

Then, and a good deal to my surprise, there came a knock at the door. Hays opened it and there stood Obregon's clerk. The first thought that hit me was that I had wasted money on powder and kerosene and derringers and sending for Lew for nothing. Obregon was going to keep his word.

Luís looked extremely nervous. He refused to come in, just stood in the doorway twisting his hands. He said, "The Señor Obregon has sent me. He regrets, he regrets—"

"He regrets what?"

He got hold of himself enough then to deliver his practiced speech. He said, "The señor regrets that there have been complications. Also at the last moment. It will be but a small delay and he begs you be patient. Unfortunately, he cannot tell you theese thengs himself because he will be from the city tomorrow. When he returns, on the day following, he bids you call on him. He is certain of success. It may require perhaps a little, a leetle, uh . . ."

I helped him. "Little more money?"

He looked grateful. "Yes. Thank you and good day, señor."

I smiled thinly at him. "What about me seeing my brother?"

"Oh!" He looked like a schoolboy that had forgot part of his lesson. "The Señor Obregon wishes me to tell you you may visit your brother at any time."

I said, "Well, you just tell the good lawyer that I appreciate his help. Tell him I will most certainly see him on his return. He will be back the day after tomorrow?"

"Oh, yes."

"Fine," I said. I gave him that thin smile again.

When he was gone Hays said, "What if he runs off with the money, boss?"

"Oh, he ain't going to do that," I said. "He'll be back

for some more milk. He's just trying to make me a little anxious is all. Figures that makes the milk easier to get.''

I settled back comfortably and poured myself a drink. For a second I'd been confused, but now I was content to know that Obregon was dependably undependable.

Hays said, "Well, what you reckon?"

I said, "I reckon some folks around here have gone to the thin edge of the outside. Only they ain't discovered it yet."

Hays said, "You sound downright cheerful."

I said, "I am. Never did like my business being handled by other people. Say, ain't you supposed to be down at the train depot meeting Lew Vara?"

"Next train ain't 'til seven an' it's jest goin' five now."

I said, "You always got an excuse, ain't you, Ray."

He left and I did some more waiting. I reckoned I'd done more waiting in the last several days than I'd ever been guilty of in my whole life before. One thing I was doing was keeping my mind carefully away from Nora and our wedding. I didn't truthfully know how many days off it was, but I knew it was getting uncomfortably close. The reason I couldn't pinpoint the time exactly was because I didn't actually know what the date was and didn't have a calendar handy to find out. Of course I could have figured it out by counting backwards to a day the date of which I knew. But I was in no hurry to do so. I figured to handle one worry at a time.

Jack and Ben came back at about six o'clock looking dusty and tired. They came in and slumped down at the table and reached for the whiskey. I let them get a drink apiece down before I asked how it had went.

Jack shook his head. He said, "Depend on a Mex to git it wrong. 'Twas more like twenty *miles* than twenty kilometers."

"Hot as hell," Ben said.

I said, "Hell, I didn't send you on no pleasure ride. Did you find the damn ranch?"

"We found it," Jack said. "Not a hell of a big spread. Not the kind of place you'd need ten men to work."

Ben laughed.

I said, "I ain't interested in Señor Elizandro's managing talents. I want to know about his men. Will they come?"

"Seven will," Jack said.

"He said he had ten."

Jack glanced at Ben and then came back to me. "Justa, I thank you ought to know this here Elizandro ain't pre-zactly what you might call in the cattle business. At least not *his* cattle. Near as I could figure out, the bunch had a run-in with the *rurales* and three of 'em didn't make it back."

"You saying Elizandro is a cattle thief?"

Ben said, "It ain't that so much, Justa. I mean he ain't no out-and-out cattle thief. Jack says he's what they call a *politico* down here. Seems he's mixing in politics at a pretty high level. Like taking on the governor of the state of Coahuila. At least that's what Jack thinks they were talking about."

I said, "Hell, I don't care if he's running for president. Or whatever. You say his men are coming?"

Jack took another drink. "Yeah," he said. "Fact of the business is they'd just about figured out where he was 'fore we showed up an' was comin' in to git him anyways. But I hope you taken note of what Ben was saying about him bein' a *politico*. I figure you're plannin' on takin' him out along with Norris in return for the use of his men?"

"Of course."

Jack shifted uneasily. "I just hope you un'erstand that it gits a mite more serious breakin' a *politico* out than if it was jest Norris. We liable to draw considerable more attention than you'd bargained for."

I said, "Hell, a jailbreak is a jailbreak. It's gonna make them hot as hell anyway. Besides, once the deed is done Elizandro is going one way and we're going the other."

Jack poured himself out another drink with a hand that was none too steady. He said, shaking his head, "Wahl, for all our sakes I hope you do be right."

I said to Ben, "His men—are they *pistoleros?*"

"They sure as hell ain't ranch hands. I'd say they're about half bodyguards, half troublemakers and half thieves. Of one kind or another."

"Are they any good?"

"Three are pretty good. The rest just so-so."

"What do mean, 'pretty good'? As good as Hays?"

He gave me a look like I ought to go back to school. He said, "Hell, no! Hell, Hays is somewhere near as good as I am. Well, not really, but kind of. They better than Norris, let me put it that way."

"The rest?"

"They're about as good as Norris. Only difference is they'll shoot without talking matters over first."

I looked at Jack. "When are they due?"

"Sometime 'fore noon. They is a place jest outsida town. Kind of a cross between a boardin'house an' a whorehouse an' a saloon where most of the Mex cowhands put up. Ben an' I is supposed to meet 'em out there. I din' know if you wanted them comin' into town an' being seen with all of us."

I said, "I didn't, Jack. You done good."

Ben said, "When do we get to know what you got planned? Some of us are gettin' a little curious."

I said, "I ain't altogether certain myself. I just know we are going to get Norris out of that jail. I'd druther wait until Lew gets here before going in to what little I got planned."

"You figure he'll get in tonight?"

I took out the pocket watch ol' Howard had given me for my eighteenth birthday. It was going on for eight o'clock. I said, "We'll know soon. Last train is due in here just about now. At least the last one due in from up our way."

Then it wasn't long before they showed up. Lew came in ahead of Hays carrying a small valise. It reminded me I'd forgot to tell him to bring his horse. It was a matter of no import, seeing we were going to have to buy a couple anyway.

It was good to see him. I had Ben and I had Hays, but it was damn reassuring to see another gun I knew I could depend on.

We shook and howdied and then he turned a chair around, straddled it and pulled up to the table. I poured him out a drink. He downed half of it and then said, "Well, I figured you couldn't get along without my help. I knowed what was in that telegram 'fore I even opened it."

I said, "Careful. You are liable to break your arm patting yourself on the back so hard."

I studied him. Yes, he could pass for Mex. And, God knows, he spoke it well enough. Plus he had that air of authority about him that would work well on the Mexican policemen.

He finished his drink and held out his glass. I poured it full and he said, "Well, what the hell is up?"

As best I could I explained what all had gone on since we'd reached Monterrey and how I didn't figure it was going to get any better.

He said, "So they playin' you for a milk cow, huh?"

"Appears so."

He drank and said, "I ain't surprised. Did you think of trying another lawyer?"

I shrugged. "I don't think it would make much difference. Neither does Jack."

They'd been introduced when Lew had come in and now Lew looked over at Jack. Jack just shrugged. "We were already in considerable money before it began to appear that Obregon was givin' us a fast shuffle. I took him on what recommendations I could git. After him we'd of just been drawin' blind."

Lew came back to me. "So now you figure to bust Norris out."

I nodded.

He rubbed his jaw. "What's the jail look like?"

It was Ben that spoke. "Like a damn fort. Enough damn police around there to hold a convention."

Lew raised his eyebrows at me. "Don't sound too good."

I said, "It ain't all that bad. Plus we got some help. Seven other guns that Ben rates fair."

"Well, what's the plan and when do we do it?"

I said, "It's not all thought out down to the last detail, but this is what I got so far."

Then I told them what I had planned.

When I was through, nobody said anything for the longest minute. Finally Hays blew out a breath and said, "Wahl, boss, it's bodacious if it ain't nuthin' else."

Lew said, "I ain't exactly sure where I come in."

I said, "Your job will be to gather up that *Capitán* Davilla. We're taking him with us the first fifty miles or so."

Lew frowned. "You sure you wouldn't rather have me at the actual jailbreak?"

Of course he was saying that I might could use his gun, but I shook my head. "I'm gonna get you a uniform. That way you'll catch Davilla off guard. Besides, you can ride off with him and wait for us outside of town without anybody thinking anything about it. Plus he's liable to be a handful.''

"How am I going to git to him?"

"We're going to do it at siesta. He'll be home.''

Jack said, "Sounds, Justa, like it will mainly be you inside that jail.''

"Me and Hays," I said.

Hays made a slight moan, but Ben said, "Like hell! Norris is my brother too.''

I said, "I know that, fool. But the most dangerous part of this whole operation is going to be when we hit the street. Ben, I've got to have my best gun out there. And that's you. You're going to have to direct the fire of yourself and those *pistoleros* and get us across that street and to the horses.''

Lew lit a cigarillo. We both smoked the same kind. He said, "I can see it all except about the money. Don't you reckon you be pushing things a bit on that?''

I said, firmly, "Nope. We didn't start this fight. And I'm damn certain we ain't going to be the loser by it. Now, Lew, I know I'm asking considerable of you. I've asked you to leave your post as a lawman back in Blessing and I've asked you to come down here and help us commit an illegal act. If you feel like you hadn't ought to have any part of it, I'll understand and they'll be no hard feelings.''

He looked at me for a moment and then laughed. He said, "Just so long as you un'erstand this be the first illegal act I ever committed. What, you gone loco, Justa? I will be awhile getting the books balanced with you.''

I said, "Well, you don't owe me nothing. But I'm still much obliged.''

Jack said, "What's next?''

"Nothing tonight," I said. "In the morning I want you and Ben to go over and meet those *pistoleros*. Tell them they got to stay put and not be seen gathered up in one bunch. In the morning Lew and I are going to ride out and look over the best escape route. Hays, Lew will have to use your horse. You just stay put in the hotel. We're going to do this little matter day after tomorrow sometime between three and four o'clock. I can't pinpoint the time exactly. I wish to hell Obregon hadn't gone out of town, else we'd try it tomorrow. It makes me nervous, those *pistoleros* hanging around town. Jack, you got to really look after them. We got a bunch of loose pieces in this plan, but they is the loosest."

Jack said, "I'll do what I can."

I sent Hays down to get another bed to be moved in with Ben and Jack, leaving Lew to bunk with me. As much as I depended on the other three it was good to have Lew with me, someone I could talk matters through with, the good and the bad. Sometimes I had to hide the risks from the others, but I could never have done that with Lew.

After the others had left and we were settled down over a last whiskey, he said, "Boy, you doin' a pretty good juggling act here. Getting me a uniform, that police captain, getting to Obregon, keepin' them *pistoleros* tied down, not to mention the actual jailbreak and escape its ownself."

I grimaced. "Don't remind me. That fucking Obregon. He picked a hell of a time to be out of town."

"Where you gonna git me a uniform, anyway?"

"I don't know," I said. I stood up. "Let's get some shut-eye."

5

Elizandro had recommended just before six o'clock because of the changing of the guards. In some ways that would have been best: it would have meant that the guards would have been less alert, that there would have been more confusion and that night would have fallen on our getaway a good deal sooner.

But it just didn't fit in with the rest of my plans. For that reason I'd chosen to act just before the end of siesta, somewhere around half past three or so. That would at least keep most of the townspeople out of the way and off the streets.

Lew and I rode out the next morning right after breakfast. Because it was the closest route from the jail, we rode out toward the west. Coming through town I was gratified to see that our way took us down a lot of narrow little streets. And some of them were crooked as a dog's hind leg. That was going to make it that much harder on a catch party to see exactly which way we'd gone.

Once we cleared the main part of town the countryside was mostly rolling, with small houses patched around here and there. But about a mile out of town was a little range of hills covered with stunted mesquite trees and cedar and high weeds and bramble. We rode into its midst and looked back after we'd topped one of the little hills. The city was nearly invisible, which meant we'd be invisible to anyone looking from the city. I said, "If we can make it up to here without being spotted they ain't going to have the slightest idea which way we went."

"Yeah," Lew said, leaning his arms on the pommel of his saddle. "If."

I said, "I figure to leave them in a pretty good state of confusion, with maybe a bunch of them shot up. I think it's going to take them a pretty good little while to get themselves a catch party put together. And then Elizandro and his bunch will be going in a different direction."

"Yeah," Lew said. He spit. "I ain't so much worried about that first mile as I am the next ninety-nine. They got telegraphs in this country, you know."

We turned and rode down the little hill. As we footed it I was grateful to see another little line running off at an angle from the ones we'd just crossed. They appeared to be about a half mile away. We put our horses into a lope and crossed the intervening plain in good speed. By veering to our left a little we could get around the little crest of hills and put them between us and any pursuit. I could see another broken line ahead, to the north. They appeared bigger, but they were also more barren. A man never wanted to take uncovered high ground when he was fleeing. He'd stick out against the sky like a sore thumb. No, we'd round that next range.

But I could see, and from what I remembered of the train ride, the further we got from Monterrey, the more desolate the country was going to get. We'd need to bring plenty of water and grub.

We stopped to let the horses crop at the burned grass while we surveyed the countryside. I said, "I know they got telegraphs, Lew. But they got to locate us first. And then we're going to have *el capitán* for trade goods when they do."

Lew spit again. "Shit. You reckon they going to give a damn about one Mex policeman when a bunch of gringos is to be had? And them carrying money? You ask me, I think dragging this Davilla along is just extra weight."

To the east I could see that the country was much flatter with less cover. Of course our main direction was north, but I figured we'd come out of town to the west, swing northwest around the growth of hills and then begin to bear up north. I said, "Yeah, this pretty much looks like the route. So you don't much want to take Davilla?"

"Don't see the point."

I laughed. "Norris might want to punch him again."

He said, "All right, we bring him a mile. Then we let Norris bust him one in the mouth. After that I shoot him. Takes care of it all."

I looked at him. I said, "You'd do it, wouldn't you?"

He said, "I've knowed hombres like this Davilla. He probably needs shootin' on about a hunnert different counts. Better late than never."

I was thoughtful for a moment. "I hear he's a pretty tough character. Second in command to the *jefe*, the police chief. But the chief is old and fat and ain't about to lead a chase. But this Davilla will."

"Just let me handle it."

"I'll think about it." I reined my horse around. "Let's get back to town. I got a bunch of details to sack up."

Ben was in the room when we got back to the hotel. I asked him where Jack was. He pulled a face and said,

"He's settin' on top of Elizandro's men. They about ready to go and blow that jail up right now. Justa, I think you better get over there and talk to them. I don't see how we can hold them down until tomorrow afternoon. And they do be gettin' liquored up."

"Oh, hell!" I said. "This is all I need." I looked around. "Lew, I reckon you better come with me. Jack speaks the lingo like you do, but he ain't exactly a commanding figure." I turned to my brother. "Ben, I want you to go and buy the three best horses you can find."

"Three?"

"Yeah, one for Lew, one for Norris and one for a packhorse. And make sure that packhorse is as fast as the rest. Country we're going to be crossing, we ain't going to be able to cut him loose if we get in a hot chase. Say that place is just south of here?"

Ben said, "Yeah, take the street right in front of the hotel. It'll Y just outside of town but just keep bearing to your right. About two miles farther on, but you'll hear it before you get to it."

Lew and I went back to the livery stable and saddled up again. As we rode out of town I pointed out Obregon's office and then, a little farther on, signaled toward Davilla's ranchero. I said, "Jack says it's back in there about a mile, mile and a half. I'm going to get him to take you there tonight so you can find it on your own."

Lew said, "This Jack, is he a pretty steady hand? He looks a little long in the tooth for this foolishness."

As best I could I explained about Jack Cole. I said, "Don't put him down because he can't take no part in the fight. Ain't nothing he can do about it and I reckon it will come to all of us. He'll be holding the horses."

Lew said, "I reckon that's square. I'd druther a man tell me I couldn't depend on him in a fight than find out about it at the wrong time."

Like Ben had said, we heard the place before we got there. It was a big, rambling, ramshackle, one-story affair made out of cinder blocks and wood and first one thing and then another. It looked like it had started out to be one thing and then just kind of growed from that.

We hitched out horses in front of what we took to be the cantina part and went in through a curtain of some kind of beads. "A hell of a front door" was what I thought. The inside was smoky and hot and noisy. We stopped just inside to let our eyes adjust from the glaring sun to the dark interior. It wasn't as crowded as I'd thought, but them that was in there was doing their part in the noise department. The bar was lined with a bunch of what I reckoned to be Mexican cowboys with here and there a *campesino* scattered in amongst them, distinguishable by them white pants they wore tied at the ankles and by them sandals, *huaraches* they called them, that they wore.

I finally spotted Jack sitting at a table along the back wall with four or five of what I reckoned to be Elizandro's men. He had a kind of unhappy look on his face, but it sort of smoothed out when he took sight of me and Lew. I give him a little wave and we made our way through the tables to his side.

He said, "I'm damn glad to see you, Justa. I was scairt Ben wouldn't run on to you in time."

"What's the matter?" I said. I was looking over the five hombres sitting there. They were about as rough a looking a lot as I'd ever laid eyes on before in my life. At least in one bunch. They were all dressed like cowboys in those *charro* britches, them leather-lined, wide-bottomed outfits they wore. And they were wearing big, wide-brimmed sombreros and short leather jackets. Now the leather britches and jackets I could understand. Mexican cowboys work cattle mostly in brambles and cactus patches and

they needed to wear leather to keep from getting skinned
alive. And they needed them big straw sombreros to keep
from getting their brains fried from that sun.

But after that any resemblance to working cowboys come
to a quick halt. Most of them were pretty dirty to begin
with and none of them looked like they'd seen a razor in
some time. But it wasn't the state of their clothes or their
personal habits that took your attention so much as the
look in their faces. Everyone of them appeared as if he'd
be just as pleased to cut your liver out as not. The one
sitting nearest Jack looked to be the worst. He was so
swarthy he damn near looked black. He had a scraggly
beard and a big bush mustache that drooped down on both
sides of his mouth. For a Mexican he was big, with big
shoulders and a big neck. He had a flat, mean-looking face
with a big nose and a jagged knife scar that ran nearly all
the way down one cheek.

Jack jerked a thumb at him. "This here is Benito. He's
kind of the boss of the rest. At least while Señor Elizandro
ain't here. He's getting a little impatient."

He just looked at me, making no sign of greeting, neither nodding nor sticking out his hand.

So I figured the hell with him. Lew and I looked around
and drug us up a couple of chairs. There was room to
Jack's right because the five Mexicans were all kind of
ranged along the long table with their backs to the wall.
Jack was sort of at the end of it. I sat down next to him.
That put this Benito right across from me. Lew sat down
to my right. He said, pleasantly, "Friendly bunch, ain't
they?"

I said, "Maybe they ain't figured out yet that we're all
on the same side."

"Maybe somebody ought to bring that to their attention," Lew said.

I leaned across toward Benito and said, "My name is

Williams. Señor Elizandro has directed that we should work together to free him and my brother."

I was about to tell Jack to translate it when this Benito said, "We doan geeve a sheet of choo brudder. You steenkin' gringo. *Esta noche* we blow the fuckin' *calabozo* all to sheet and keel all the *policía.*"

I was plenty surprised he spoke English. He didn't even much look like he could speak Spanish for that matter. But I heard him say "this night" and I knew that wasn't going to work. I said, "Naw, you ain't. I got a plan that is going to use all of us. You are going to take your orders from me. *Sus ordenes con mi. Comprende?*"

He spit, barely bothering to turn his head. He said, "Ah doan take sheet from choo. *Adiós,* gringo. Maybe I blow choo head off."

I leaned toward him and inched my chair closer to the table. As I did I eased my revolver out of its holster and held it between my knees, mostly pointed toward Benito. I knew Lew had seen the motion. I figured he was doing the same. I said, low but hard, "Listen, *el stupidio,* anybody gets their head blown off it's going to be you. Right now I got a gun under the table pointing right at your *cajones.* And the gentleman sitting to my right is doing the same thing. You or any of these other hombres do much more than breathe and you ain't gonna be so popular with the *señoritas. Comprende?*"

I heard the clank of their big roweled spurs as several of them involuntarily moved their legs to protect their vital parts. But all Benito did was stiffen up and narrow his eyes.

I said, "Now you listen because I've had about all the shit I'm gonna put up with in this piss-ant country. I've been lied to, robbed, insulted and now you've taken to threatening me. Now you are either going to do what I tell you or you are going to get the hell out of the way. You *comprende?*''

I didn't know if the others were understanding what I was saying or not, but there was no mistaking that Benito was taking it in. He looked at me, his face working.

Jack said, "Careful, Justa."

I figured he was plenty scared, but, to his credit, he hadn't made any move to back out of the line of fire.

Benito and I just sat there staring at each other. Both of his hands were on top of the round table. Very slowly his right hand began to move backwards, as if he meant to let it dip under the table and perhaps find a pistol. As his hand got to the edge of the table I cocked my revolver. The sound of the cocking, the *clitch-clatch,* was very loud, louder than the noise of the crowd, of the music, of the drunken shouting.

His hand stopped.

Lew said, "I got the three on the end. You ought to be able to get the blowhard an' the one next to him."

We sat that way for another ten seconds or so.

I said to Benito, "Now you got a choice. You can either call for us a drink or you can walk out in the street with me. But I tell you truly that I am a badass hombre and I will kill you. Savvy?"

Lew said, lowly, "You better let him save some face, Justa. Else we gonna have to kill all five and they ain't gonna do us much good dead."

I smiled, thinly, and said to Jack, without taking my eyes off the big Mexican, "Tell him in Spanish so that the others can hear that we are all of a common purpose and should be friends. Tell him I am acting on orders from Señor Elizandro. Tell him that I am asking him to be my lieutenant and am planning on assigning them the most heroic part of this daring adventure we will undertake to free the captives."

I heard Lew laugh ever so slightly.

Jack's voice betrayed how tensed up he'd been. He started off in a kind of high squeak and then had to recover and start over again.

It seemed it took him a good long while to say what I'd directed. Maybe he was flowering it up a little, which ain't no bad idea with Mexicans. But whatever he said seemed to go down pretty well because most of the hombres started nodding their heads and looking a good deal less fierce. Finally, Jack finished. Benito stared at me for another second and then slowly began to smile. He said, "Aw, sheet. *Mi borracho poquito. Es hokay. No le hace. Es nada.*"

He put out his hand. It took me a second to transfer my revolver to my left so I could shake. Yeah, he was a little drunk and it didn't matter and it was nothing and it was okay, but I was still going to keep a close eye on the son of a bitch.

After we'd shook he sent one of his men running to bring me and Lew a glass. Then he poured them full for us with tequila and we saluted each other and took down the raw, fiery stuff. I tried not to choke, but it was a near thing. It's not polite to cough over another man's whiskey.

I looked over at Lew; his eyes were watering. He said, "Damn! I've drunk plenty of tequila, but this stuff needs straining. Reckon this was what they were going to blow up the jail with?"

Well, we all got on pretty good after that. After about three drinks I asked Jack what had taken him so long to translate my message. He looked embarrassed. Finally he said, "Hell, I couldn't think of the Spanish word for lieutenant. I finally give up and made him a captain."

I just looked at him. We might have all been killed because of his Spanish. I said, "That's wonderful, Jack."

He said, "Dammit, Justa, I told you my nerves wadn't what they were."

I reckoned that matters ended up on about as good a foot as could be expected. We had about three or four more drinks with Benito and his *compañeros* and then I had Lew explain to them what we wanted. What I emphatically wanted was for them to stay out of town until the next day and not to call any attention to themselves. Then I wanted them to meet us at the livery stable behind our hotel at two o'clock on the morrow. I said to Lew, "Tell them it is most important that they come in to town in ones and twos, not in a whole bunch, and that they are to do nothing to give notice to the *federales*. Make damn sure they understand that. And I assume they've brought an extra horse for Señor Elizandro. Tell them I'll explain what they are to do at the livery stable. And tell them it is very important that they follow my orders exactly as I say."

Lew told them all that and they seemed amiable enough about it. So we made our *adiós*es and rode on back to town.

Jack seemed to still be showing a little of the strain of the meeting between us and our *compadres*. I said, "Hell, Jack, buck up. They can't do no more than get us kilt."

He said, "I thought you was about to do that back yonder in that cantina. Pushin' a drunk Mex is one thang, but pushin' five of 'em in a saloon in Mexico is another. Them boys don't keep regular attendance at Sunday school, you know."

Lew laughed and I had to smile a little myself. Jack wasn't exactly knowed for making jokes.

But Lew said, "I hope you ain't countin' on them boys too heavily, Justa. I'm with Jack on they character. They may or may not be there and they may or may not do what you say. They just as likely to get drunk tonight and forget all about tomorrow as they are to try and blow up that jail tonight."

I said, in a kind of weak voice, "I know. You don't got to remind me. But I got to play the cards I was dealt. Even if they all are jokers."

Truth be told, I was plenty worried about Elizandro's men without any supporting opinions from anybody else. Just about our whole escape depended on them and how well they did their jobs. If they didn't lay us down a good covering fire there was a damn good chance we were going to catch a few bullets ourselves whether them Mexican police could shoot or not. My main hope had been that Ben could direct the fire in such a way that the police outside the jail would scatter and go to ground so that it would take them some time to get up a chase party. But, more to the point, I was hoping the fire would scare them off so that we wouldn't actually have to kill anybody. I figured the less dead policemen, the less hard they'd pursue us.

But I doubted I was going to be able to get that fine point across to Benito and his boys.

Well, it was about as confused a mess as I'd ever tried to organize and about all I could figure to do was roll the dice and hope for the best.

That night I took a piece of the primer cord, measured off six inches and then lit it while I counted, "One thousand and one, one thousand and two, one thousand and three . . ."

It burned at about the rate of two seconds per inch.

Hays was watching me intently. He shook his head slowly. "Boss, I don't know 'bout this. Foolin' 'round with dynamite cain't lead to no good end."

"It ain't dynamite," I said. "How many times I got to tell you that? It's black powder and kerosene. The black powder is cordite, like mining engineers use."

" 'At's what I mean. Gonna blow up, ain't it?"

"Yeah. I hope so."

"Wahl, ain't that what dynamite does?"

"Listen—"

"An' me an' you in there in that there jail! Gawd-a'mighty, boss, ain't they another way?"

"Oh, shut up, Hays," I said. "You sound like some-body's grandmother. Now go downstairs and get me a candle."

Later that evening we carefully uncapped a dozen bottles of beer, poured the beer out in a bucket then washed each bottle out with kerosene. After we'd done that Lew and I carefully poured each bottle about half full of the black powder. Then, using a funnel I'd made out of a rolled-up newspaper, we filled out each bottle with kerosene. I held one of the finished products up to the light. It looked pretty good. The bottles were of dark glass and the Mexican beer was dark. Stuck down in the ice in the bucket that we intended on taking them into the jail in, they'd look just like ordinary bottles of beer.

Lew said, "Do you really have any idea of how big a explosion this stuff is gonna make?"

I was supposedly an artillery officer in the Texas militia, but I'd never had a great deal of experience even though we still used black powder. I finally admitted that I wasn't real sure what my little bombs were going to do. I said, "Best I'm hoping for is they'll make a hell of a bang and spread some confusion. Only thing I don't know is if the glass will break. The cap is the weak point and it might just blow the cap off and fizzle out."

Lew said, "That ain't gonna do a hell of a lot of good."

Ben said, "They'll break when you throw them, won't they?"

I said, "I ain't gonna throw them so they'll break. I want the explosion to bust the glass so that kerosene will throw fire all over the place."

"Why don't you just use dynamite?" Lew said. "Like we done before with that herd of cattle with tick fever?"

I looked at him. Normally Lew is a pretty solid thinker. I said, "In that jail? In those close quarters? I don't reckon I will. I'm trying to rescue my brother, not blow him up."

We spent the next hour putting the caps back on the bottles, crimping them carefully with a pair of pliers. After that Ben took his pocketknife and bored a hole in the middle of each cap just big enough to take the primer cord. But I wasn't putting it in just then. And wouldn't be until we actually entered the jail. Instead we plugged each hole up with candle wax and then rubbed the wax with tobacco ash so the hole wouldn't be noticeable.

After that we put the bottles in the galvanized bucket we regularly took to the jail.

We sat back and had a drink. I said, "Now what have I forgot?"

Jack said, "You arranged fer grub an' water?"

I slapped my thigh. "No. I nearly forgot that. We'll do it in the morning. But we'll get canned goods out of the mercantile. I don't want none of this junk outen this hotel café. Maybe bread. *Pan* they call it."

Hays said, "Boss, how many days you figure to the Texas border?"

I said, "Can't be many. I'm due at a wedding."

Hays gave a kind of groan. "I sure hope I'm there to do a little dancin'. An' in condition fer it."

I went over the plan once again and what part each would play. Hays would be responsible for the grub and plenty of water, Ben the horses. Jack would take Lew out to Davilla's ranchero and show him where it was. Then we'd all gather back up at the hotel around noon and go over the show for the afternoon performance.

Lew said, "You still ain't got me no uniform."

I said, "Yeah I do."

"Where is it? Damned if I see one."

I said, "Well, I was thinking about sending Ben and Hays over to that alley next to the saloon to knock the first drunk policeman over the head that staggered in there to take a piss. Say about midnight."

Hays sucked in his breath.

I said, "But then I suddenly realized wasn't no need for that. Got a uniform all ready for you and it ought to just about fit from what I hear."

"You going to tell me where it is?"

I leaned back in my chair and put my hands behind my back. I said, "Well, if he's a tidy man, or if his wife is tidy, I figure it'll be hanging in his closet. Or whatever they call where they keep their clothes down here."

Lew said, with what I took for just a trace of sarcasm, "Yeah, ain't no use complicating the matter. I'll just saunter up and ask the good *capitán* to give me the loan of one of his uniforms. Then I reckon I'll mention I'm taking him prisoner right after he gets me outfitted. That about the size of it?"

I said, "If it was me I'd put on my sheriff's badge—you are a sheriff, you'll remember—and go up to his door as one lawman to another. Ought not to be no trouble gaining access to the house. After that I figure you know what to do."

Lew smiled faintly. "Justa, if you wasn't so damn smart somebody—not talkin' about me, you understand—might take you for a smart aleck."

Ben said, loud enough to rouse the whole hotel, "I would!"

They were nervous and I didn't blame them. Hell, I was nervous too. What we were about to attempt was getting on toward being dangerous. It wasn't just the job of actually getting Norris out of the jail and getting us all out of town safe and sound, there was still that little matter of a hundred miles overland to the border. That was going to be a hard three-day ride at best, and that on good horses. God only knew what kind of stock Ben had been able to pick up for Norris and Lew and the packhorse. I turned around to where he was sitting on the edge of one of the beds and asked after his luck. He just kind of shrugged. He said, "It's fair. We wouldn't have it on the ranch, but I figure it'll make the trip."

"How bad will it slow us up?"

"Against our horses? Some."

I thought for a moment. Then I said to Lew, "Listen, I understand that this Davilla fellow mainly raises horses. While you are getting him ready for his little trip, run your eye over his stock and see if he might not have a couple of extras that look like they might be worth taking along."

Lew raised his eyebrows. He said, "To all them other things you askin' me to do you now want me to add horse stealin'? Is that right?"

I said, "As I recollect . . ."

I'd said it because it had been his first brush with the law when he'd been up in the Oklahoma Territory. He hadn't been guilty, having fallen in with bad company as a lad, but he'd had a pretty warm time of it extracting himself from trouble without getting hung or going to jail. I'd said it partly as a joke, but partly because I was worried about the poor quality of the stock Ben had just described. You didn't fool Ben about horseflesh. If he said the ones he'd been able to buy weren't up to the quality of the animals we'd brought from the ranch, that meant we'd be slowed up to the speed of the poorest of the horses.

I said to Ben, "How much did you pay for those three?"

"Hunnert apiece."

Well, that was just some more added to the price of that worthless five thousand acres Norris had come down to save. Hell, if we didn't get out pretty soon we were going to have to run those nesters off and take up residence on the place ourselves because we'd have to sell off the Half-Moon just to pay off what this jailbreak was costing.

But I said, "A hundred dollars each for genuine Mexican plugs?"

Ben shrugged. "They was the best I could find, and you didn't give me a whole hell of a lot of time."

Which was true.

He said, "I just took the best the local corral had to offer. They're stabled with our horses. Another hunnert for two saddles, a pack saddle, and the other gear."

I took a drink. Boy, I was starting to boil, but I knew it wouldn't do any good so I just said, "Reckon we ought to start thinking about going to bed. Might get a little busy tomorrow."

I lay awake long after I heard Lew snoring, running everything through my mind, mostly about what could go wrong. The more I pursued it, the more it seemed there was a heap more that could go wrong than could go right. I was at one slight disadvantage in the whole business. I knew about cattle and I knew about horses and I knew about fights, but the one thing, outside of women, that I didn't have much experience at was jailbreaks. I finally figured out I'd just have to make it up as I went along.

Then, just about the time I was starting to relax and get ready to go to sleep, another thought came across my mind. I played around with it for a time, dismissed it as trying to bite off more when I'd already bitten off too much, and settled down to go to sleep.

But the thought wouldn't go away. Finally I sat bolt upright in bed, lit a cigarillo and stared out the casement window at the Mexican night. It was another risk, albeit not a very bodacious one, especially in light of the ones we were already taking, but it was just adding more to the load. But, I thought, what the hell? We were already in over our heads in deep water so what difference did one more foot make? It was, however, not something I was going to tell the others about. They might not understand. In fact I was pretty sure they wouldn't understand. But Howard had always told me, ''Son, if you're going to build a fence to hold cattle, make sure you get all four sides up before you drive the cattle in.''

Well, we'd come down to do a job and it was my job to protect the interests of the Williams family. I figured I'd try for the whole hog.

After that I lay down and went to sleep.

6

In the morning, right after breakfast, I made my way over to the jail. The others of our party were bent on their chores, but I was on a more delicate errand. I had no trouble getting back to Norris. Lord, I'd spread enough grease around that jail I could have slid back to his cell on my boot heels. But just to keep everyone sweet on me I laid a few more twenty-peso notes around. It was *"Gracias"* this and *"Gracias"* that and Lord knows what else. Going into the jail I took note that even though it was as late as eight in the morning nearly everyone looked asleep. It made me wonder if we were setting the hour for the jailbreak at the right time. But it was too late to reconsider. Plans were afoot.

As I made my way down the hall of cells the *caballero*, Elizandro, noticed me first and came to the front of his cell. I just tipped him a wink and kept on walking. Behind me were the two jailers, both yawning, both having just come on duty. They'd given me no more than the perfunctory shakedown I'd had on my last couple of visits.

When I got down to Norris's cell he was laying on his back staring up at the ceiling. After a moment he rised up and gave me a look and sort of grunted. He was continuing to look better. On his little table I could see a basin of fresh water, the steam still rising from it, and he was shaven and dressed except for his tie. His clothes appeared clean but wrinkled. I just stood there looking at him, waiting for him to quit feeling sorry for himself and get up and face me.

Finally he stood up. I said, "Norris, if it wouldn't trouble you too much, how about you coming over here and us talking?"

He walked slowly toward the bars. He said, almost defiantly, "Well, have you made any progress in your way?"

I said, "That ain't the point of why I'm here."

He put his chin up. "Then what is?"

I said, "Have you got the metes and boundaries of that property?"

"What property?"

Hell, if he'd of been close enough I'd of reached through the bars and punched him. But I said, as calmly as I could, "Why, that property across the river in Laredo. What else? Do you have those metes and bounds?"

He said, looking like I didn't know what I was talking about, "You mean the survey?"

"Yes, dammit!" I was getting a little impatient.

"Well, yes," he said. "I have them here. I have the title."

"Where?"

"Why, in my valise." His chin went up again. "Rightful property that was returned to me, no doubt, because of your bribe money."

I was getting tired of it. I said, "Goddammit, Norris, if you have the title just give it to me."

He give me a long look and then finally turned back to that sagging bunk of his. Reaching under he pulled out the scarred remains of what had once been a fine piece of pigskin luggage. He opened it, sitting on his bunk, and rummaged around for a moment. Finally he come out with a piece of paper and handed it to me through the bars. Without unfolding it I could see it was a title of some kind. I said, "This the whole thing? This do it?"

He got that look on his face again. He said, "Yes, if you know what to do about it."

I just gave him a long gaze and started to turn away. He said, "What about me? What are you doing about me?"

I said, "Well, Norris, what do you want me to do?"

He said, "Get me some qualified representation. Some legal counsel. Somebody who can make these courts work!"

He was gripping the bars with both hands so hard the white was showing in his knuckles. I said, "We have sent to Washington, D.C., for the best legal counsel we can get."

And then, for maybe one of the first times, I heard my brother swear. He said, "Goddammit, you better get me out of here!"

I looked at him. I said, "I am. Be ready."

His face got molten. He said, "Not that way! Not that way! No bribes!"

I turned and walked away.

As I passed down the line of cells, the jailers still in tow, keys jangling, Señor Elizandro was still at the front of his cage. I stopped and took out a cigarillo and offered it to him. I struck a match and lit it for him. As he got it drawing I made little shooing motions to the jailers. They withdrew toward the main door. I said to Elizandro, "I bring you greetings from Benito."

His face lit up. He said, "Aaah, yes. A good man."

"In some ways a very good man."

"A leetle hard to handle, perhaps?"

"Yes, but we reached an agreement."

"That is good."

"Perhaps we will see you this afternoon."

"At *seis*? *Perdone usted*. Six?"

"Earlier, I think. Maybe siesta?"

"Aaah," he said, understanding. "Yes."

"You will be ready?"

"But of course."

"Will you do as I ask?"

He shrugged his shoulders. "Must you ask?"

"No. But I wonder which way do you ride from here."

"Which way do you suggest?"

"We will go northwest. If you went the other way it might confuse our enemy."

The *caballero* smiled. He said, "Yes, it is hard to chase two coyotes at the same time."

I said, "That's what I was thinking."

The guards were making motions at me. I gave the *caballero* the pack of cigarillos and the remains of my matches and said, "Until later."

He said, "Yes. And tell Benito I will kill him if he doesn't do as you direct."

"I already did."

After I got out of the jail I sauntered over to lawyer Obregon's office. Luís was on duty at his accustomed post in the outer office. It was going on for ten o'clock, but I wasn't certain the señor would be in. By a lucky chance he was, and by the slick transfer of a fifty-peso note from my hand to Luís's I was able to get in to see him right away.

He was about the same—sitting behind his desk, looking well satisfied with himself and eyeing his pigeon with relish. He bade me sit down and offered me coffee. I said that I reckoned I was about coffeed out and sat down across from him. Luís stayed in the room to translate. I brought out the title to the land in Laredo and explained, as best I could, what the problem was. I asked if there was anything he could do about it that might be handled quickly. I didn't have much hope but he surprised me by laughing and saying that it was a matter of the slightest effort. In fact his clerk could bring me the necessary document from the courthouse.

Well, I wasn't that surprised. I asked him what he reckoned the cost would be. He pulled a face and said, through Luís, that he would gladly do it for me as a favor, but, unfortunately, the people at the courthouse were not quite so generously disposed and if I wanted the matter handled quickly and with dispatch he thought a small fee—for the clerks, of course—might speed matters along. I asked how much and he said he thought about five hundred pesos would do the job. I done a little quick arithmetic in my head, knowing the peso was running about eight to the dollar, and come up with about fifty-five dollars. That was pretty good pay for a small favor from some clerk who probably never saw that much money in two months.

But I outed with my wad and slid the money across to him. Then I sat back in my chair and waited to see what he'd do with it. On a past occasion, just as we'd been leaving the office, I'd chanced to glance back to see him turning toward a little curtain that hung down in the corner. He'd had my wad of bills in his hand and had been bending over as I passed through the door and lost sight of him.

Now he did nothing, just let the bills lay there. He said, through Luís, that if I cared to come back in an hour he would have the Spanish grant title all ready for me. I got up. I said, "No, I don't reckon. I've got some business around town. How about if I return around two o'clock?"

He rose, formally, with me and came around his desk to shake my hand. He said that the hour would suit him perfectly and he also wished to add that he was very sorry about the difficulty about my brother but he was sure I, a man of the world, understood and he hoped I realized he was doing everything in his power.

Luís said, formally, "Señor Obregon is much troubled by this business and regrets with extreme the sorrow it has caused you. But he hopes that you have been somewhat comforted by the freedom of access to your brother that he has personally arranged."

I said, just as seriously, "Yes. Tell Señor Obregon that I am in his debt but expect not to be for too much longer."

They bowed me out formally, Señor Obregon even going so far as to pat me on the shoulder. He assured me once again that the document would be ready at two o'clock.

I left there cursing Obregon and cursing Norris. I had no doubt the clear title would be ready by that afternoon. Hell, that was a very small bone to throw to a dog you were trying to take the hind leg off of. He'd do that little favor just to keep me well hooked, keep the cow up at the trough for milking. And if that damn Norris hadn't been so pigheaded the matter could have been handled with just as much ease.

Back at the hotel I found Ben and Hays. Jack and Lew hadn't come back so we settled down to wait for them before making a noonday meal.

I asked after the work they was supposed to have done that day. Ben said the horses were standing saddled, loose-cinched and ready. Hays said he'd laid in just about all the grub he figured the packhorse could handle along with about six gallons of water. He said, "It's all done, boss. All we got to do is skedaddle."

About a half an hour later Lew and Jack came in looking sweaty and dusty. They sat down and we poured a drink out all around and then knocked them back "for luck."

I let the whiskey get settled and then looked at Lew. He shrugged, and said, "Don't look too tough, Justa. Best sight I had of Mr. Davilla—pardon me, *Capitán* Davilla— was him sitting out in his front yard with his shirt off and a bottle of tequila in his hand. Didn't see nobody about the place except a couple of peons and a few women. I figure he ought to come along pretty easy."

"What about his horses?"

He made a face. "Didn't see nothing worth bothering with. If he's got any good stock he's got 'em hid somewheres else."

"All right. That horse Ben got you, what do you think?"

He took a moment to answer, glancing over at Ben first. He said, "Well, he wouldn't be my first choice in horseflesh, but I ain't seen nothing better around here. I reckon Ben knows as much about horses as anybody, and I reckon he got the best he could find."

"But will he last the distance?"

Lew said, "Depends on how hard we have to push. Hell, Justa, they ain't going to be exactly chasing us on no purebred stock, you know. You got some idea they issue racehorses to them ordinary *federales*?"

I stood up. "All right," I said. "Let's go down and make a meal. Liable to get a little busy around here before long."

We made the best we could out of the poor fare in the hotel dining room. I urged everyone to just keep on chewing and swallowing. I said, "Likely to be a good little bit before the next meal and that will be out of a can."

After that we went back upstairs. Wasn't too long before we were going to have to meet Benito and his men but I wanted to be sure everyone knew his job exactly. On a piece of foolscap I drew up a rough sketch of the town, where the jail was, our escape route and where I wanted each man positioned.

The jail sat at a sort of a Y in the middle of the main street. One road ran off to its southeast. That was the road I expected Elizandro and his men to take. Directly across from the jail was a line of shops and cantinas and the usual scuffle of businesses you'll find in most of the larger Mexican towns. I had scouted the area right across from the jail and I liked it. It wasn't but about ten yards from the front of the buildings to the front of the jail. And there were some nice concrete columns in front of one store that would make good cover. That was where I wanted Ben to position Benito's men. I said, "You can have them hold their horses just right around the corner here. My deal with Elizandro is that he is going to give us plenty of covering fire in return for me breaking him out. Ben, you and Jack will have the horses. You'll both be mounted."

I pointed to a location a little behind the block of buildings that faced the jail, back toward our hotel. I said, "Jack, here is where I want you to pull up with the horses. Just enough behind the corner of that building to be out of sight." To save his feelings I said, "I don't want to take a chance of any of the horses catching a stray shot. But as soon as you see me and Norris and Hays come running across the street you get there right smart with our mounts. We ain't going to much want to hang around that area longer than we have to."

Ben said, "What are you going to do about your handgun, Justa?"

"You'll have it," I said. "Soon as I get near enough pitch it to me and hope like hell I catch it."

Lew said, "Sounds like I drawed the easy job."

"Not so as you'd notice," I said. I made a mark on the paper about a block from where I'd told Jack I wanted him and the horses stationed. "I want you and the good *capi tán* about right here. I want you to tie him on his horse. I don't want his hands free, I want them tied down to the saddle horn. As we come by you take his horse on lead so he's the last member of the parade. If they come after us shooting I want him to be the first one hit." I glanced up at him and give him one of his own crooked smiles. "Of course, then, you'll be next. You'll be the rear guard, so to speak. Still think you got the easy end of it?"

He said, "Well, since you put it like that, I'd just as soon swap out with Hays."

Hays made a little gulp. "And I'd just as soon swap out. *You* go in that jail with the boss. Hell, I'll get that Mex and dress him up in rope."

Which suddenly reminded me of something I'd forgotten. I said, "Ray, run around to that mercantile where you got that powder and get me about twenty feet of quarter inch cord. Sash cord, if they ever heard of such a thing."

"What would you be wanting with that?"

"Just go," I said. "And be quick about it."

After he was gone I sat, thinking, trying to figure out what I'd forgotten. I could feel an edginess coming over me. Maybe there are those men who can go into a dangerous situation without some fear but I wasn't one of them. I had no qualms about the necessity of what we were about to attempt, but neither did I have any illusions. It was going to be dangerous work and no mistake. We were about to attack a small fortress that was swarming with armed men. That sort of foolishness can get you killed.

Ben said, "Justa, it's going on for two o'clock. That's

the time we're supposed to meet them *pistoleros* over at the livery stable.''

I sighed. ''Yeah, I know. Let's have one more drink. Time's getting close.''

I poured out all around and then we knocked them back. I said, ''Ben, you and Lew and Jack go on over there and get them *pistoleros* lined out. If they're drunk or trouble-some let Lew handle them. But make sure they understand one damn thing. Every one of them *federales* they kill is one less that's gonna be chasin' us or them.''

Lew laughed. He said, ''Oh, I don't reckon we have to reinforce that idea. I reckon they already thought of that they ownselves.''

I said, ''Luck.'' They filed out. I called after Ben, ''Be damn sure you watch yourself. Them Mexican bullets kill just the same as the ones on the other side of the Rio Grande.''

He turned and gave me a look. ''Don't tell me. You're the one going to be closest to the fire. If you weren't the boss I wouldn't let you do it.''

Then they were gone and the wagon was in motion. All I could do was sit there and hope it didn't run off a cliff.

Just when I was starting to get nervous about the time Hays finally showed up. He came in carrying a coil of sash cord. He said, ''This what you had in mind, boss?''

I stood up. ''Yeah,'' I said. ''Your saddlebags packed?'' ''Yeah.''

I reached into mine and took out the two derringers. I handed one to him. ''Here, stick that in your boot. It's loaded. Two shots.'' I shoved the other one down in my right boot. After that I took the wad of primer cord I'd cut up and shoved them down in my pocket. They were cut to different lengths, all the way from two inches to ten inches. Four seconds to twenty seconds. I shouldered my saddlebags and then looked over at Hays. "We forgetting anything?"

He shrugged, looking nervous. "Not so that I taken notice. 'Cept the bucket."

I said, "Pick it up." It was the bucket with the twelve innocent-looking beer-bottle bombs that I hoped would work. After he had it in hand I said, "Well, let's go."

On the way out I stopped at the desk and paid us out. It came to a little over fifty dollars, which I considered excessive, but I wasn't in a mood to argue. Hays and I stepped out on the street. He said, "Where we headed, boss?"

I said, "Going over to the jail, but first we're going to do a little bill collecting."

He said, "Huh?"

I said, "Never mind. Just follow along with me."

When we got to Obregon's office Luís was smiling. He said, in his accented English, "We have done the job, Señor Williams. The matter of the deed is cleared up. Señor Obregon has it ready for you. I will show you in and come along to help with the translation."

"Mighty good," I said. Hays and I dumped our saddlebags by the door. The twenty foot of sash cord had been shoved down into one of the pockets of Hays's saddlebags. We followed Luís into Obregon's office. The little fat lawyer rose as we entered, all smiles. In Spanish he said that all was well, that he had managed to prove up our Spanish land grant. Some of it I understood; Luís translated the rest. Then Señor Obregon handed me my original title and some document in Spanish. Luís said it was proof of the land-grant title. I smiled and thanked him through Luís and took the two documents and folded them carefully and put them in my pocket. After all, they were what the whole business had been about. Then I said, casually, to Ray Hays, "Ray, put a gun on that boy so he don't make any noise."

Then I pulled out my pistol and stuck the business end right between Señor Obregon's eyes. He'd been standing up, but with the gun in his face he slowly sank down into his chair. I just let the end of my gun follow him. His bottom jaw dropped so I took the opportunity to stick the barrel of my revolver in his mouth. Out of the corner of my eye I could see Luís, frozen stiff, Hays standing just behind him with a drawn pistol in his back. That was one of the reasons I valued Hays; he might argue from time to time, but he reacted when you needed him to without question.

I said to Señor Obregon, "Listen, lawyer, you got seventeen hundred and forty dollars of my money which you took without doing me a damn thing. I ain't counting that fifty-five dollars I give you this morning, but I intend on having that money back. *Comprende?*"

His eyes were wide and staring and he commenced making little gurgling sounds. Hays said, "Boss, I don't think he can talk with that pistol in his mouth."

I took the revolver off his tongue and shoved it back up between his eyes, but kept leaning across his desk. I figured he'd enjoyed the taste of cold steel enough to get my message. But I said, "I know you don't speak English, but I have taken notice that you have a safe over there in that corner behind that curtain. Now I want you to open it and give me back my money, else I'm going to pull the trigger on this heavy-caliber pistol and splatter your brains all over this nice office. You *comprende*?"

He just sat there shivering and shaking, his eyes still wide, his mouth still open. I said, "I reckon you better tell him, Luís. He's got about a minute to make up his mind." For emphasis I cocked the hammer of my revolver. The sound echoed off his tonsils in the quiet room.

Luís let go a high, nervous torrent of Spanish at the lawyer. When he was finished Obregon started shaking his head. Luís said, "He says he has no moneys in the safe, that he has transferred them to the bank."

I sighed and said, "Well, tell him that's his hard luck. I'm going to count to ten and then I'm going to shoot him. After that we'll have to shoot you too because we can't have no witnesses. You ready, Ray?"

Hays said, "Yeah, boss."

I started counting. I didn't even bother with the Spanish. I just held up my left hand and started ticking off fingers. I said, "One, two, three, four, five, six, seven—"

Luís said, suddenly, "Señor, I have admittance to the safe. Please don't shoot me." His voice was high and hysterical. I didn't blame him. Hell, if I'd had an unknown gun in my back and a long life ahead of me I'd of done the same.

I said, "All right. Then open it."

I could see him look fearfully back at Hays before he moved cautiously around the desk and toward the corner. As he went he said, respectfully to Obregon, in Spanish, something like, "Forgive me, *patrono*. It is necessary. It will mean our deaths otherwise."

But Obregon didn't like it one damn bit. He started to turn his head and say something to the young man but I tapped him hard across the forehead with the barrel of my pistol; he let out a little scream and collapsed across his desk. I hadn't meant to hit him so hard, even though I was a little sick of his ways, but it seemed I'd managed to give him a pretty good cut and knock him out a little.

Luís had drawn aside the curtain and was working the dial of an old-fashioned combination safe. He said, "It is all in here, señor. Señor Obregon does not put his money in the bank. Do you want it all?"

"No," I said. "Just seventeen hundred and forty dollars American. Only what I've give this thief. If it's in pesos you make sure you get the right amount. I ain't going to count it but I'll be back if you short me.''

I saw him swing the door open and begin to work feverishly with stacks of bank notes. When he was done he stood up and solemnly held out a wad of money at me. I tilted my head toward Hays. I said, ''Give them to him. Ray, stick those in one of the saddlebags out by the door and then bring that cord back in here.''

While he was gone me and Luís stood like a couple of statues. I was sorry to be scaring the boy, but I really hadn't had no choice. When Ray came back, carrying his saddlebag, I directed Luís to lay facedown on the floor. Obregon was making little moaning sounds. I went around the desk and jerked him out of his chair and threw him facedown on the floor. Then I said to Hays, ''Take that cord and hog-tie them both. Make sure you do a good job of it.''

He got the cord out of his saddlebags, took out his knife and cut the twenty feet into proper lengths. When he was finished they were both laying back down on the floor with their hands tied behind their backs and their feet drawed up toward their hands. They looked mighty uncomfortable. Hays straightened up from his work and said, ''That good enough, boss?''

I said, ''Yeah. You got any socks?''

''What?''

''Socks. What you wear on your feet.''

He looked a little dubious. ''Yeah,'' he said, ''but they ain't too clean.''

''Never mind,'' I said. ''Stick one in each of their mouths.''

He went into his saddlebags and came out with a couple of bedraggled-looking objects I wouldn't have let a cat bed down on. I said, ''Luís, you got a handkerchief?''

With a little effort because of the position he was in he said, "Yes, señor. It is in the pocket of my suit coat. On the right side."

"All right," I said. I nodded for Hays to accommodate Señor Obregon with one of his socks, but I knelt down by Luís, found his handkerchief and stuffed it in his mouth. Then I went over to Obregon. I said, "You son of a bitch, you thought I was easy. You might want to think again before you try some of your tricks on the next sucker that walks through your door."

After that Hays shouldered his saddlebag and I done the same with mine as we got to the door. There was a key on the desk usually occupied by Luís and I used that to lock the office door. Anybody coming by would simply think they'd left for siesta. Hays had the bucket containing what I hoped were bombs. I'd put tenpenny nails in a few of them, but I didn't really think they'd be very effective except as a diversionary tactic. Hays was mumbling something about what he was supposed to do with just one sock. I told him to shut up.

But as we stepped out of the office he said, kind of hesitantly, "Boss, you know, I ain't real sure you ain't part crazy."

I was watching the street, looking for Ben and Jack. I said, "Why is that, Ray?"

He said, "Well, here we are, fixin' to try and break your brother outen a Mexican jail and you take time off to fix things square with a lawyer. Boss, that don't make no sense. Most folks would be content with just the jail-break."

I said, still searching for sight of Ben as we walked toward the jail, "That's because you ain't ever had to be responsible for running an outfit. Do you know how many cowhands wages you can pay with seventeen hundred and forty dollars?"

"No," he said.

"I do," I said. "And once you let folks start getting to you they'll think the bank is open twenty-four hours a day. Look, yonder comes Ben and Jack with the horses. From this instant on you do exactly what I tell you, when I tell you."

"Ain't I always?" he said.

We were almost at the corner of the street opposite the jail. Ben came riding up with Jack lagging back, leading three horses. Hays and I tucked our revolvers into our saddlebags and handed them up to Ben. He took them without a word and then wheeled back toward Jack. There just wasn't anything left to say. Hays and I, him carrying the bucket, started across the street toward the jail. There was a little wind blowing and it raised some of the dust of the street so that I was able to get a good noseful of just what a Mexican town smelled like.

Maybe it was just apprehension, but there appeared to be considerable more police hanging around the front of the jail, either sitting on benches or leaning up against the granite wall. All of them had those Sam Browne belts with the strap across the chest and they were all wearing the khaki uniform of the *federales*. And all of them had a carbine either hanging off his shoulder or near to hand. All I could think was that Elizandro's boys had better do some damn good shooting or we'd never reach the horses. I glanced over at Hays and he gave me a kind of nervous little laugh. I didn't blame him; I wasn't feeling all that calm myself. And it wasn't even his brother. I said, "Remind me to give you a raise if we get out of this."

He said, "I appreciate it, boss. I just hope I git a chance to spend it."

He sounded about as sure as I felt.

The *federales* glanced at us as we pushed the big door open and entered the outer office. It all looked the same

but, in light of what was to come, very much more threatening. The same sergeant was sitting at his desk by the
door that led back to the cells. By now he and I were old
buddies on account of all the *dinero* I'd passed his way.
His eyes lit up and he smiled when he saw us come in. I
figured he was thinking, ''Here comes Santa Claus again.''
I went up to his desk and made application to see my
brother, meanwhile slipping a fifty-peso note across the
desk to the sergeant. He took it without a word and folded
it carefully and put it in his shirt pocket. I taken notice
that he had his police revolver laying on his desk where it
would be right quick to hand. That was something I'd have
to keep in mind.

About then my two jailer friends came up, jangling their
keys on their belts and smiling big. One of them had a
gold tooth and I was surprised somebody hadn't killed him
for it. They were just as glad to see me as the sergeant
had been, naturally expecting another payday. Well, it was
payday all right, but not the kind they were expecting.

One of them opened the big door that went back to the
cells and we went through. Gold Tooth went first, then
me, then Hays and his bucket, and then the second guard.
Jailers, or anybody that goes near the prisoners, don't carry
weapons for the simple reason that they're running the risk
of having one taken away from them. Not that that mat-
tered because I had no intentions of giving them time to
use them. We walked down the hall between the line of
cells on both sides, heading toward the end where Norris
was bunking. About halfway down, just as we came opposite Elizandro's cell, I stopped and bent over like something was bothering my boot. I slipped my hand inside,
and when I straightened up I was holding the derringer.
Gold Tooth had stopped also and turned back to face
me. I let him see the little gun, then rammed it in his belly.
As I did I held a finger of my left hand to my lips indi-

cating he should not make a sound and emphasized it by prodding him a couple of times with the derringer. His eyes got big in his brown face and his gold tooth was showing but not because he was smiling. To my left I heard a quiet chuckle and, out of the corner of my eye, I could see Señor Elizandro standing at the door of his cell smoking a cigarillo. He said, *"Muy bueno."*

I said, "Hays, you got the other one?"

He said, "Got his hands over his head, boss. He's quivering a little, but all in all he's being right nice about matters."

I said, "Take his keys and hand them to Señor Elizandro." Then, to the *caballero*, I said, "Señor, as soon as you can find the right key and get yourself out of your cell I want you to take this derringer from me and put these two in your cell and keep them quiet."

He said, "I thenk that will be very possible."

I heard a lot of jangling and rattling of keys and then Elizandro was beside me. I felt his hand on my gun hand and I let the derringer ease into his grip. He said some words in Spanish to Gold Tooth and he moved with good speed into the cell that the señor had lately been occupying. I turned around. Hays was herding his man in behind Gold Tooth. I said, "Just keep these two quiet. Don't shoot unless you have to."

Hays said, "We better hurry, boss. Somebody is likely to get curious what we doing back here."

I took the keys off the belt of Hays's jailer as he passed, picked up the bucket of beer-bottle bombs and hurried back to Norris's cell. He was sitting on his bunk, staring down at the floor, seemingly unaware of all that had transpired. I fumbled with the keys until I found the right one, unlocked his cell door and swung it wide. He looked up. He said, "What's this?"

I said, "I think they call it a jailbreak."

"Oh, no!" he said. "Not on your life!"

I had reached into my pocket and come out with the primer cord fuses and was starting to fit them into the holes in the top of the bottles. I glanced up at him in some surprise. I said, "What?"

He was just sitting on his bunk shaking his head. "Oh, no. I'll be no party to a jailbreak. I'll have my day in court and show how wrongfully I've been treated. I'm not going to be a party to an illegal action."

I was still busy stuffing the fuses through the waxed-over holes in the caps of the bottles, trying to vary them so some would go off in a second, others two seconds, others longer. My intent was to keep up a continuous run of explosions as we were trying to race through the office of the jail. I stared at him. I said, "Are you crazy?"

He crossed his arms and leaned back against the wall of his cell. "I certainly am not. I know my rights and I will have my due process of law. I'm considering legal action against these people for false arrest."

I said, "Norris, this is Mexico. They *ain't* got no due process or whatever you call it." I could feel the seconds ticking by and knew that time was running out. "Norris, we have pulled guns on two Mexican jailers. We are in too deep to back out now. Get your ass up and get out of here. This thing is dangerous enough without you costing me time."

"No, sir," he said.

I couldn't believe it. I said, "Four men are risking their lives to get you out of here. Now get off your fat ass and move it!"

"Nope," he said, still with his arms crossed resolutely.

I was squatting down by the bucket, still inserting fuses. I looked behind me. Hays and Elizandro had the two guards inside the cell with the door shut and locked. The guards had their hands on the top of their heads, but they were being helped to behave by the two derringers pointed at their bellies. There were no prisoners in the few cells near Norris, but I could see several on down the line. They were up against the bars watching, in some fascination, what was going on. Most of them appeared to be peons, probably arrested for being drunk or for petty theft or because some *federale* wanted a shot at their wife without the old man interfering. I looked at Hays. He had a most anxious appearance about his face and he made little hurry-up signs to me with his free hand.

I turned back to Norris. "We are out of time. Are you coming?"

He took a deep breath and began, as if he were explaining to a child, "I have told you I have been wrongfully arrested. I am going to insist on my rights. I am going to stay in this jail cell until I get redress of the wrongs that have been done me. My position . . ."

He kept going, sounding like a Philadelphia lawyer, but I wasn't paying him any attention. I took out the ten-inch fuse, rammed it into one of the bottle bombs and then got out a lucifer match. I struck it on the sweaty concrete floor and lit the fuse. Then I rolled the bottle bomb across Norris's cell floor until it came to rest under his bunk. He looked up, startled, stopping his lesson in constitutional law. He said, "What's that?"

I stood up, grabbing the handle of the bucket. I said, "That's a bomb, Norris. It's going to go off in about five seconds. You go ahead and sit there on your principles if you want to but I'm getting out of here before I get mine blown off."

Then I turned and started running up the walkway between the cells. As I passed Hays and Elizandro I said, "Come on!"

Behind me I heard Norris yell, "Justa!"

By then, though, I wasn't paying him a whole hell of a lot of attention. I reckoned him to maybe have more sense than to sit on a bomb.

7

We got to the door. Hays and I knelt by its left side. We both got a match lit and then I bade Señor Elizandro to push the door open as far as he could without exposing himself. I said to Hays, "Light the short fuses first and then work your way up. We want to keep them going off in a steady run. And roll the damn bottles along the floor. Don't throw them."

About then I felt a breath on the back of my neck and Norris saying, "Goddam you, Justa! I'm never going to forgive you for this. You—"

But his words were drowned out by the explosion of the bomb I'd rolled under his bunk. It went off much louder than I'd expected. It went *"KA-BOOM!"* making the granite walls echo and reverberate like a thundercloud had turned loose in their midst. Unfortunately it was one of the ones I'd put the nails in and I could hear them singing around and wanging off the bars and the granite walls. I hoped none of the peons would get hit. I would have liked to have freed them, but it would have just complicated matters.

By now Hays and I had both got a cigarillo lit and drawing and we commenced lighting fuses and rolling the bottles out into the outer office. I saw the desk sergeant turn, startled, and look toward our door. But it was a little late for his curiosity. While we were rolling out the last of the bombs the first began going off and I was considerably stunned by the effect they were having. The black powder would blow up, igniting the kerosene, and then you not only had an explosion, you had a sheet of flame rising up in all directions. On top of that there were the nails and the splinters of glass flying around.

I was still crouched down. I said, "Get ready. Norris, the horses are across the street. Follow me and Hays."

I took the derringer out of Señor Elizandro's hand. I had retained two of the short-fused bombs for the work at the outer door. Elizandro said, "You have my thanks, señor."

I said, "I just hope your men have started their work." They were supposed to start firing at the troops outside as soon as they heard the sound of the first bomb.

I waited another second for the flying nails and glass to subside a bit and then I went charging through the door. The outer office looked like hell. It was brighter than any room I'd ever seen. There was smoke and fire everywhere. I could see a few indistinct forms through the fog of cordite, but they looked confused and uncertain.

But the desk sergeant was still standing there, his mouth open. I shot him twice with the derringer, then dropped the little gun and grabbed up the sergeant's service revolver that was still lying on his desk and took several shots at some of the forms I could see through the smoke.

We ran toward the front door. I had the two remaining bombs in my left hand and the lit cigarillo in my mouth.

Hays shoved the big front door open as I lit one of the
bombs, tossed it along the front of the building to my left,
lit the other and tossed it to the right. Behind me I could
hear a few gunshots being fired but none were coming my
way. Through the open door I could hear the sound of
heavy firing and I hoped that Elizandro's men were doing
a good job of covering fire.

I waited an instant more until I heard the bombs go off
and then I said, "Go!" and ran crouching through the
door that Hays was holding open.

I didn't have to tell anyone to stay low. There was smoke
and flames on both sides of me and I had to step over the
body of one of the *federales* as I ran into the street. Across,
I could see Elizandro's men firing steadily at the front of
the jail. I was running too fast to get a clear view, but
I had the distinct impression of terrible carnage. Mostly I
saw bodies laying in front of the jail, but here and there I
caught a glimpse of a *federale* down on one knee, carbine
to shoulder, firing back. In the middle of the street I
stopped, letting the other three go on past me, and whirled
and fired the last three remaining cartridges at the policemen. Then I threw the gun down and ran toward the
corner where Ben was supposed to be.

He was there, carbine to his shoulder, firing at the federal militia. He saw us coming and stopped long enough
to pitch a pistol to Hays and then to throw my gun to me.
I turned, knelt, and fired the full chamber of bullets at the
remaining riflemen. When my revolver was empty I
jammed it in my holster and whipped around to get horseback. I felt something hit my boot and felt a slight pain
in my ankle, but I had no time for that. I could see that
Jack had brought the horses up, rounding them off and
pointing them north. I could see Norris and Hays getting
mounted. Hays had turned in the saddle and was firing
back over my head as I sprinted toward my own horse.

Off to my right I could see that Señor Elizandro had made it to the safety of his own men who were continuing to faithfully lay down covering fire. There would be no one coming out of the front door of that jail unless they were crazy.

I reached my horse and swung into the saddle on the jittery animal. Ben was coming behind me. I said, "Let's get the hell out of here!"

And we began pounding down that dusty main street with onlookers lining the sidewalk gawking and staring. I heard what sounded like a few gunshots and felt the zing of something going over my head. I didn't know if them nonparticipating parties along the way were stupid enough to get involved, but I pulled out my saddle gun and fired a few shots over their heads just to give them fair warning that we weren't just funning.

A block ahead I saw Lew with this *Capitán* Davilla. They were both in uniform. As we closed on them I could see Lew take Davilla's horse on lead and begin slowly loping past. We came up to them and then he clapped spurs to his horse and fell into our rear at the same dead run we were going.

The little street that turned west came up before I'd expected it, but I reined my horse in and swept us around its corner, still going almost full tilt. A few peons were lazing their way across the street, but they heard the thunder of our hooves, took one startled look and got the hell out of the way. In point of fact it was a wise decision on their part because we weren't stopping for anything.

I could not remember all the little twists and turns that Lew and I had mapped out, but I just kept us racing down those little narrow streets, turning this way and that but always heading west. The sound of gunshots was long past and all I had to do now was concentrate on getting us into open country and heading for cover. When I could I took a quick glance back over my shoulder, half dreading I might see an empty saddle. But they were all there, Hays and Jack just behind me, Norris behind Ben, and, bringing up the rear, Lew with Davilla on lead. The *capitán* was hunched over, looking mighty uncomfortable tied in his saddle the way Lew had trussed him up. I wasn't shedding no sympathy on him.

At long last we left the town, passed a few lonely looking adobe shacks, and then we were in the open country. I pulled my horse down, intent on saving him after the long run he'd had, and put him into a ground-eating lope. The rest behind me did the same except Norris who spurred his horse to come even with me. I took one look over at his face and I didn't like the look of it. He was saying something to me, leaning toward me out of his saddle. I pretended not to hear. I looped the reins around the saddle horn and then twisted backwards to reach into my saddlebags for spare ammunition. Still going at a pretty good lope I took the time to reload my .42/.40 and my saddle gun. When I shoved the saddle gun home in its boot I waved Norris back. He wanted to say something else but I just kept my gaze straight ahead, calculating the ground and the direction we had to go.

I turned us straight west, whipping my horse through the stunted underbrush and the rocks and the cactus. I was careful of my animal, but I was more careful of what I knew were the inferior beasts that Ben had been able to buy in Monterrey. Off to my right I could see the first of the little line of wooded ridges that I was counting on for cover. I gradually turned us northwest. Calculating the time and the month of the year we were in, I figured we didn't have much more than three hours until dark. I wanted to make as many tracks as possible before the moon got up. We may have shot the hell out of the *fed-*

erales at the jail but there was a whole bunch more around and available.

And then there were the *rurales* to consider. Of the two, I didn't prefer either one. All I knew was that I had a hundred miles of ground to cover before I could bring my people to safety.

We kept riding, taking a pace that the horses could stand across the sometimes green but most often barren landscape. After two hours I called a halt and ordered everyone out of their saddles to walk their mounts. Of course that did not include *Capitán* Davilla, whose poor animal would have to put up with whatever it could bear. We had no intentions of untying the good *capitán*.

As we walked, leading our horses to give them a much needed blow, Norris came up beside me. He said, "I just want you to understand that I'm doing this under protest. I want you to know that I could have won my legal way out of that jail without you resorting to tactics equivalent to theirs."

My ankle was hurting and I was weary and still a little scared. My patience was short. I said, "Oh, shut up, Norris. I don't want to hear any more of this foolishness. Now drop back and keep out of the way."

He said, "No, we'll discuss it now."

I had been kind of glancing around. Looking to my right, just past Norris, I suddenly saw a small band of riders coming toward us at a gallop. I yelled, "Company coming. Mount up!"

I was amazed they could have gotten after us so fast. Hell, as far as I was concerned we'd left that jail in a shambles. But then there must have been a police barracks somewhere near who'd been able to get up a catch party Johnny Quick. But as I swung my leg over the saddle I took another look at the intruders. They were no more than a half mile away and coming fast. Near as I could tell there weren't but about five of them and it would have been the last word in foolhardiness to have attacked an equal party such as ours on an open plain. Hell, in another moment we'd have been able to start picking them off with our lever action Winchester carbines. I sat my horse for a second, watching them, then put him into a slow walk. I kept seeing them get closer. They did not look like *federales* or *rurales*. I wished mightily for the old ship-captain's spyglass that my father kept in his room, but that was a good three hundred miles away. I would have to content myself with my own eyesight.

I looked ahead. The nearest cover, the little scrub-covered ridge, was too far off to break for. We were out in the middle of a flat, barren plain with an unknown enemy bearing down on us. When they were about a quarter of a mile away I called for a halt. I said, "Dismount. Put your rifles across your horses' saddles and get ready to fire. But no man shoots until I do."

Looking down the line I yelled for Lew to lead Davilla out between us and the advancing party. I watched them coming on, wrinkling my brow as to who they could be. They were near enough now for me to get a count; it appeared to be six men. What six men would be foolish enough to charge down the guns of an armed and hostile group of men as desperate as they must have known we were? That is, if they knew who we were and they were chasing us.

I kept watching them come on, their horses' hooves raising a small dust cloud as they galloped over the plain. They grew bigger and bigger. I started to tense up and carefully took aim over my iron sights. Then I relaxed as I recognized the lead rider. I said, "Oh, hell!" I took my rifle down and swung into the saddle. I said to the others, "Never mind, it's Señor Elizandro."

Ben said, "Is that the *politico*?"

"Yeah, only he was supposed to have gone the other way."

Ben said, disgustedly, "Ain't that just fine. And I imagine he's brought some company right behind him. Goddammit, Justa, what does he think he's doing?"

All I could do was shake my head. We stood steady watching them come on. Ten yards away they came to a jolting and shuddering stop as they pulled their horses up. Their animals were good and lathered up and their flanks were heaving. A man with one eye could see they'd been put through a hard run and they weren't the quality of horseflesh could stand much hard usage. Señor Elizandro put his hand to a sombrero he'd got somewhere. He said, "Well, good day, my good friend. We have the good fortune to meet again."

I said, "Señor, what the hell are you doing here? You promised me you were going southwest."

"Aaah, yes," he said, smiling. "That was the plan. But by bad chance we ran into a large party of *federales* who had heard the shooting and were coming to the jail for the rescue." He shrugged. "We had no choice, since they outnumbered us to a great extent, except to turn the other way."

"Well, did you have to come straight to us?"

He smiled and swept his hand around. "Was there any other way for me to turn? Besides, you seem to have excellent luck, Meester Williams." He gestured toward the little ridge in advance of us. "I think perhaps we should progress forward. I think maybe there are some *policía* coming."

I looked off in the direction he'd come from. Far off in the distance, maybe several miles, I could see a thin column of dust rising toward the sky. I said, "Well, that is just wonderful. I break you out of jail and you bring the police down on me."

He said, gently, "Did you not think they would chase you anyway? Your leetle bombs did much work. An idea, by the way, on which I congratulate you. It was excellent planning."

"Let's move," I said, with no attempt to hide my ill temper. I looked back to see how Elizandro's men had fallen in with my party. I saw Benito. He gave me a big smile and a wave. Then I saw Jack sort of bending over in his saddle. Then I saw the red splotch on his white shirt near his left side. I said, "Jack! What the hell's the matter?"

"Nothin', Justa," he said. "Little nick. Don't amount to a hill of beans."

I swore. "When did you get hit? You were supposed to be back out of the way."

Ben spoke up. "He wouldn't stay back. He come up by me to give more fire."

"Damn you, Jack!" I said. "You wasn't to have any part of the gunplay. Now you've gone and got yourself shot. You told me you was too old for this sort of thing! Why didn't you listen to yourself?"

Before he could answer, Señor Elizandro said, gently, "I think it would be good if we moved." He pointed toward the dust cloud. It was visibly larger. "I think they come pretty queek."

"Let's go," I said.

We set off at a canter, aiming for the corner of that low ridge. I yelled back, "We're going to take it slow. I don't want to raise any dust. Lew, how's your man?"

Lew said, "He ain't real happy right now. I think he's got a busted wrist. Don't know how that could have happened."

I had originally estimated the ridge as being some two miles distant. But it seemed the more we rode the further away it got. Heat shimmered off the barren plains making it difficult to see clearly in that westerly direction. I took a squint at the sun. It was coming down toward the horizon and I calculated there couldn't be much more than an hour and a half before it started coming twilight. Dark was our ally; it would cover our dust and disguise our intentions.

Elizandro said, politely, "Perhaps we should go a leetle more *rápido*."

"No," I said. "We're doing just fine. By the way, what the hell is your calling name? Your first name? I'm getting tired of calling you señor."

He said, "Miguel. Until my father's death I was called Miguelito because, as you say it, Miguel was also his calling name."

"We do the same thing in Texas," I said. "Except we refer to them as Junior."

"I know," he said.

"You know a lot about the United States and you speak damn good English. How come?"

He said, "I lived in San Antonio for some time. I went to school there at the small college they have."

"Yeah?"

He was looking off in the distance, watching the advance of the catch party that was beginning now to almost grow visible as mounted horsemen. "Yes," he said. He hesitated, then said, "Perhaps I came this way because I will have to leave Mexico for a time. I have some very powerful enemies in the government. I think I will do better across the Rio Bravo, or the Rio Grande as you call it."

That alarmed me. I said, "Listen, Miguelito, I've got my own troubles. I got no time to be messing in Mexico's politics. If you've brought a hornet's nest down around our ears on account of your business, I ain't going to take that too kindly."

He smiled. "I will ask you again if you do not think they would have chased you anyway?"

I said, "Maybe not as hard as they're going to be chasing you."

He said, "My men and I will take the hard parts. We will fight the rear-guard action if it comes to that."

Which made me think of something that had been on my mind. I said, "You should have been eight. What happened to two of your party?"

He made a motion with his hand. "They were killed. Mexican politics are very violent. It is difficult to last long as a politician in these times."

I said, "The same can be said for your horses. Looks like you rode them pretty damn hard. You're liable to be fighting a rear-guard action, all right, but that will be because your horses have played out."

Miguel smiled and said, "Oh, no. It is a well-known fact that Mexicans are the best horsemen in the world. We know that because we keep telling each other. We've been killing horses since the time of the *conquistadores*, but we are still the best horsemen in the world."

I just gave him a look. Then I glanced toward the horsemen that were quartering toward our right flank. The ridge had mercifully drawn a little nearer. I waved my arm forward and touched spurs to my gelding. He responded even though I knew he had to be damn good and tired. I put him in a gallop, Señor Elizandro keeping pace beside me. I looked back. Our little band was strung out with Lew and his *capitán* bringing up the rear. Jack was still hunched over his saddle horn, but he seemed to be riding easy in the saddle. I could just hope he wasn't too bad hurt, but I wouldn't know about that until I got a look.

I kept watching the catch party coming up on our right. They had the angle on us, but they were a good deal too far off to present an immediate threat. As we swept around the west end of the little ridge I calculated the police party was still a good two, three miles away.

Ahead of us there were other ridges and I debated about going on further, perhaps forting up behind the second in the line, or perhaps the third. They weren't ridges exactly, not what I thought of as a ridge. They were more little long, narrow humps of sand and rock and cactus and brush with every kind of thorn you could imagine. They didn't seem to have much order or much reason; they just seemed to rise out of the floor of the plain more or less as an afterthought. I knew, of course, that they stepped their way toward the distant mountains but they were so far off you didn't immediately connect them with the little humps that looked so friendly to my eye.

I decided to take a stand behind the first knoll. I knew the horses needed rest badly and I knew that standing at the first ridge would leave the *federales* unprotected on the flat plain. We might be able to deal them considerable discouragement with some well-placed shooting.

We swept around the end of the ridge and I led us to a halt about halfway down its quarter-mile length. I yelled back, "Take the bits out of your horses' mouths and loosen their girths, but don't unsaddle. Lew, you better get your prisoner off that animal's back before he craters. Just hog-tie him and lay him on the ground. And hurry! We haven't got much time."

I dismounted, pulling out my carbine as I did and digging down in my saddlebags for a handful of extra ammunition. I said, "Miguel, tell your men to take their rifles and get up on the ridge. Tell them no one fires until I do. Make that very clear to them."

He let loose a volley of Spanish and his men began swinging out of the saddle and doing as my party was doing. "Jack," I said, "you stay down here and look after the horses. Rig you up a picket rope if you feel up to it. But stay down here!''

He didn't say anything. I thought he looked a little drawn and white-faced, but I was in too big of a hurry hustling people up on the top of the ridge. I had let my horse's reins drop. He would ground halt, being trained not to walk far trailing his reins because he'd found out the hard way that he would step on them and that would bring a result not to his liking. I had my carbine in my hand and I scrambled up the little slope, dodging through the brambles and briar bushes. My ankle was hurting pretty good and I had no doubt that I'd caught a slug through my boot, though just how bad it was I didn't have time to look into. I went up toward the crest yelling for Ben. I wanted him beside me. If any delicate shots had to be made, he was the one that would make them.

When I got to the top I collapsed behind a bramble of greasewood and peered out. I could see the riders now. There appeared to be about thirty or forty of them. A voice to my left said, quietly, ''*Federales* and *rurales*. See the difference in the color of the uniforms? The *federales* are tan. The *rurales* are green. Fortunately for us I see more *federales*.''

I looked over. Señor Elizandro was lying just to my left. He had a rifle laid out before him. I said, ''They're still at least a mile away. But riding hard.''

''They have good horses,'' he said. ''They will come straight on. They are not very intelligent. They will have expected us to do what they would do—keep running. They would not have considered the ambush.''

I said, ''Then they got a hell of a shock coming.''

Ben had come up to my right. He flopped down and looked at the oncoming riders. He said, ''They keep coming like they are, I'd figure about five minutes.''

I raised my head and looked down the line. Señor Elizandro's men were deployed to the left. Counting Norris, we were five of our party anchoring the right side, the side the catch party would try to flank. Lew was at the very end. I called down to him and asked how the *capitán* was doing. I still hadn't made up my mind as to how best to utilize my hostage.

He called back, "Got him tied down on the ground. Jack's watching him."

"How's Jack?"

"Little unsteady, Justa."

I said, because they were getting a little too close to be talking out loud, "Pass the word—nobody fires until I do."

The word went to my left in Spanish and to my right in English. Then I said to Ben, "Tell me when you think you can hit your first target. I'll wait about a half a minute after that for the rest of us."

Ben said, "We're going to kill an awful lot of horses."

I knew how he felt about that but it couldn't be helped. Horses just made much bigger targets than men and, at the range we'd open up at, there was little chance of just hitting men. But a dead horse was just as good as a dead man so far as their pursuit went. They weren't going to be able to ride double and catch us. I said, "Forget it, Ben. I never taught you it was easy doing these matters."

"Yeah," he said. He licked his lips, watching the riders coming on. They sure as hell weren't saving anything for the next day. Ben said, "What the hell, we'll probably be doing them horses a service by shooting them. God knows they is fixing to get rode to death."

I looked down the line. Norris was laying next to Hays. I could dimly see a rifle in his hands through the underbrush. I didn't know where he'd gotten it; borrowed it off of Jack, probably.

The light was starting to go. I figured it wasn't more than a half an hour to good dark. I tried to think of the date, trying to figure how much moon to expect, but all that did was bring on guilty thoughts of how near the date was and how little time I had left. But, hell, I couldn't blame the woman. She'd put up with my foolishness about as long as any mortal woman could. She wanted a husband and a settled life; she didn't want to be married to some wild man that was always chasing around the country getting into trouble. She couldn't have cared less that I was laying on a lonely hummock in Mexico fixing to shoot it out with the police troops. As far as she was concerned I should have been at home seeing to getting our house built and picking out my best man.

Ben said, "Getting pretty close." He shifted his rifle into a firing position. "You might want to tell these folks that at the distance we'll be shooting they need to aim low. Us up above them is likely to make for high shooting."

I passed the word down. Ben knew how to shoot and there was no mistake about that. He'd learned from Buttercup, who might have been the worst cook God ever invented but who knew more about shooting than anyone I'd ever met.

I waited a minute more. They were closer. The time was coming. From my left Señor Elizandro said, "Are you puzzled why they should ride so straight into an ambush?"

I said, "Yeah."

He said, with almost amusement in his voice, "Because they must keep their jobs. And because they know there are thirty more coming behind them. And because they do not believe they will be the one that is shot." He paused. "I do not think you understand the mind of the Mexican, Señor Williams."

"I reckon not," I said. My mouth was starting to get a little dry.

He said, "I do not know about this 'reckoning' business, señor. But I do know about shooting men. I think you are feeling bad about shooting at these men as they come after us."

I turned my head left and said, in a hard voice, "Look here, you are the *jefe* with your men. Right now I'm the boss. Just keep your damn opinions to yourself."

Ben said, "I could hit one right now."

I sighted my rifle, concentrating on the leader. He grew ever larger as they closed toward our position. But Señor Elizandro's words were bothering me. I said, out of the corner of my mouth, "What do you mean talking to me like that? Hell, you ain't even supposed to be here."

He said, quietly, "I was only complimenting you on your sense of honor, señor. I meant no insult. And I apologize, once again, for my presence and that of my men. But you must admit that we might prove valuable."

I said, "Just shoot when I do."

By then the party was no more than two or three hundred yards away. They were already taking the bend to outflank us to the right. I sighted again on the leader of the catch party. Ben said, "Dammit, Justa, shoot! They going to be in our back pocket in another minute."

Coming out of the jail I had shot the desk sergeant without a qualm. And I had perhaps shot one or two others in the smoke and confusion. But that had been in hot blood. Now I found myself reluctant to shoot men who'd done me no harm and were simply exercising their jobs.

The lead rider grew bigger in my sights. I aimed for his chest and squeezed the trigger. He flipped off the back of his horse like he'd run into a clothesline.

At my shot the others began to fire. At first it was sporadic, but then they got in unison and began to lay down a deadly and devastating barrage. At first the whole crowd continued to come on but then the leaders began to falter and turn back. After about four or five volleys I could see the terrible effect our fire was having. Horses and men were down all over the place. Occasionally I would see a man who'd had his horse shot out from under him catch on with a *compadre* and swing up behind him and ride hell-bent for the rear, racing to get out of the range of our fire.

It was all over within two or three minutes. I could see a few wounded men crawling around on the floor of the plain. I'd stopped firing, as had my people, but to my left rifles still exploded, aimed at the wounded men. I said to Señor Elizandro, "Dammit, tell your men to quit firing. We don't shoot the wounded."

He shrugged. "It is perhaps an act of mercy. But as you wish." He raised his head and yelled, *"Alto! Alto!"*

The firing ceased. Not a single shot had come our way. To my right Ben said, "I think we thinned them out considerable. I reckon they lost fifteen horses and upwards of ten men."

Now twilight had asserted itself and dark was not far off. I waited, watching as the policemen pulled well back out of range. There was no distinct place for them to huddle up, it being that worthless plain. But it appeared that they drew back something like a mile. I could see them circling their horses around them and grouping together as if they were taking counsel with each other. I said to Señor Elizandro, "Will they try us tonight?" I couldn't see him, but I felt the shrug in his voice.

"Who can say? They are not cowards, but neither are they stupid. My guess would be that they won't, but then again they might."

I said, dryly, "Thanks for the answer. I know less now than when I asked it."

He said, "If you ask a difficult question, expect a difficult answer."

"Yeah," I said. I waited another half hour, waited until it was good dark and I could no longer see the party that was chasing us. Then I said to Ben, "I want you to stay up here and keep your eyes open. You got the best eyes of any of us, but I got to get these men fed and get this mess organized. I'll send you something up."

"Water," he said. "My mouth is dry as a bone."

And so was mine. Gunfighting is mighty thirsty work. I said to Señor Elizandro, "Miguel, leave two of your men up here to watch. We're going down to the prairie floor and figure things out. You know this country. I've got to have your advice."

He softly hollered down a little volley of Spanish. After that he got up, as I did, and started down the little incline in the dark. Ben was passing the word down to the others and I commenced to make my way through that tough underbrush. Me and Señor Elizandro arrived at the bottom at about the same time. Dark shapes were looming up all around me. I picked out Hays amongst the bunch and told him to start getting some of the canned goods and water off the packhorse. "And as soon as you've passed it around down here I want you to get some provender up to those who are still on the ridge."

He had about a half dozen gallon canteens of water that he was passing around. On top of that he had two big earthenware jugs carrying about five or six gallons apiece, but there was no water for the horses. You can fill men up with water, but if they are depending on horses you better have water for the horses or else the men ain't going to make it.

Señor Elizandro and I sat down on the ground, cross-legged. I got out my big jackknife and cut about half the top out of the can Hays had handed me. Then I took a good suck at it. It was canned tomatoes. I don't like canned tomatoes, but it was something so I made do as best I could. I passed the knife to Elizandro and he done like I had. I said, "What'd you get."

"Apricots," he said. "Or peaches. Who can say? It all tastes like tin."

"How much damage you reckon we did them?"

I could feel him shrug in the dark. "Perhaps a dozen men. More horses."

"Oughtn't that to slow 'em down some?"

He shook his head. "Not really. Remember, they are not like your police in Texas. They are more like soldiers."

I didn't know what time it was but the moon was starting to get up. It was a three-quarter moon, on the wane, and the soft light cast little shadows here and there in our ravine. Now and again I could hear a horse stamping his feet and low murmurs in Spanish and English as the men talked amongst themselves. I said to Elizandro, "What about water? We've got what I figure to be about eighty-five miles to go to the border and these horses ain't going to make it without water. You know of any water holes nearby?"

He shook his head slowly. "Nooo. But then you must realize I am from the south of Monterrey. This is not my part of the country. I do know there is a river some forty miles distant."

"Forty miles?" I said. Hell, it might have been a thousand for all the difference it made.

Just then I heard the soft sound of someone calling my name. I looked back up the slope. It was Ben who'd come about halfway down. He said, "You better get the folks up here. They is fixing to give us another try."

I jumped swiftly to my feet, calling urgently to my party as I did so. Señor Elizandro was doing the same. In unison we raced up the incline and flopped down on the crest. By the light of the moon I could see the large party moving toward us, angling off to come around the other end of the ridge, the easterly end. Behind them they had left several fires burning, sagebrush and mesquite I reckoned. Of course that was to make us think they'd settled in for the night.

I watched them moving. They were still well out of range. I wanted them within at least three or four hundred yards. I said, "I thought they wouldn't attack at night?"

Ben said, "That's Indians, Justa."

I said, a little irritably, "I know that. I just think it's kind of damn foolhardy to attack a fortified position when you can't see what you're shooting at and you're in plain sight."

Just beyond Ben I heard Norris's voice. He said, "Everyone is not as smart you you, Justa. And they *are* the law. This *is* their country, you know."

I didn't say anything. I knew that sooner or later me and Norris was going to have to have a real good talk and get matters straightened out, but I didn't see any point in rushing it.

Ben said, "Any time now, Justa."

I said, softly (because sound carries so much better at night), "Just fire into the bunch. It's too dark for individual targets. But watch your elevation. Shoot almost over their heads."

Then I sighted down the dark barrel of my carbine and squeezed the trigger. The gun boomed in my ear. I saw the mass of men and horses go into sudden confusion but I couldn't see well enough to tell if I'd dropped anyone. On my shot guns began to boom all around me. I fired my magazine empty and was in the process of reloading when I heard shouting off to my right. "JUSTA! JUSTA! JUSTA! DAMMIT, JUSTA!"

I looked. It was Lew, anchoring the right side of our firing line. He was gesturing behind him. He yelled,

"RIDERS! A HALF A DOZEN! MAYBE MORE! COMIN' OUR WAY!"

So that was their attack. A diversion and then a flank attack. Sacrifice a few of your people to take your enemy from his blind side. I jumped up. I said, "Come on, Ben! Hurry!" I waved at Lew to come with us and then started scrambling back down the ridge. Fortunately few of the other men had seen what was occurring and so didn't try to follow. I scrambled down the bank, still cramming cartridges into my rifle as fast as I could. Ben and Lew and I all hit the floor of the ravine at about the same time. It was a good two hundred yards to the end of the ridge. I desperately wanted to catch the ambush party as far up the line as I could. I didn't want shooting in behind my men and I didn't want a gunfight anywhere near our horses.

"Hurry!" I said, and began to run as fast as I could toward the end of the ridge, the direction the riders would be coming from.

We had run and staggered our way for about one hundred yards when I suddenly saw dark shapes rounding the end of the hummock. They were clearly outlined against the moon-bright sky.

I didn't have to say a word. Like one we all dropped to a knee, finding what available cover we could behind the brush and brambles of the ravine floor. I waited, sighting on the riders. I couldn't get a clear count but there appeared to be about eight of them. I waited and then I waited some more. They were not coming very fast, more in a slow canter than anything else. I figured they were unsure of themselves—unsure of where we were exactly and unsure of the terrain. They'd probably gotten a pretty good count on our number by the muzzle flashes earlier and they probably knew they couldn't afford many mistakes. Well, they'd already made one. They'd started too early and they'd ridden too wide of the ridge's end. If they'd hung closer Lew might never have seen them and they could have got in behind us and caught us in some kind of cross fire. The only man we'd of had watching our back was Jack, and he was hurt. I was going to have to see to him at first light, but meanwhile I had this other business to tend to.

I sighted in on the lead rider. Just before I squeezed the trigger I said, softly, "Fire!"

We levered and fired, levered and fired. I had expected the police to turn and run at the first volley, but they had stubbornly stood their ground, firing back. Most of the shots went singing over our heads, but then I felt one play its way through the little bush right beside my ear.

I emptied my rifle and then pulled my revolver and continued firing. At last they began retreating. It appeared to me that only two men rode away though it was difficult to tell because the horses of the downed men were stampeding along with the others.

Slowly I stood up. I said, "I've got to get back up on that ridge. But some of those hombres may be playing possum. Ben, you and Lew stay here and watch. I got to get back up there and see what the hell that main bunch is doing."

I turned and limped back up the ridge. In the excitement of the moment I had run with no thought of my ankle but now, in the aftercalm, it was aching and hurting.

I got back to my original position and flopped down. The rifles had stopped firing and, in the eerie quiet, I could see the main party of the police galloping back toward the light of their campfires. I couldn't be sure but I thought I could see a few dark shapes on the ground. I caught sight of one horse loose, but I figured the *federales* were pretty careful to gather up any strays that might have lost their riders.

I had no earthly idea what time it was. I glanced up at

the sky and saw the moon was up considerable more than I'd expected. I got out my watch and struck a match and was amazed to see it was going on for eleven o'clock. It didn't seem like it but it appeared we'd been in a three-hour gunfight, off and on. If somebody had asked me to give a time I'd of said no more than fifteen minutes.

I said to Señor Elizandro, "Leave one man up here to watch. We are going to go back down and prepare to pull out."

I got to my knees and called softly to my men to move to the ravine floor. "Don't make any noise. Take it slow and quiet."

We gathered up at the base of the ridge behind a bunch of rocks that had rolled down the incline. I directed Elizandro to have his men gather up as much brush as they could and build three or four fires. I wanted our pursuers to think we'd settled in for the night.

I was concerned about Jack Cole, but first I had to get Lew and Ben back. Just as I was about to send for Hays to send him after them I heard two shots ring out down the ravine. I started hobbling that way, going as quick as I could. I wanted to call out, to yell to Ben to see what had happened, but I dared not. I just kept going, hoping they hadn't gotten themselves suckered by a couple of Mexican police crawling up on them through the bush. But I couldn't help my misgivings. There had been two of them and there had been two shots.

I had gone perhaps fifty yards in the dark, making my way slowly, when I saw two shapes loom up in the dark. I dropped to one knee and leveled my rifle. Then I heard English being spoken. I said, "Ben! That you?"

He said, "Yeah. Me and Lew."

"Y'all all right?"

"Yeah, but you were right about them Mex soldiers. A couple of them were playing possum."

"What happened?"

I heard Lew chuckle. "They ain't playin' possum no more."

As we walked back the fires were starting to be lit. It made an eerie sight, horses and men milling around in that little ravine, their shadows dancing off the rocks and the side of the ridge.

We walked into the light. Jack Cole came up. He didn't look good, but he didn't look as bad as I'd feared. I asked after his condition. He said, "Best I can figure the slug went on through. I ought to be all right. Lost some blood is all. But the worst part is we lost two horses."

"What!"

"Yeah. That little gunfight y'all had down the draw there. Bunch of bullets got to whizzing around down here and hit a couple of horses."

I said, tensely, "Good horses?"

He shook his head. "Mex horses. But I can't see none of these animals carrying double, not as give-out as they are. Not to mention short of water. So what it comes down to, the fact of the business is, we is two horses short."

I set about getting matters organized. It was difficult because I had to give orders to Señor Elizandro's men through him. I got him aside and said, "Look here, we're trailing out of here tonight. These horses won't stand much hard pushing so we are going to walk them."

Then I gave him the bad news about the two horses we'd lost. I said, "They may be yours or they may be a couple of mine. But I can't walk and Jack Cole can't walk and I won't let my brother or Lew Vera walk. They are too important. Now, how you want to handle it?"

He said, simply, "We will switch off walking, my men and me. Do you have a plan?"

I said, "Right now the only plan I got is to put as much distance between us and them *federales* as I can."

In the flickering firelight he said, "Of course you know that will not help."

I was hot and thirsty and damn tired. I said, "What are you talking about? We get away from them and we got a clear run to the border. All we got to do is find water for these horses and we'll make it."

He shook his head. "You forget the telegraph. They have such equipment that they can come to the telegraph line and make it work just as if they were in a telegraph office."

I said, incredulously—not because I'd never heard of such a thing but because I didn't expect it of the Mexican police—"You mean they can tap into the line?"

"Yes," he said, gravely. "That is what I was trying to express. You must realize also that there are several *rurales* stations between here and the border. We will have the ones behind us and perhaps a hundred in front. This is not as easy a matter as you thought, Señor Williams."

"Son of a bitch!" I said.

At my shoulder an irritating voice said, "If you'd have acted in this matter as I wished, none of us would be in this fix now. But oh, no, you knew best. Well, let's wait and see if you knew best."

It was Norris. I said, with cold heat, "Get the hell away from me, Norris. You and I are going to come to terms. But that will be later. I don't think you're going to enjoy it."

I said to Señor Elizandro, "Where the hell is this telegraph line?"

He pointed east. "In that direction. I do not know how many miles. It runs beside the railroad track."

I said, grimly, "Then we better get started. We got to beat those bastards to the line and cut it before they can telegraph ahead."

"That," he said, "would be a wise plan."

I said, lowly, "Pass the word, everybody mount up. Miguel, you see to your men. I recommend everyone drink their fill of water right now. We ain't going to be doing a lot of stopping. We'll be heading northeast but mostly east."

I stopped to take a look at Lew and his prisoner. Davilla looked pretty beat. Lew had untied him, but he still looked like a man that hadn't been very comfortable for a considerable amount of time. I said to Lew, "Let him walk at first. Elizandro's men are going to have to trade off. Let him trade off with them."

I didn't know if Davilla understood me or not but he give me a sullen stare and mouthed something in Spanish I couldn't understand. I asked Lew what he'd said. Lew said, "Well, I don't reckon you want to know. I don't *think* you want to know. I figure ol' Davilla here ain't real well acquainted with your temper else he might have kept his mouth shut."

"Just let him walk awhile," I said. "If I thought he could stand it I'd have Norris walking too. It's him and Davilla that has got us all in this pickle. But you stay in the saddle. If any trouble comes up I want you and Ben and Hays mounted."

I swung into my own saddle, noting with what difficulty Jack got mounted. I hoped he wasn't just being brave to save me worry. If he was bad hurt I wanted to know about it.

My horse was some rested though I knew he would have admired to have a good drink right about then. But there was nothing I could do about that. I rode to the front of my little caravan and said, quietly, "Let's go."

We went trailing off across the plains, skirting the little hummocks, traveling by the moonlight and generally heading for the railroad tracks and the telegraph line.

8

All through that long night we trailed east by northeast. I didn't want to head directly east because that wouldn't have taken me a mile closer to the border. I wanted to make every mile north I could while at the same time angling toward that telegraph line.

The trek was wearing us all down. We hadn't ate, we hadn't slept and the horses had had no water. I could tell they were suffering badly, especially the Mexican horses, who were simply not as strong as the stock we'd brought from home.

We kept trailing through the night. Occasionally I would drop back to see how Jack was doing. He was suffering and there was no mistake about that. Lew had untied *Capitán* Davilla's hands because his wrist was swollen so badly. I asked Lew how it had come to be broken and Lew said he thought someone had whacked the good *capitán* across it with a pistol when the *capitán* was slow putting

down a gun. I said, "You wouldn't know who that someone was, would you?"

He said, "Oh, just someone who was there at the time.
The *capitán* got confused. He was told to fetch this person
one of his spare uniforms and he must have misunderstood
because he fetched out a revolver instead. Reckon his
hearing had gone off."

I inspected Lew in the poor light. But I had taken note
earlier that he looked mighty authentic in his uniform. It
was even a pretty good fit. I said, "Well, how does it feel
to be a *capitán* in the *federales*?"

He said, "Well, it's kind of funny. I have to catch myself every once in a while to keep from arresting the lot
of you sorry *bandidos*."

Once Norris rode up alongside me and said, deter-
minedly, "I want to talk to you."

"Not now, Norris," I said. "My poor tired horse is
having enough trouble carrying me without that extra load
of righteous bullshit you are dying to load on me."

About four in the morning we struck a wide-open stretch
of salt flats. It made the going easier, but it also made us
more vulnerable to attack. Having the strongest horse, I
dropped back, telling Ben to take the lead and keep pointed
in the same direction we'd been going. I wanted to see if
there was any pursuit behind us. I waited a good half hour.
Nothing showed up. And they would have been easy to
see with the moon glinting off the white of the salt flats.
I gave it another quarter of an hour and then put my horse
into a canter to catch up. He didn't much like it but he
was game and he was a stayer.

So we went on. I taken notice that Señor Elizandro did
not exhalt his position. He changed off walking just like
the rest of his men. Ben and Hays volunteered to do the
same but I wouldn't have it. Fortunately for the Mexicans,
they were wearing low-heeled, calvary-style boots. Next

to our high-heeled Texas boots, that made walking a near-bearable chore. A Texas cowboy wears those high-heeled boots so as to have an excuse to never do anything on foot that he can do on a horse.

I was worrying considerable about Jack. He was looking worse and worse, and every now and then I'd see him sway in the saddle. Norris had taken to riding alongside of him, putting out a comforting hand every now and then to steady him.

Finally, just about the time I was ready to give up on it, the sun started putting in an appearance. I looked at my watch. In the dim light I could see it was just after six o'clock. We'd been trailing for nearly seven hours. I didn't know how many miles we'd made, not as impeded as we were, but I had to figure it was close to fifteen.

At seven I called a halt. I didn't like our position. We were out in the middle of a broad-ass plain with the nearest cover a good two or three miles away. But there was nothing I could do about it. I had to take a look at Jack and I had to see to my ankle. It wasn't throbbing worse than I could stand, but it was getting a good deal of my attention.

And the horses had to have some rest. The Mexican horses were standing splay-legged, their heads down, their flanks heaving even though they hadn't been doing nothing but walking. A man can go longer without water than a horse can, and these horses had been sweated up a bunch. I doubted the Mexican horses had been heavily watered, as ours had, before we'd departed Monterrey in haste.

We crawled out of our saddles, most so weary they just sat down where they stood. I went over to Jack and helped him down. When I got him on the ground I saw immediately he was pretty sick. I felt his forehead. He was burning up. I said, ''Well, Jack, we've let this go too far. At least I have. You've got yourself a pretty good infection.''

Ben and Hays came over to see if they could help, but
I ordered them back to the head of the line. I said, "I'm
fixing to get kind of busy. So, Ben, it is your watch. I
don't want anything slipping up on us."

Señor Elizandro's men were out to one side, watching,
hunkered down on their heels. Miguel had come to my
side offering his assistance. I said, "You can build me a
little fire. Won't take much. I can already tell I'm going
to have to use a knife."

I got Jack's shirt off and it was about as bad as I'd
thought. I yelled at Hays, who was officially in charge of
the supplies, to bring me the last bottle of whiskey. Then
I took a closer look at Jack's wound. If we'd have got to
it right away it would have been nothing. The slug had hit
him in the meaty part of his side and passed on through
without touching any of his vitals. But in the time that had
passed, the wounds had scabbed over and set up an infection inside. From both wounds, the entry point of the bullet and the exit, little red lines were running out and the
flesh was puckered and inflamed around the holes. I was
going to have to open him up, let the infection drain, and
then stick in some whiskey-soaked tents to keep it draining
and keep down the infection. Jack just sat there, his head
down, his hands in his lap. He said, "'Twas my own damn
fault. I knowed I wadn't no gun hand no more."

"Let that be," I said. "Can't be helped now."

Señor Elizandro had a small blaze going in front of us
from some dried brush he'd gathered up. He said, "How
else may I be of assistance?"

I said, "You might want to hold his shoulders when the
time comes. But mainly you can tell me where the hell
that telegraph line and that railroad is."

He shrugged and pointed east. "It is over there. I know
not how far. Perhaps just over the next rise, perhaps a
mile."

"That's just dandy," I said. "Here I am with a wounded man and worn-out horses and we don't even know where we are."

Jack said, "Justa, I'd appreciate it if you'd git on with it."

I could hear the hurt in his voice. I said, "Here comes Hays with the whiskey." I took the bottle out of Ray's hand, uncorked it and held it out to Jack. "You better take a pretty good slug of this. I reckon this little bit of foolishness might smart some."

He tilted up the bottle gratefully. His throat worked several times and then he took it from his mouth. He said, "Aaaah."

I said to Hays, "I've got a clean shirt in my saddlebags. Take and rip off a couple of rags from it about two inches wide and about six inches long."

"Huh?" he said. "A *clean* shirt?"

I said, "Don't stand there gawking and mumbling. Do like I tell you."

While I waited I got out my jackknife and began to heat the tip in the fire. Ten yards away I was aware of Elizandro's men. They were watching us but they were having a hell of a palaver in Spanish. They were speaking low, too low for me to hear at that distance even if I could have understood them. Benito seemed to be doing most of the talking. We were along toward the middle of the line, sort of strung out in the same fashion we'd traveled. Ben was up at the front and Lew and his prisoner were at the end. Norris was lurking somewhere behind the horses and Hays was running to get the rags. All of a sudden Benito and two of the other three got up. The fourth just stayed hunkered down, staring at the ground. Benito and the other two drew pistols. I was so startled I just stared at them. But it didn't matter. Where I was placed and the position I was in there wasn't a damn thing I could have done. All three pointed their revolvers straight at me. I stared at them.

Benito said, "Hey, choo *pinche* gringo. We want choo *dinero* and choo horses. *Comprende?*"

I shifted my eyes left to Elizandro. I said, "You got a funny way of thanking a man for getting you out of jail."

He said, quietly, "This is none of my making, señor. But I will attend to it."

Benito cocked his pistol. He said, "Ah doan want none of choo chit, Señor Williams. Choo git up an' han' me choo money."

I stood up slowly, the hot knife still in my hand. But Señor Elizandro was already walking toward Benito. Perhaps fifteen to twenty yards separated them. He said, in Spanish, "You will not do this thing, Benito. These are our friends. You will not rob them."

Benito said, in Spanish, "Get away, Don Miguel. You have nothing to do with this. I am dealing with this gringo. I am tired of being chased and shot at. He has enough money in his pocket and good horses on which we can make our getaway and have no more trouble. We cannot win your way." He pointed the revolver toward Elizandro.

I said, "Miguel! Leave him alone! He's loco. Don't fool with him."

But Elizandro kept walking and kept talking in that calm voice. He said, "I am not going to let you do this. These people have helped us. Is this the way you want to repay them? I thought we were working for the cause of a better Mexico. Now I want you to put that pistol away and obey orders."

"The hell with you!" Benito said. By now all three guns were trained on Miguel.

He was perhaps five yards away when Benito shot him. The bullet took him high in the left shoulder, flipping him sideways and down.

But almost as an echo to that single shot there came a fusillade so fast I couldn't count. All three of the Mexicans went staggering backwards, falling after one or two faltering steps. I looked to my left and there was Ben with his revolver drawn and smoke issuing out the end. He had shot all three faster than you could have thought, faster than Señor Elizandro could hit the ground. He was some quick, that Ben.

The fourth man of the group got quietly to his feet and put his hands above his head. I looked around quickly for the fifth man. They had been six in all. He was standing by the packhorse, by Hays, staring in disbelief and wonder.

I ran over to Señor Elizandro. He'd caught a bad one. He was on his back, bleeding from his left shoulder. After all the explosions of the shooting, the morning had got suddenly quiet. I ripped open his shirt. The ball from Benito's revolver had hit him square in the bone of his shoulder. There was no exit wound. It was clear the slug was in the complicated apparatus of bone somewhere around the upper reaches of his arm. I closed his shirt gently. I said, "Miguel, there is nothing I can do for you. This is work for a doctor. All I can do is pour a little whiskey in there to try and keep the wound from festering. Meanwhile, I must attend to my own man, Jack Cole."

He said, through clenched teeth, "I beg your humble pardon for bringing men such as Benito and the others down on your troubles. I had never thought they would behave in such a manner."

I said, "Rest as easy as you can."

I glanced up. Norris was there. I said, "Try to make him as easy as you can." Then I added, bitterly, "He'd of never of got shot without your help."

I got up and went over to the three dead Mexicans. Ben was standing there, reloading his revolver. Each of the

three had caught two perfectly placed bullets in or near
the heart. Ben said, "I was slow, Justa. I'm sorry. I should
have pulled the minute I seen this son of a bitch"—he
tapped Benito with his boot toe—"come out with his. Hell,
it could have been you they shot."

I give him a look. He was a pretty good kid.

But I still had Jack to worry about.

The fire had burned down but there was still enough
blaze to get my knife tip a glowing red. I advised Jack to
take another long hit off the whiskey bottle. The first one
was already beginning to work and he was glad enough to
have another drink. I let it soak in while Hays brought me
the strips of cloth off my clean shirt, the tents, as they
were called, to keep the wounds draining. After I'd given
him a few minutes I had Hays get around behind him and
hold his shoulders while I took after the two punctures
with my hot knife. Lord, what blood and gore poured out
of those two holes. I was amazed the man could still be
alive with so much poison in him. He done a good bit of
squirming and smothered curses, but all in all he took it
pretty well. When I had let both holes drain as best they
could I took the two pieces of cloth, soaked them in whiskey, and then prodded them into the holes with the point
of my knife. The idea was to make them heal from the
inside out rather than to have them seal off and then pu-
trefy from within. When it was over Jack was just about
spent from the pain. I gave him another drink of whiskey
and then carried the bottle over to Señor Elizandro, who
was lying on his back staring up at the sky which had now
turned a merciless blue with that hot summer Mexican sun
bearing down on us.

I hunkered down beside him. I could see he was in
considerable pain. I pulled his shirt back to expose the
ball of his shoulder. The bullet couldn't have taken him in
a worse place. I poured a little whiskey into the opening

the slug had made. He winced and jumped enough to tell me it had done some good. Norris was beside him, down on his knees. He looked a little pale. I said, "Fun, ain't it, Norris?"

He didn't say anything.

Señor Elizandro said, "How many—" Then he gasped a little as some of the whiskey trickled on down into his wound. After a few seconds he got control of himself. "How many of my men were involved?"

"Just the three," I said. "They are dead. My brother shot them."

"Gracias, mi Dios," he said.

I said, "But we got trouble. We got to get you to a doctor. I just can't help you. And that is a bad wound you got. Miguel, I got to tell you, right now I don't know what to do."

He said, trying to struggle up, "I can ride."

I stood away from him. Hays came over at that second. We looked around. Ray said, simply, "Well, at least we ain't short no horses no more."

I yelled, "Lew!"

He was there in an instant. I said, "Take *Capitán* Davilla and ride east. That son of a bitch has to know where the railroad line is. And the telegraph."

He said, "He wants to see you. By the way, the bastard speaks English. Some, not much."

I said, "Get him over here."

After a moment or two Lew appeared with *Capitán* Davilla. He didn't look real spruce. His wrist was swollen about twice the size it ought to have been and his uniform was dirty and stained. He walked with the gait of a man who had either drank too much whiskey or had been tied in a saddle for too many hours. I knew which one was the truth. He stood before me, giving me a sullen look. I said, "I hear you speak English. Tell me what you have to say."

He said, without too much disguise for the contempt he felt, "You let me go. I make ever'body go back."

I said, "Now, *Capitán,* don't bullshit an old bullshitter. I let you go, you are going to bring rain around our heads and it ain't going to be the kind that makes crops grow. Not unless lead is good for corn."

He said, "You make big meestake."

I said, "No, you made a big mistake when you treated my brother as you did. Now the best thing you can do is to cooperate with us. Help us. That is if you want to get out of this alive. Do you want to get out of this alive?"

For answer he spit on my boots and said, "You gonna feed some crows. And maybe some wild dogs. Or coyotes."

I didn't do a thing. I just said to Lew, "I don't think you've got your prisoner in hand. Y'all take off and find us that railroad as fast as you can and get right back here."

Well, we were in a hell of a mess. I sat down and eased off my boot. I was expecting the worst but it was nowhere near as bad as I'd thought it would be. The bullet hadn't even made a hole in my boot, just a deep crease in the leather. There was no wound in my ankle, just a bruise caused by the passage of the slug. Still it hurt like hell and I realized it might handicap me if I had to do any great amount of walking. And it was so considerable better than what Jack and Señor Elizandro had suffered that I gave a silent prayer of thanks. All we'd have needed at that point was for me to be hurt to the point where I couldn't lead.

I watched Lew and the *capitán* taking off across the plains at a slow lope. I turned around to Hays, who was standing by my shoulder, and said, "Let us hope we are close. We are damn near out of options."

Lew was gone a good solid two hours. The passage of so much time made me nervous as hell and I kept an apprehensive eye on our back track, but nothing showed up. Actually, the time was handy because it gave Jack some room to get over the shock of what I'd done to him and gave the horses a little rest. It didn't help Señor Elizandro, but then nothing was going to help him except a good surgeon. And he was about seventy-five miles short of one. I didn't see how he was going to last that long. Studying him, seeing how he was laying on his back with his hurt arm cradled in to his chest, seeing the pain in his face, I couldn't see him riding five miles a-horseback let alone the distance to Laredo, which was the nearest help.

And then there was the matter of the horses. They'd been rode hard for twenty-five miles without benefit of feed or water. And out there on that barren plain there didn't look like hope for neither one.

Lew was mad as hell when he got back. He had Davilla riding beside him, the *capitán*'s bridle tied to his, Lew's, saddle horn. He said, jerking his thumb at Davilla, "This son of a bitch just took me on a wild-goose chase. That railroad line ain't no more than a mile east of here. But this bastard—" He paused to strike Davilla a backhanded slap across the mouth. "Wanders me all over hell and back like I ain't smart enough to see what he's doing." He raised his hand again. "I ought to beat him half to death."

I said, "Wait a minute. Don't kill him yet. We might can still use him."

It was a chore getting loaded back up. Everyone was nearly give out, and then there was the problem of getting the two wounded men astride their mounts, especially Miguel Elizandro. Some color had started coming back into Jack's face, but the señor was looking mighty weak and peaked. But he made no complaint or sound as we put him on his horse. I had taken the remains of my clean shirt and made a bandage of sorts, soaked in whiskey, to place over the wound. After that we'd taken some soft rope we had and bound his injured arm to his chest as tight as we could without it cutting off the circulation. When you lead a rough life in rough country you either learn how to take care of injuries and wounds or you and the people around you just don't make it. I figured I'd treated just about every kind of hurt that could be done to a man over the long years, but I shore didn't care for the way Miguel was looking. It made me feel frustrated not knowing what to do. I'd dug a few bullets out in my time, but that had been out of flesh. Near as I could figure that bullet was somewhere in the bone of his shoulder, and that was about three steps beyond me. Nevertheless, if it began to look like he wasn't going to make it anyway, I figured I might give it a stab.

We left out, leaving the three corpses of Señor Elizandro's men buried under a pile of brush that his other two hands had gathered up and covered the bodies with. It wouldn't have fooled a schoolboy, but we didn't want the *federales* or the *rurales* to know we were reduced in force by the three men, and if they didn't come right by they'd be none the wiser.

I had asked Miguel if he thought I could trust the other two, but his embarrassment about the betrayal of Benito and the two that had joined him had been so great that he excused himself from making such a judgment. He'd said, "How can I apologize? How can I say what I am sure of? I would have wagered my life on Benito and then he acts thus. He became afraid because he thought the long odds had gone against us. He became a coward. I can tell you no more."

We rode, about as sad a looking crowd as you'd ever want to see, across the alkaline plain under the unmerciful Mexican sun. I could feel the weakness in my horse. I was racking my brain, trying to think of something to do, some way to improve our position, when Ben rode up beside me. He said, "Don't look so good."

"No," I said. "Don't."

He was quiet a moment and then he said, "Trying a getaway on horseback may not have been the best idea. Especially us not knowing the country."

I gave him a look. "What'd you have in mind, taking the train back? Reckon those police would have been polite enough to have waited for the conductor to have boarded us and give us a good start? I reckon we ought to have planned the jailbreak around a railroad timetable."

He said, "No. But I think we could have figured something else."

"Just what?"

He studied for a moment and then he said, "Well, we could have scouted the country out and had us a place to go to ground so that when we run from Monterrey we'd have been damn hard to find and we wouldn't have worn the horses out or had a running gunfight across this bad terrain. Then, when matters had cooled off, we could have eased on out for the border and nobody the wiser."

It was good thinking and I told him so. Then I said, "First off you forgot a couple of small items. First, we didn't go to Monterrey to break Norris out. You'll remember we were going to try and buy him out. Once we see that couldn't be done we didn't have much time because, if you'll remember, I'm due at a wedding. Mine. And I intend to make it. To do what you figured out would have taken about a week longer and, for all you know, they might have moved Norris to someplace like Mexico City. You think we're having hell now you figure out what it would have been like to break him out of one of those prisons in the big capital."

He thought on it for a time, turning it over in his mind. Then he nodded. "I reckon you're right. I reckon we've just got to make this one work."

"That's about the size of it," I said, dryly. "And right

now nearly the full ownership of the Half-Moon Ranch is in one hell of a mess out in the bald-ass middle of nowhere. You can't look back to the last hand, Ben. You got to play the cards you were dealt.''

''Was I sounding like Norris?''

''Just a little more than I care for right now. He ain't my most popular person at the moment.''

''Justa, he feels terrible about all this. He says you won't talk to him. He says he wishes you could see his side.''

I said, ''He better leave me alone right now. I'm in the mood to see his side, all right—his insides.''

Ben shrugged. He said, ''Don't be too hard on him, Justa.''

We kept going. I don't recall ever riding a longer mile in my life, but before much longer I could see the railroad. As we got closer I could see that the bed for the tracks had been graded up some three feet off the floor of the plain. I didn't know how many *campesinos* with pick and shovel it had taken to dig up that caleche soil and elevate that rail bed, but I knew why they'd done it. Country like we were in might not get rain but about once every six months, but when you did get it it might come a gully washer and you could have a flash flood before you could blink an eye. And then there would go your railroad—tracks, ties, gravel and everything else that might be in the way.

We got to the rail bed. I pulled us to a stop and looked up at the telegraph line, a copper wire running from post to post and sailing off into the distance as far as the eye could see. I dismounted tiredly. Everyone else, except for the two wounded men, got down. We stood there looking up at our problem. The posts were a good foot in diameter. We weren't going to cut them down on account of having nothing to chop with. And I couldn't see how any of us were going to be able to climb up to the wire even if we'd had something to cut the wire with. I said, trying not to sound so tired, "Ben, you are going to have to shoot that wire in two. A bullet ought to cut it, but I reckon you'll have to hit it where it's nailed to the post."

Lew came up. He said, "Justa, have you got any idea how sound will carry in this kind of country? Hell, why don't you just send up smoke signals and let them know where we are?"

I shook my head. I said, "Lew, you make a good point. But I got to get that wire cut and I don't know no other way to do it. If you know, then go right ahead."

He was silent for a second and then he shook his head and turned away. "I guess," he said. "Hell, you're the boss. Something I'm glad I ain't right now."

Ben had gone over to get his saddle gun. I stood in front of the post and gave him a shoulder for a rifle rest. It wasn't going to be any easy shot. That wire wasn't more than a quarter of an inch thick and, even as close as we were, it was going to take a hit dead center to cut it.

Ben got behind me and rested his rifle on my right shoulder. He said, while he was sighting, "Hell, hold still. You are trembling."

"Tired," I said. "Let me take a deep breath."

I sucked in a lungful of wind and Ben sighted carefully up at the wire. The sound of his carbine going off right next to my ear almost deafened me. I looked up. The wire was the same, undisturbed. "Try again," I said. "Maybe I moved."

He fired again and I could see the wire tremble.

"Getting closer," he said. "I think I cut it about half in two on that shot."

The wire fell on his third shot. A sort of ragged cheer went up from around the assembled party as Ben's shot severed the wire. Lew said, "Doubt that it makes much difference. I reckon word has gone out some time back."

I let us all rest for a few minutes and then I made a resolve. I said, "Hays, pass out the food and water. I know you must have some canned meat and beans or something like that. Surely to the gods you didn't just get canned apricots and canned tomatoes?"

He said, earnestly, "I got what they had, boss."

I said, "Well, pass them around. And I want everybody to take one hell of a drink of water, whether they are thirsty or not. We've got to do something about these horses."

Hays said, "I got some bread, boss."

I gave him a sour look. "Then don't keep it to yourself. Pass out everything you got. We are fixing to have to start traveling fast."

We ate, sitting around on the iron rails, looking off into the distance for any pursuit that might have been aroused by Ben's three shots. Of course, thinking back, I didn't see what difference it made. Not much more than a mile from where we sat Benito had loosed off a shot and Ben had followed with six more. Hell, if they were on to our whereabouts all we could do was fight anyway. I had four good guns, including myself and not including the two remaining men of Señor Elizandro. If we were attacked in force, given the terrain and our position, we weren't going to have much of a chance.

I looked down to where Norris was sitting. He had his head down, eating out of a can of beans with a spoon I figured Hays had rustled up for him. He looked jail-weary and trail-worn. I figured he wasn't altogether too happy with himself right then and there. It come to me to make a sort of gesture toward him that might buck him up a little, but then I hardened my heart. The time was not yet ripe.

I had beans and then I had a can of some kind of stew. I hated to think of what was in it. It might have been all right or nearly edible if it had been heated up, but we had no time and no inclination to make a fire.

When we were through I stood up. I called Hays. I said, "I want you to get them water jugs off the packhorse. Then I want every man to take his hat and fill it up with water and give his horse as much as we've got while it lasts."

Hays protested. "But, boss, what about us?"

I said, "Those horses go down, we go down. You understand? We can stand a little thirst for a few more days, but those horses are packing us, not the other way around. Now do like I tell you."

I set the example by taking my hat and pouring it as full as I could get. My young bay gelding took after it with eagerness and appreciation. I yelled down the line, "Get as much water in them as you can. It could be forty miles before they water again."

Off to the north, through the shimmering heat waves, I could see the track running straight as a die toward the Texas border. I thought, what the hell, we might as well follow it. At least we wouldn't get lost. We were about to run out of the little hummocks and ridges, and the only protection left was the stunted underbrush and small trees and our own guns.

I looked down the line of horsemen. Some of them were still watering their horses. Hays come up to me with a worried look on his face. He said, "Boss, I hope you know what you are about. We got exactly two canteens left. Two gallons of water."

I patted him on the shoulder. "Don't worry, Ray. You'll probably be dead before you get a chance to be thirsty again."

He said, "Oh, well, then I—"

Then he stopped and looked at me. I yelled out, "Mount up. We got to get this caravan moving." I took a look at

Jack and Señor Elizandro. Jack appeared to be picking up, but the señor was going the other way. Well, there wasn't a thing could be done about it. I swung in the saddle.

Just about the time I was set to move out on my refreshed mount I heard Ben say from behind me, "Justa, take a look to the west, to your left. Breaking out from behind that brushy *barranca*."

I wheeled in the saddle and looked where he was pointing. A half dozen men had broken clear of the scrubby underbrush a half mile to the west of us. They were coming full tilt. Even as I watched I saw another small party come from around the other side of the little hummock, another half a dozen men, and come charging.

I stared, not quite knowing what to make of them. From behind me, sounding like he was speaking through clenched teeth, I heard Miguel say, "*Rurales*. Very bad. Very bad. They won't stop."

"Lew!" I yelled.

9

Lew was beside me even as I was dismounting. I said, "We got to lure them on. There are too many of them and if we get caught in a running fight they'll dog us all the way to the border. We got to lure them, decoy them."

"What you want me to do?"

I said, "Get up there in the middle of the tracks with Davilla. Get behind him and get a pistol in his back but not where it can be seen. I want him to wave those riders on in. I want them close enough so that we can take the biggest part of them out with our first fusillade." I looked at Lew. "I know I'm asking a hell of a lot. I'm asking you to expose yourself to extra danger."

He spit on the ground as if to say it didn't amount to that much. "Hell, I'll have Davilla in front of me. They ain't gonna shoot at him. And I got a uniform on. Them *rurales* will just think we're a couple of *federales* officers with the prisoners. If we get lucky they'll just come riding right on in."

I said, "We'll be sheltering down behind this grade. We can't get the horses down, but they ought not to be too exposed. When we let go with that first barrage you jerk Davilla down and get behind cover yourself."

The others were already dismounting. Ben and Hays were helping Señor Elizandro off his horse and propping him up against the bank of the railroad grade. Lew was forcing an unwilling *capitán* of *federales* up the steep slope and onto the railroad tracks.

The *rurales* were coming on, converging as they did until they were just one group. I estimated they were still a good quarter of a mile off. I yelled out, "Men, you got to make these first shots count. We got to get all of this bunch. I mean every damn one of them."

But I didn't know if I had the guns for it. With Lew more or less out of it there was only me and Ben and Hays. I didn't know how well Señor Elizandro's men could shoot but I damn sure knew about Norris, even though he had a rifle in his hands.

I saw Lew jab Davilla with his pistol in the back. They were just over my head and to my left. With obvious reluctance Davilla began to wave to the *rurales*, making come-on-in motions. I could see but couldn't hear Lew talking in his ear.

Then it seemed to me as if the riders slowed up, became more cautious. They were only a couple of hundred yards away, but it was still too far for really accurate and rapid firing. Finally they came to a halt a full one hundred yards away. One of them yelled something in Spanish at Davilla. Davilla didn't reply. Lew jabbed him with the pistol and talked in his ear. My heart was in my throat. If they got spooked now they'd lay out on our flanks and pick us off at their leisure. I prayed for Lew to do something, but I didn't know what he could do. If Davilla didn't say something soon it would be too late.

Then Lew stepped out from behind Davilla. He was still holding the pistol in Davilla's back but it wouldn't have been apparent to the *rurales*. He yelled something in Spanish. It was too fast and too complicated for me to follow, but it got the *rurales*' attention. Their leader shouted something back and then Lew fired something back at him. Finally the *rurales* started forward again. Only this time they appeared to be coming with greater caution, coming at a walk. Lew shouted something else at them and I was wishing mightily that he'd get back behind Davilla where he'd have some cover. I knew the officers could see the backs of our horses and they must have wondered who else was in the party. Lew kept up that taunting kind of hollering. It must have been working, for the party broke into a trot. They were seventy-five yards away, and then fifty, and then forty.

At twenty yards, with them almost in our laps, I suddenly raised up, rested my rifle on the near rail, and snapped off a shot at the leader. The others had seen my motion and they were doing likewise. Our fire was having a deadly effect. The *rurales* were dropping like a giant hand was sweeping them off their horses. I felt a motion to my left and Lew came tumbling down the embankment dragging a screaming *Capitán* Davilla after him. With one swift motion he hit the *capitán* over the head with his revolver, grabbed up his carbine, and joined me at the top of the grade.

Riderless horses were running everywhere. A few *rurales* were on the ground, trying to return fire. But their positions were totally exposed and they didn't last long. Then two riders suddenly broke from the rapidly diminishing pack and headed back from whence they'd come. I tried a shot but they were quickly getting out of range. Ben raised up, sighted a long second and then fired. One fell but the other kept going. In a moment he was well out of range.

We stood up to look. I counted eleven men down, including the one Ben had shot at long range. A couple of them were moving. I did not know what to do about that, but Elizandro's two men quickly resolved it for me. Standing up, they quickly—before I could say a word—pumped bullets into the two men until they were still. I wanted to stop them, but, to my shame, I was glad they'd done it. I had no idea what I would have done with two wounded policemen. I had enough wounded to worry about as it was.

Lew said, shouting into my ear because of all the noise, "We ought to try and ketch some of them horses."

But I didn't know about that. They were scattering in every direction, some of them galloping in fright from the noise of the guns, some trotting, stepping on their trailing bridles every so often. I said, "We'd just wear our animals out trying to chase them. Besides, they are a pretty poor looking lot as it is."

Lew said, "Well, we better figure to do something plenty fast. That one that got away is going to have a mighty pretty story to tell. We ain't seen the last of these boys. I guarantee you we ain't got enough ammunition to kill all the *rurales* in this state if they was to line up for us."

I looked down to where *Capitán* Davilla was sitting on the ground with a dazed look on his face. I said, "Looks like your friend didn't want to help."

"Yeah, he taken a bad case of the tongue-tied at the wrong time."

"What was that you were yelling at those boys to get them to come on?"

Lew shrugged. "The *rurales* and the *federales* hate each other, mainly because the *federales* think they are the superior bunch. So I yelled at them that they was just the two of us plus one more had captured all you prisoners and would it be asking to much, considering we was out of food and water and I knowed their bellies was stuffed with beef and beans, for them to give us a little help. He yelled back to ask if I was begging for help and I said if I was to ever beg for help it would be from some quarter where I might expect to get some, not from no *pinche rurale*. And so on like that. The more I jawed, the closer they come.''

I nodded. It had been about what I'd expected. I said, ''Well, y'all better get mounted up. Like you say I reckon we ought not to homestead this place. Every mile we make north today is one less we got to make tomorrow.''

He left, but I just stood there staring at the dead men and horses. After a moment Ben joined me. He said, as if he knew what I was thinking, ''You didn't have no selection, Justa.''

I sighed. ''I know that. This just ain't my kind of fighting.''

''What choice did you have? They'd have shot the hell out of us or throwed us in a prison somewhere. And like you say, the majority of the Half-Moon family is here.''

I shook my head. I said, ''I hate it about those two wounded men.''

''C'mon, now. That wasn't your doing. And even if it had of been, what could you have done, taken them with us? Don't talk loco. And they'd have died a hard death on that desert floor before any help came from their people. Hell, Justa, life's cheap in this country or haven't you taken notice?''

I said, ''I guess.'' I turned and started down the embankment. ''Let's get mounted up and get moving.''

We trailed down the east side of the railroad tracks, keeping the embankment between us and where I expected trouble to come from. Miguel was looking worse and worse, but there wasn't much I could do about it. For that matter wasn't any of us looking all that well. I glanced up at the sun; it was nearing its highest place in the sky, beating down on us like a boiling rain. I had dropped back in the pack so as to better observe horses and men. Hell, nobody had to lead, all we had to do was follow the damn railroad tracks. Looking at our party I could see the damage the sun and the miles and the hard use was doing. I could see the way the men were slumping in the saddles; I could see the sag in the horses' backs and the way they drug their legs. About one more day of such going was going to finish us.

Ben dropped back and rode alongside me for a moment. He glanced up at the sky. It was coming one o'clock. He said, "Ain't we better call a halt and take a rest, Justa? Get some water and what food we got left?"

I shook my head. My mouth was so dry I didn't want to waste saliva talking. We had planned our water and provisions for just our party. We hadn't planned on the surprise visit of Señor Elizandro and his boys. But who was going to deny them out in the big middle of nowhere?

I said, "In a bit. Maybe an hour. We got to make some distance."

So we kept riding. About three o'clock I called for a halt. It didn't matter where I did it; the terrain was the same in all directions, just barren plains covered with nothing much anyone would want. Even the horses, hungry as they were, just nosed at the greasewood and bramble bushes and mouthed a little bit of it for moisture without really swallowing. There wasn't a tree in sight.

We had no more water for the horses, but Hays passed around one of the two remaining canteens and we all had a drink. Canned tomatoes were all that was left of his stock, but I didn't hear nobody complain. I certainly didn't.

After we'd rested for a time I called a conference between me and Ben and Lew. It was mean of me to leave Norris out, but I did it. He took one look at us palavering and then turned his back. I knew he felt the slight and I intended it. I said, "Anybody know what date it is?"

They both shook their heads. Ben said, "Feels like about a week since we run out of Monterrey with the devil chasing us. But I know it hasn't been."

I looked around. "Gentlemen, we ain't equipped for this kind of country. Much longer and we ain't going to have to worry about the *rurales* getting us. This goddam barren son of a bitch will do us all in."

Ben said, "I don't think Elizandro is going much further. He's got a fever, I reckon."

"Already?"

"Feels like it. Anyway, he ain't going to be sitting a saddle a hell of a lot longer."

I said, "Well, anybody got any ideas?"

Lew shrugged. "I don't see what we can do except keep plugging away."

Ben looked around. "I can't believe there ain't a goddam village or at least a little *ranchito* somewheres around here."

Lew said, gesturing, "There are, but they're back toward those mountains, back where it rains every once in a while."

"But all those peons getting on and off the train coming down here. Hell, they got to live somewhere."

Lew gestured again. "They do. Back up near the foot of those mountains."

Ben said, "But, hell, those mountains must be fifteen, twenty miles away."

"They are," Lew said. "Which is about what a peon

can do in a day on a mouthful of water and a handful of
corn. But even if we reached one of those *pueblos chiqui-
tos*, those small villages, it wouldn't do us much good.
They ain't got no horses and they ain't got a hell of a lot
of anything else. Boys, you better face it, this is rough
country.''

I said, ''Well, I don't know what to do—push the horses
and have them crater or have the *rurales* catch us up by
going slow.''

Lew let a handful of dust run through his fingers. He
said, ''The *rurales* are going to catch us anyways because
they is in front of us. All they got to do is wait. They are
strung out from here to the border and I don't reckon you
got that line cut in time to keep them from being notified.
We going to have to fight our way through.''

I sighed and shook my head. ''Don't try to cheer me
up, Lew. You know I never cared for that sugar-tit way of
thinking of yours.''

He laughed. ''Might not be so bad. Maybe you'll get
kilt in the next couple of hours. That way you won't be
thinking of how thirsty you are.''

We kept going as afternoon stretched into night. I knew
I should have rested the horses but I figured it took less
out of them to plod along through the night than under
that relentless sun. Though, truth be told, there wasn't that
much difference between the night and the day except you
couldn't see as well at night.

If there had just been some kind of shelter—some small
trees, a shack of some type. But there was nothing.

The only advantage to that was that you could see the
enemy coming as far off as he could see you. But through
the balance of that afternoon and on into dark we fortunately did not catch sight of another living soul. Hell, we
didn't even see any buzzards. I figured that was because

there wasn't enough life on that desert to die and feed them. It wasn't a handy thought.

Somewhere around nine that night I called for a rest. I asked for volunteers to stand guard while the rest caught a few hours of sleep. Norris immediately struggled up. I ignored him. I said, "I'll take the first watch. Ben, you've got a timepiece. I'll wake you in an hour. Then you do the same for Lew. After that comes Hays. We ain't going to be overlong in this one place."

We made a cold camp, without a fire and without any food. Hell, even if we'd had wood to make a fire we wouldn't have needed one because there was nothing to cook over it. Everybody made do with a good drink of water and turned in. I helped Miguel to get as comfortable as he could on the hard ground. Jack Cole was doing better, but Miguel wasn't. He felt mighty warm to me. I took a look at his shoulder by the light of a match. It was swollen all to hell, but the outside didn't look too infected. I figured what was killing him was the inside damage that bullet had done to the bone in his shoulder. He whispered to me, "Can you not do anything?"

I shook my head. "Miguel, this is more than I can handle. There's a slug in there. You want me to go burrowing around in your busted-up shoulder bone looking for it?"

"Yes," he said. But it come out like a sort of gasp.

I said, "Then you got more guts than I do."

On the first watch I laid on top of the railroad grade, staring off in the distance in all directions, looking for movement of any kind. I wasn't particularly sleepy, but I was so weary I could have laid down and not got up for a week. Looking down on the hard clay floor, I could see the rest of them jerking and shuffling around trying to get comfortable. We had the horses all tied to one loose-ended picket rope. But even that was unnecessary. Those poor beasts were so give out they wouldn't have walked away

if you'd taken after them with a bullwhip. I had no earthly
idea how much longer they could last. I'd rode horses before with little water, but that had been in country that
had some moisture in the air. Where we were the air just
seemed to suck the fluid right out of your body. And the
bigger the body, the harder it sucked.

I tried not to think about Nora but she kept sneaking
into my thoughts. For all I knew it was practically my
wedding day. I hated to think what sort of thoughts she
was entertaining about me at that instant. If I ever got to
see her again, let alone have her marry me, I'd have to
count myself lucky. Well, my duty to the family had come
first, but, then, hell, she was family too. What I should
have done was let Norris enjoy the comforts of Monterrey
while I got myself hitched, took my honeymoon and then
leisurely slipped on down and straightened out his trouble.

But I hadn't done that. I'd been so sure I could make a
quick trip down, bluff me out a few little Mexicans and
then be back home without supper even having a chance
to get cold.

Only it just hadn't worked out that way. I didn't know
who I was madder at—me or Norris.

After about two hours I went down and woke Ben up.
He yawned and looked at his watch. "Went a little over
your time, didn't you?"

"I'm too tired to sleep," I said. "Call Lew next."

We didn't have any blankets or bedrolls. There was
nothing to do but take my slicker, lay it on the hard ground
and rest my head on my saddle. I didn't figure to really
get all that much sleep.

Next thing I knew Hays was shaking me awake. Anybody that could have slept under those conditions must
have needed the sleep mighty bad. I sat up rubbing my
eyes and tasting the cotton in my mouth. Hays said, "It's
goin' on for four of the mornin', boss."

I got up swearing. "Dammit, I didn't want to dally this long. Rouse everybody. Pass the canteen around for a short drink of water and then let's get saddled up and start moving. Goddammit, what do you mean waking me up so late? Did you go to sleep on watch?"

He shook his head. "Not me, boss. It's just the way it worked out."

Well, it couldn't be helped now and it was probably just as well. God knows, everybody, especially the poor rode-down horses, could use the rest. I said to Hays, "You got any provisions left?"

"Nary a thing," he said. "Cupboard is bare."

"Then strip that pack saddle off the packhorse and put him on lead. He's got a fresh back and we might need it before the day is over."

All around me men were getting up groaning and swearing. They eagerly took the canteen as it was passed around. Hays followed, making sure nobody got overly ambitious with the last of our water. I went over to Miguel Elizandro about half dreading what I was going to find. I don't like to break a man out of jail and then have him die on me. But the *caballero* was sitting up and struggling to reach his feet. I took two quick steps to give him a hand. I'd just thought he'd had a fever the day before. Now there was no doubt. The heat just radiated off him. It was a sickening thought but I knew I was going to have to cut into him before the day was out or he wasn't going to make it. I said, "Can you ride?"

He gave me a look, sick as he was. It had been a damn-fool question. He didn't have much choice. He had to ride unless he wanted to leave his bones to bleach where we stood.

One of his men had saddled his horse and brought it over. Together we assisted the don into his saddle. He made it without a lot of cries or moans, but a blind man could have seen the pain in his face.

After that I went to see about Jack Cole. Norris was helping him to mount so I hung back until Jack was in the saddle and Norris had gone on about his own business. I tell you, I was getting madder and madder at Norris. It's one thing to be a damn fool where you've only got yourself to hurt; it's quite another to endanger a whole lot of other people by acting like one. Of course his answer would be that nobody asked me to come down and rescue him, or to even get involved for that matter. Well, me and Mr. Norris Williams was going to have an accounting and in the not-too-distant future. That is if any of us made it out of the mess alive.

Just as I was about to go to Jack I saw one of Elizandro's men strike a match to light a cigarillo. I struck it out of his hand as quick as I could. "You damn fool!" I said lowly but with as much force as I could get in my voice. "No lights!"

Then, just in case anyone else was about to get the same harebrained idea, I said, "No lights! No matches! No smoking!" I was going among them, whispering but making it urgent. "And be as quiet as you can. Sound carries a long way on this desert at night. Now let's move out. We got miles to make."

I swung into my own saddle and got us started down beside the track. After a little I reined back to where Jack was riding sort of hunched over in the saddle. I asked after his condition. He gave me a kind of wan smile. "Tell you the truth," he said, "I been better."

"That gunshot kicking up?"

He shook his head. "Naw, since you reamed it out it's been considerable better. It's just sore now. Onliest thing I can figure out is wrong with me right now is I'm gettin' too old for this foolishness. Been a long time since I was this give-out an' thirsty and hungry."

I said, knowing I was lying, "Well, it won't be long now."

He just gave me a little smile and said, "Bullshit, Justa. You better go kid somebody else. I *live* down in this country."

Sometime before dawn we saw a light far off in the distance. Lew said, "Train's coming."

"Everybody get away from the tracks," I said. "Hurry! That thing might be full of soldiers." I led them in a shambling trot a hundred yards until we were far back in the darkness. The train suddenly came roaring past us, rattling and shaking the earth. A few of the horses skittered and trembled but they were too tired to do much of anything.

It was just an ordinary passenger train and we watched in envy as the lighted windows flew past. One in particular took my eye. It appeared to be the dining car and I could see people through the lighted windows eating breakfast and drinking coffee. Coffee! God, I reckoned I would have killed for a cup of coffee and a drink of brandy.

After the train was gone we stared after it in envy. Ben said, "Don't you wish you were on that?"

I shook my head. "Going the wrong way."

But it had put a thought in my head, one that I couldn't do anything about right then but that I might could make use of if we got lucky and the right set of circumstances happened. We rode on.

The sun got up and began to beat down on us. But, mercifully, the broad plain remained empty of uniforms. Once I thought I saw a little file of white-clad peons but they were too far away to be sure. And even if we could have gotten to them they wouldn't have had anything we could have used.

About nine of the morning I halted us and went to the rear where Lew was riding with his sullen *capitán*. Though by now the *capitán* didn't look so much sullen as desperate. I think he'd already figured out that whatever happened to us was going to happen to him and he'd better hope we did good. I said to Lew, "Listen, that packhorse is about the freshest animal we got. I want you to put your saddle and bridle on him and scout on up the tracks. I'm going to stay here and rest these horses and men for about an hour and then we'll follow along slow."

He swung out of the saddle and started undoing the cinch. He said, "Got any idea what I'm looking for? *Rurales?* Water? Food? Shelter?"

"Yeah," I said.

"How far you want me to go?"

I shrugged. It wasn't a question I could answer. I said, "That will pretty well depend on your horse. Say you can get five miles in an hour and a half. With us coming your way that'll give you an hour back to us. I don't know what to tell you if you run into any police, but you got the uniform for it."

He was starting to saddle the packhorse. He said, "Hell, I'm a *capitán*, ain't I? Maybe I'll order them to give me their horses. Who knows?"

I said, "Just don't take any chances."

He laughed. "Aw, no, I wouldn't do that. It's so damn safe and secure back here with y'all."

As he rode away I yelled for Hays and detailed him to take over the watch of Davilla. Then I directed everyone to get out of the saddle and take a rest. "Now you can smoke," I said. I sat down by the embankment and leaned back against it, my horse's reins in one hand, and lit a cigarillo. It was a poor substitute for food and drink, but it was all I had.

My thinking, in sending Lew on ahead, was that there

had to be some way to service the rail bed and somebody to do the servicing. At least that was the way it was around Texas railroads. Maybe he'd find a little crew bunkhouse that had stores in it. Maybe he'd find one of those little pump carts that crew people used to get by rail from job to job. Hell, I didn't know what he was likely to find; I was just hoping he'd find something that would give us a little relief. The shape we were in we could have used week-old water and two-week-old bread. But looking at the horses, I figured we weren't long from being afoot. But at least that way we'd have something to eat.

After an hour I mounted up and directed the rest into their saddles. It was painful watching Señor Elizandro being helped astride his horse. But I didn't think it was yet time to take desperate measures.

We trailed north for about half an hour. I taken notice that the roadbed was starting to get lower and lower, a situation I didn't much care for. I could see the country falling away to the north and I guessed the railroad builders had figured there was less chance of disastrous flooding with a drain plane rather than the flat way it had looked some few miles back.

But I still didn't like it. That embankment was the only cover for twenty miles and I hated to see it dropping away to nothing.

After about a quarter of an hour I saw a dim speck coming toward us. I held up a hand and halted the party. Ben rode up beside me. "Reckon that's Lew?"

"Should be," I said. "But let's wait a bit and see."

We watched as the dot grew larger and larger until it turned into the figure of man and horse. After a few more minutes I could see it was Lew. I urged my horse forward, the rest following. It took about ten more minutes, but we finally closed on one another. The first thing I noticed was the sort of satisfied look on Lew's face and the fact that his horse didn't look nowhere near as drawn and worn down as he had when Lew had taken out two hours earlier. Near as I could figure, two hours riding in that heat had never done a horse no appreciable amount of good, especially without feed or water. Also, Lew was chewing something.

I said, watching him closely, "Find anything?"

For answer he reached into a cloth sack he had tied from his saddle horn. He held out a handful of flour tortillas. He said, "Care for a bite?"

"You son of a bitch," I said. But I took me a couple and passed the stack on back to the rest. The tortillas were tough and hard to swallow but the finest light bread had never tasted so good. I said, "Where'd you get these?"

He jerked his head back in the direction he'd come. He said, "They's a water tank, a railroad water tank, the kind with a spout that they use to fill up a railroad engine's boiler, back up yonder about a mile."

"My God!" I said. "We can finally water these horses. Anything else? Is it guarded?"

He said, "Well, it's supposed to be but it didn't work out that way. They is a little crew bunkhouse there. Whatever you call it. Was two ol' boys that work for the railroad there. But they ain't guarding it right now."

"You kill them?" I was about to get sick of the depredations we'd done in a country we didn't have no standing in.

He shook his head. "Tied 'em up. They was pretty gentle. Thought I was a *capitán* of the *federales*. They was plenty helpful. Even give my horse some water and feed and give me all sorts of useful information."

"They got a telegraph there?"

He shook his head. "We ain't talking about the kind of hired help that can run a wire key. They more what you might call caretakers."

"But there's feed and water for the horses there?"

"Oh, yes," he said. "Not a hell of a lot, but they is that big water tank and they got a well. Also got some beans and some dried beef. But I reckon we ought to kind of get in a hurry."

"Why? If you've got them tied up."

He gave me a wink. "We've got a train to catch. In just a little over two hours."

I stared at him. "A train? How we going to stop a train, much less catch one?"

He said, "I think I've got a way. How'd you like to be in Laredo by this evening?"

Wasn't much I needed to say to that. The men were crowding around, demanding to know what was going on. I told them that I didn't know but that Lew had reported some help up ahead. Just how much I couldn't say.

We hurried that last mile, spending the last of our strength and the last of our horses. As we rode I asked Lew for more details.

He said, "Well, they is a train coming in. And it's a short train, a cattle train, so there will be room for the horses. And should be water and feed aboard."

"I don't believe this," I said. "I can't believe our luck finally changed."

Lew said, "And they will stop for water at that water depot."

"Lord," I said. "This get's better and better."

"Just the one thing, though," Lew said.

"What?"

"Train's going the wrong way. It's headed for Monterrey."

10

We pulled up about a hundred yards short of the place so I could look it over. Like Lew had said, there was a hell of a big wooden water tank up on stilts so its spout would be over the boiler of the railroad locomotive. Then just beyond and behind that was a little shack. Behind that was a corral with a few sorry-looking nags standing around, their heads drooping.

I said, "What time is that train? That train that is going the wrong way?"

Lew consulted his watch. It was just quartering eleven o'clock. He said, "A little over an hour and three quarter. 'Course these damn Mexican trains never run on time."

I give him a look. "How you know so much about it?"

He shrugged and said, "A man gets around."

I studied the shack. "You sure you got these two railroad workers fixed where they ain't going to give us any trouble?"

"Guarantee it," he said.

The hot afternoon wind was starting a little early that day, stirring up dust so that it swirled between us and the water tank. My horse was mouthing his bit, smelling the water. I wanted to go in, but I wanted to go in cautiously. I said to Lew, "Let's go take a look." Then I motioned the rest of the party to hold their ground.

Lew and I rode slowly forward. The late morning air was still and quiet, the little swirling winds having died for the moment. I eyed the shack. It was a gray adobe affair with gray tiles for a roof and poles sticking out of the sides for rafter supports. The windows were small slit-like affairs. I could hear small insects buzzing around. Other than that there was no sign.

We pulled up at the water tower and tied our horses to the stilts that held up the huge wooden drum. My horse nickered at the horses in the corral back of the shack. They just raised their heads and switched their tails and made no other sign.

Lew said, "Ain't you being a bit overcareful?"

"Quiet," I said.

We walked toward the door of the shack. I had drawn my revolver. Lew, after a shrug, had done likewise. The only sound was the slight *ching-ching* of our spurs on the hard ground. When we got to the front of the shack I tried to see through one of the slitlike windows but it was covered with some kind of material. I walked over to the wooden door; I motioned Lew to the other side of it. He shrugged and took up his position.

All of a sudden I jerked up the wooden latch and shoved the door open. There was a sudden loud *BOOM* and a slug came whistling through the opening. Without hesitation Lew and I jumped into the door frame and fired two or three shots apiece into the gloom of the inside. I heard a few go whining around, but I also heard several strike something solid, like the person that had fired the shot.

We rushed into the room of the shack. Laying on his back was a workman-looking fellow in some sort of a worn-out blue uniform. Laying between his legs was an old black-powder-firing muzzle-loader. I looked around. There was a chair laying on its side, busted. Around it were ropes. Against a far wall was the match to the fellow laying on the floor, except he was still roped to his little wooden, cane-bottomed chair.

I gave Lew a glance. He leaned down and picked up the old black-powder rifle. He said, "Justa, I swear I tied these boys up and then searched this place for weapons. I swear I done it. I just didn't know he had Grandma hid out here somewheres. Hell, I may have seen it but I would have never thought it was anything anybody would actually shoot."

It was easy to see what had happened. The dead man had tipped his chair over and the old, lightweight framework had busted, practically freeing him from all but the last of the bonds. It had taken him time, but then he'd had time, the time it had taken Lew to fetch us. Once he'd got his hands free it had been but the work of a moment to free his ankles. He'd probably looked out the window, saw us coming and realized he didn't have time to free his comrade, just time to load the old muzzle-loader. The only question was why. I put it to Lew and he put it to the fellow that was still tied to the chair. They spoke together in Spanish for a moment. Lew shrugged and turned to me. "The fellow hates *federales*. They killed some of his family. He saw me alone and thought I was a *federale* and that it was a good chance to get some revenge."

I looked at the dead man and shook my head. "I ain't never been much of a promoter of Mexico, but we better get out of this poor country whilst a few of them is still alive."

"And us, too," Lew said.

I went outside and hailed the others to come on. They came up with relief and excitement on their faces. They were all for coming inside and having a bite to eat and something to drink, but I bade them help Señor Elizandro into the room and then take their horses around to the corral in back and get them watered and fed before they taken care of themselves. I said, "You better watch your animals. You know better than to let them drink too much in one go. Hays, you and Ben take my horse and Lew's. We got some planning to do."

I went back inside. They'd laid Señor Elizandro just inside the door. Lew was at the little coal stove stoking up the fire under a huge pot of what smelled like beans with chilies. He had a stack of tortillas warming and softening on another part of the stove. With his other hand he was eating an orange. I pulled Miguel's shirt back. Well, the wound was good and infected. I may not could dig for those slugs but I could at least open the wound up and let it drain. If I didn't he was going to die before we could get him to a doctor just as sure as shooting. I said, "Lew, those coals in that stove hot? I mean real hot?"

He opened the grate. "Not yet. But I can get 'em like that. You fixing to do some more surgery?"

"Yeah. We are out of whiskey, ain't we?"

"Far as I know. But they ought to be some around here somewhere." He spoke to the man bound to the chair. I saw the man nod his head toward some cupboards near the stove and say something. Lew opened the door of the cupboard. "They got tequila," he said. "Will that do?"

"Going to have to," I said.

He handed me the tequila and I handed him my knife. "Fan up them flames real good and then get the point of my knife nearly red."

He said, "You do mind that we ain't got all that much

time, don'cha? That train is going to be here in less than an hour and we got a bunch of stuff to get ready.''

I said, "Does that train automatically stop here and take on water?"

Lew nodded his head toward the man in the chair. "Pancho don't think so. But the other one told me it didn't, that it was one of the newer locomotives of a bigger class and didn't have to take on water so often. Train has to be stopped.''

I looked down at Miguel. He was breathing heavy and his eyes were closed. Hell, I couldn't figure out how he'd made it as far as he had. I reckoned the coolness of the shack was some relief to him. After the merciless pounding we'd taken from the sun for two days, the dim interior of the little building felt like the inside of one of them icehouses I'd been in once in Houston. I said, "Miguel, I'm going to open you up. You'll feel better. You understand?"

He nodded, pretty tight-lipped.

I said, "I got some tequila here and I want you to take down as much as you can. I figure it'll be pretty raw stuff but do the best you can with it.''

He nodded again and I put one arm under his shoulders and raised him to a sitting position. He opened his eyes and I guided the bottle into his right hand. Trying to make a joke, I said, "Now really put it down, Miguel. The more you drink means the less I got to.''

He tried to smile but it didn't come to much. Then he put the bottle to his mouth and took several swallows. When he took it away he was gasping. He said something I couldn't hear. I put my ear close to his mouth. I said, "What?"

He whispered, "I think I prefer to be shot."

At least the man could joke. I had to admire him for that. I got the bottle back up to his mouth and forced a few more swallows down him. Then I laid him on his back and poured some of the tequila right over the wound. But it was so closed up he didn't even flinch when the raw stuff hit it.

Lew brought me over the knife. He said, "That about right?"

The point was glowing a cherry-red. I said, "Well, you've taken the temper out of a damn good blade, but it will do Miguel a world of good. Hold his shoulders hard. He ain't going to enjoy this overmuch."

While Lew got at the *caballero*'s head and put his weight on Miguel's shoulders, I took the bottle of tequila in my left hand and my knife in the other. With a quick movement I punched the hot blade into the point I took to be the bullet entry. As I did I began pouring on the tequila. Miguel moaned and thrashed his legs, but he didn't move his upper body and he didn't call out.

The results were about the same as they'd been for Jack Cole, although the knife had been so hot with Miguel that I figured I'd cauterized the wound while I was opening it up. I said, "Sit him up. Let him suck down some more of this tequila. He's got to be hurting like hell."

Elizandro took two hard sucks off the bottle then pushed it away and sighed. He was still pale, but it was a different kind of paleness. His eyes fluttered open. He said *"Gracias"* in almost a whisper.

Lew lowered him back to the floor. I said, "Just lay there, Miguel. I know you're hurting, but there's not a damn thing I can do about it right now."

He opened his eyes again. "It's not so bad. Do you have a cigarillo?"

I lit him one and stuck it between his lips. Then I got up, leaving his shirt laying open. Lew said, "Ain't you going to bandage him up?"

I shook my head. "We ain't got nothing clean enough

to use for a bandage.'' And I wasn't going to poke a tent in either. If we were able to get hold of that train we'd be in Laredo before the wound could close again and he'd be under a surgeon's care. If we couldn't . . . well, it wouldn't make much difference either way. He'd never last to the border horseback.

Lew and I went back to the main part of the adobe shack. The beans were starting to smell. I said, "They got any coffee?"

Lew spoke to the man in the chair again. "Hey, Pancho, *tiene café?*"

The man shook his head. Lew shrugged. "He's probably got some hid away. That's pretty rare stuff for these kind of boys." He looked around. The little shack wasn't more than twelve or fourteen foot square. He said, "Ain't that many places to hide it. We could probably root around and come up with it."

I shook my head and went over to the back window slit to see how they were doing in the corral. They were just starting to lead their horses out. I taken note that Hays had a lariat rope around Davilla's neck and was leading him like a dog. The *capitán* looked mighty run down. He didn't appear to have an ounce of fight left in him. Of course that's when you wanted to start watching somebody like him the closest. I said to Lew, "Looks like company's coming. You better start setting the table."

Lew was rummaging around on a table. "Hell!" he said. "These cheap bastards ain't got but four tin plates and just a few spoons and forks. What are we going to do?"

"Eat in shifts, I reckon," I said. "Now where the hell is that water? Is that it in the corner?"

"Yeah. An' it's good water too."

I took the lid off a big earthen crock, got the dipper and drunk my fill of the cool, fresh well water. I don't reckon

I'd ever tasted anything better. But I no more than got my thirst quenched when I commenced wanting a drink of whiskey, good whiskey, not that rotgut tequila. I reckon such is the nature of man. When he's starving to death he'd eat an armadillo raw, but once you get him satisfied he won't settle for anything but the best. But we didn't have any whiskey, mainly because Ray Hays hadn't seen to it. Not that it would have done us much good crossing that hot plain. The last thing a man needs that's short on water is whiskey. It just dries him out further.

There was a rough wooden table in the middle of the shack. I said, "Well, here comes the crew. You better go to ladling out beans and handing out tortillas before we have a riot on our hands. Then you and I better talk."

When Lew and I had eaten we stepped to the door. Señor Elizandro seemed to be going easier. One of his men was helping him with a plate of beans. The railroad track was just outside. By now the grade was barely a foot high. I said, "All right, just how do we stop this train? You and Davilla? In uniform? Standing on the tracks waving your arms?"

"Something like that," he said. "But also with these." He stepped back into the crowded room, full of men refreshing themselves after several days of hardship and danger, and returned with a couple of items. He held them out. They looked like a pair of sticks of dynamite with tenpenny nails in the bottom.

I said, "What the hell you got there?"

"Flares," he said. He tapped the nails at the end. "You use these to jam 'em into a cross tie so they'll stay upright." He gestured at the tops which appeared to have some kind of little cardboard caps over the ends. "Then you yank these off and they shoot out a red flame and black smoke. Engineer sees them and he stops."

"I've seen them," I said. "Just never up close. Why do they use them?"

"Might be they's trouble ahead on the track. Might be this station has passengers or freight. But they'll stop."

"Then what?"

Lew grinned. "Then me and the good *capitán* step up in the cab of the locomotive and commandeer the damn train in the name of the *policía federal*. We're hot on the trail of some gringo *bandidos*."

"Thought you said the train was going the wrong way."

"It is. But hell, Justa, them damn things run backwards. Ain't you ever seen one backing on to a siding?"

"We are going to back all the way to Nuevo Laredo?"

"That is unless you want to wait for one along about eleven tonight. Personally I don't recommend it. Far as I'm concerned I can feel the hot breath of them *rurales* on the back of my neck right now."

I shrugged. "Let's hope it works. I've had about enough of that desert. And so has my horse. You sure this train ain't guarded?"

He shook his head. "Naw. They got a brakeman and a conductor. At least according to Pancho in there. But we ought to be able to handle them."

I said, "Well, you go in there and question the hell out of that son of a bitch. Make it clear we're going to let him go when we leave. That is if he hasn't lied to us. If he lies . . . well, you know what to tell him. I'm going out and look around."

I walked on outdoors and taken a long look down the rails that led to the border. They just seemed to stretch out forever, running across that plain straight as an arrow and seeming to come together far off in the distance to merge into one rail. All around me I could see the heat waves shimmering off the basin floor and just a few minutes back outside was sufficient to remind me of just how miserable and uncomfortable and dangerous that barren plain was. Well, that train was going to have to stop. That was all there was to it. We had to stop that train somehow because I couldn't see us making it another sixty miles, not even with the horses watered and rested. And I couldn't see us dodging the *rurales* much longer.

I heard a step behind me. It was Norris. He had a very determined look on his face. He said, "I want to talk to you and I want to talk right now."

"All right," I said. I looked him over. He was pretty bedraggled-looking, nowhere near our usually neatly dressed and groomed family businessman. I said, "And I got a few things I want to say to you, also. So start talking."

A little zephyr had come up and we stood there facing each other in the heat and the swirling dust. I was good and angry and it appeared he was too, though he'd always prided himself on not losing his temper—a claim I'd always thought was somewhat disputed by a certain amount of facts. I saw Hays come to the door of the shack, sucking on his teeth and drinking at a dipper of water. With a motion of my hand I waved him back. I reckon he understood quick enough because he suddenly disappeared and shut the wooden door after him.

"Spit it out," I said. "Before it poisons you." I had taken note of where my horse was hitched next to the shack on the shady side. There was something in my saddlebags I was mighty interested in showing Mr. Norris Williams, but I wanted him to get all his licks in first.

Norris put a finger out at me. He said, "Let's get something quite straight here. No one asked you to come riding to my rescue like Sir Galahad. I was quite capable of attending to my own business." His face was starting to flush. "You seem to have this inherent feeling that none of us can function without your benevolent supervision.

Well, I am here to tell you that in my case that does not apply. I did not approve of your arrival, I did not approve of your leaving business matters back home, I did not approve of your approach and language to me, and I *certainly* did not approve of the unlawful method you took to free me from my illegal incarceration!''

''You through?'' I asked him mildly.

He drew himself up. ''I am just beginning. For most of my adult life you have taken the presumptuous and uncalled-for assumption that I could not handle myself in any situation outside of one where books and papers and bankers were involved. Well, let me make it clear to you that I had that situation well in hand. I had been falsely jailed and through some contacts I'd made with my jailers—by the way, the sympathetic jailers that you drew guns on—I was in the process of availing myself of some legal counsel that would have settled the whole misunderstanding without your untimely interference.''

My hackles starting to rise a little sooner than I'd meant, I said, ''How much did you give them?''

''How much did I give who? What are you talking about?''

''Your goddam sympathetic jailers. Them two peons that was going to get you legal counsel. Come on, how much money did you give them?''

He stiffened. ''I don't believe that's any of your business.''

I said, matter-of-factly, ''Oh, yeah it is. Because it is all going on your bill and I want to know how much more to add. If you were stupid enough to give a couple of jailers what little money they hadn't already stolen from you then you ain't got the sense God gives a piss ant. Them two old boys couldn't spell *lawyer* much less get in to see one, even if they had been so disposed to do so in your behalf.''

He put out his finger again. ''Now you look here! I'm tired of your high-handed ways. I am tired of you treating me as if I could not manage my affairs in your so-called rough-and-tumble world. If you'd of stayed out of it I'd of come home with clear title to that land and had it cleared of nesters. But oh, no, you had to barge in!''

I said, ''How much money you leave home with?''

''That is none of your business.''

''I can find out damn quick when we get home. *If* we get home. Now, how much? Two hundred? Three? Five? All I got to do is go the bank or look at your accounts.''

He stared at me a long moment. He finally said, ''Around six hundred.'' He said it in such a still voice I couldn't quite hear him.

I said, ''How much?''

He glared at me. He was flushing and no mistake. He yelled, ''SIX HUNDRED! ARE YOU SATISFIED!''

''And how much of it have you got left?''

He glared at me, his mouth a thin line.

''How much?''

He said, bitterly, ''You know how much. Nothing.''

''You get the clear title?''

Boy, his face was blazing. He said, ''You know damn good and well I didn't. Justa, I warn you, I'm about to take a poke at you. You have insulted me, degraded me, avoided me and I don't know what else.''

I said, ''Well, get ready for a little what else.'' I walked over to my horse and rummaged in my saddlebags until I located the clear Spanish land-grant title Luís had gotten for me. I went back and waved it in his face. I said, ''You see this? Take a look at it. Take a damn good look. It cost me fifty dollars and about fifteen minutes of my time. Do you have any idea what it cost to have you go after the same goddam thing? Would you like an itemized account?''

He had taken the paper and was looking at it. All the injured pride and anger were rapidly running out of him. He kept looking at the paper as if he didn't believe it. Then he said, with some heat, "Well, maybe you didn't have the same difficulties I did."

I pointed at the shack. "You mean Davilla? I didn't have any trouble with him. You want me to fetch him out so you can punch him in the mouth again?"

He said, "He's got a broken wrist."

I said, "Hah! I recall an occasion that didn't stop you from kicking a guy in the balls who was shot all to hell just because he'd kicked you in the balls some days previous."

At least he had the good grace to look ashamed. He said, "I'm not proud of that and I'd thank you to quit bringing it up." Then he looked at me, trying once again for righteous indignation. "But that ain't got nothing to do with you butting into my business. I was getting matters handled."

I said, "Let me tell you, Norris, you are my business. And everything else that has to do with the family is my business. I'm the goddam boss, or have you forgot?"

Looking away he said, "No, I haven't forgot. How could anybody forget around you. But I wanted to go on record as saying I was doing fine on my own."

He was starting to exasperate me. I poked him in the chest. I said, with anger, "Listen, Norris, you are my brother and I care about you. We got the same blood and the same mother and dad, but I swear if you don't stop that you-was-handling-matters bullshit I'm going to knock your goddamn head off. Listen, you dumb shit, you couldn't have got out of that jail with ten Mexican lawyers and a Gatling gun because you don't know how they operate in Mexico. You don't know nothing about it! And that's you all over. You ain't content to know books and business, you've got to mix in with things you don't know the first thing about! You could have got your sorry ass killed!''

He said, "Don't you yell at me!"

"I damn sure will yell at you! Do you have any idea how many men you got killed over your stupidity? Fortunately none of them were mine or I'd beat you within an inch of your life!"

He said, "You rolled a bomb under your own brother's bunk! A bomb!"

"It appeared to be the only way to move you. I'm just amazed you weren't pigheaded enough to just sit there and let it blow the ass off you. We didn't have no time. Do you understand that? I didn't have time to sit there and debate the question with you. A lot of men's lives were on the line! Every son Dad has was either in that jail or right outside. And there you sit like some frog on a log. *Aaaah!*"

I'd never wanted to hit anybody as bad in my life. It was taking every bit of self-control I had to just content myself with jabbing him in the chest. I finally got to doing it so hard he had to fall back a step.

He said, "Given time—"

I cut him off. "And another thing. Considerable money has been lost on this affair, both as cash outlay and as time lost from the ranch. I can guarantee you are going to pay back every cent. You can look to have deductions made from your salary and from your share of the profits until you pay back the business what your harebrained actions have cost it!"

A voice at my elbow said, "Justa, quit yelling! Shut up!"

I looked around. It was Ben. I gave him an amazed glance. I said, "Who the hell you think you're talking to?"

"You. Everybody in the shack can hear you. It ain't fitting."

I said, "Let them. I don't give a damn."

He pointed off to the southwest. "Then maybe you'll give a damn about them."

I looked where he was pointing. Outlined against the gray of the far-off mountains I could see a string of little black dots. I could not judge how far off they were. The heat waves and the sameness of the country made it difficult to read distances. I said, "Send Lew out here and tell the rest of the men to commence cinching up their saddles and collecting provisions and water. We may have to make a run for it."

"What about Señor Elizandro?"

I just shrugged. There was nothing I could say. If we had to ride for it he was dead either way, whether we left him to the *rurales* or took him with us. Ben went inside and, as I turned to go to my own horse, I said over my shoulder to Norris, "And if I miss my wedding and lose Nora on account of you, you're going to wish you had stayed on top of that bomb."

Lew came out as I was finishing with my horse. We walked around to the other side of the shack and I pointed out the dots. Lew shaded his eyes with his hand and squinted. He said, "Hard as hell to tell. I'd make it maybe three miles. But that's a guess. It could be two."

"When is that train due?"

He jerked his head toward the shack. "Timetable they got tacked up says one-thirty."

I looked at my watch. It was two minutes after one. I said, "I hope to hell a miracle happens and they are on time."

Lew give me a glance. He said, "You loco? This is Mexico. The only thing you can depend on being on time around here is bad luck."

I put my watch away. I said, "Then it's going to be a near thing."

He was studying the riders in the distance. "One thing, they can't make no time in this heat. They appear to be walking their mounts. I don't think they know we're here. I figure they're just from a station back in those mountains that have been sent to cut our trail. Maybe we moved a little faster than they thought."

"It's still going to be close," I said, grimly. "I don't see how we can make it horseback, not if these patrols keep popping up all the way to the border. We ain't got that many guns left."

I had Lew assemble everyone in front of the shack. I pointed out the danger presented by the *rurales* and told them what we were going to do about the train. I said, "It could be a tight thing. It could be that some of you are going to have to lay down some covering fire to keep the police back while we stop the train and ready a cattle car to take the horses. The horses are important because we will have to stop short of Nuevo Laredo and cross the river on horseback to get to the Texas side. I cannot promise you what is going to happen. All I can tell you is that you'd better do your best if you want to see another sunset."

After that Lew translated for Elizandro's two men. I'd stepped into the building to check on Señor Elizandro. He was looking better, having lost a considerable amount of his infection and having eaten and drunk water. I explained the situation to him and asked what he wanted to do should we have to leave on horseback. He said, "I ride." He said it weakly, but he said it with conviction.

I was kneeling by him. I rose to my feet. "All right," I said. "I will see that you are put on horseback."

After that I went to the man still tied in his chair. I didn't know if his name was Pancho or not, but I got

another bottle of tequila out of the cupboard and assisted
him with drinking as much of it as I could get down his
gullet. I wasn't going to kill him to keep him from telling
the *rurales*, but I was going to try and get him in such a
shape that he wouldn't make much sense. He was a willing
participant.

After that I went back outside. Everyone was milling
around, looking up the track and then turning to trace the
progress of the rural police. I took Ben aside to give him
his instructions. I said, "Lew and I, along with *Capitán*
Davilla, are going to take the cab of the locomotive. But
Lew says the man inside has told him there will be a conductor and a brakeman on the train. They'll be at the rear.
They are your job. I would prefer you didn't shoot them
unless you have to. If you can, I want you to put them in
the caboose and keep them still and not let them cause
any trouble."

He shrugged. "Hell, I can do that, Justa."

I said, "But now comes the hard part. Let's figure we
stop this train and get it going in the other direction before
those *rurales* get here. It's a good bet they'll be able to
tap into the telegraph wire and we'll have hell all the way
to the border. If we get this train, I'm going to have us
stop after about a mile. Be sure you have your carbine
with you. You've got to shoot out another wire so they
can't telegraph ahead and have a train of soldiers coming
to meet us."

He turned his head and studied me for a considerable
moment.

I said, "What?"

He spit in the dust. He said, "I never reckoned I'd tell
you this, but I might as well now." He paused as if sum-
moning some kind of strength. "You better not ever tell
anybody I said this but I've bragged on you on occasion.

On the way you think. Not often, you understand, but I've done it.''

I looked away. I was plenty embarrassed. I finally said, ''Well, that makes us even. I've bragged on you too. On the way you say foolish things.'' Then I turned around and walked off.

Norris came up to me. He said, stiff-lipped, ''What can I do?''

I studied him a moment. I didn't see no remorse in his face, but then I hadn't expected any. I said, ''Well, first, you are liable to be firing through one of those windows at the *rurales* while we're getting the train stopped. Once we do that I want you to open the door of the first car behind the coal tender and get all those cattle out of there. There'll be a ramp in there they use to load and unload the cattle. Get that in position to load the horses. And get the men in. Have Señor Elizandro loaded in. Reckon you can handle it? You like danger. Might be a few bullets whizzing around.''

He looked at me and then stalked away. Norris was going to learn or he wasn't. It was up to him.

After that there wasn't much to do except stand out in the heat and look up the tracks and then back at the advancing rural policemen. The only sounds were the dancing of the dry wind and the occasional buzz of a fly trying to find his way into the coolness of the shack.

Lew was standing by me. I said, ''You like cold buttermilk and them little garden onions? Them little green onions?''

''Yeah,'' he said. He wasn't paying me the slightest bit of attention.

I said, ''That's what I'd dearly love to have right now— a big glass of cold buttermilk and some green onions.''

He looked around. ''What?''

"Never mind," I said. "How close you figure they are?"

He rubbed his bewhiskered jaw and said, "Maybe twenty minutes away, maybe more. Hard to tell. I got to figure their horses are rode down by now. They won't come in a charge, not unless they all of a sudden want to be afoot."

I looked around. *Capitán* Davilla, along with the rest of the men, was resting in front of the shack in what little shade he could find. I said, "How's your *compadre*? I assume by now he knows what we're up to."

"Oh, yes. He understands." Lew looked back at him. "He is sulking, but he and I have had a talk and he understands the consequences if he gives trouble. I've promised to release him when we hit the Rio Grande."

"Does he believe you?"

"Who knows?" Lew shrugged. "They are not used to people keeping their promises."

I looked at my watch. It was just coming one-thirty. I looked up the track. The train was due at that second. I sighed. I said, "I guess we're in for another fight." I was on the point of ordering the men inside to take up firing positions when Lew said, "Wait! Look!"

Far off in the distance I could see what looked to be a puff of smoke. I watched. After a moment the smoke got more distinct and I thought I could see a solid something-or-other below it.

"Is it the train?"

Lew said, "It damn well better be."

We stood there switching our gaze between the rural police and the train. The train was traveling much faster. In another minute it had clearly materialized into a locomotive with cars behind it. I said, "Quick, everybody inside! Ben, you know to be near the door. You come out right behind me. Norris, have you explained to the rest what is to be done about the cattle and the horses?''

"Yes," he said. He said it evenly, with no sarcasm or malice.

I looked at Lew. I said, "Okay, it's your show."

He had the two flares in his hand. We all ran back into the shack. Lew walked out into the middle of the tracks and stabbed the two flares into a cross tie. He stood there, watching the train come on. I could see him out the door. *Capitán* Davilla was still leaning against the front of the shack. He was a haggard-looking wreck, and that untreated wrist was going to give him trouble the rest of his life. I reckoned he was going to have to beat prisoners with his off hand in future.

The train was now no more than a mile away. It might have been planning to stop for water or it might not have. But Lew had figured there was no point in taking a chance. I agreed with him, especially with the *rurales* bearing down on us.

Lew bent down and jerked the caps off the two flares. They immediately erupted like two Roman candles, sending up smoke and flame. Then Lew raced for the front of the shack, grabbed Davilla and went to stand by the tracks waving with both arms.

I held my breath. For a second it seemed the train was just going to keep on barreling through. Then, just barely, it began to slow. I couldn't reckon how fast it was going, but it was hitting a pretty good clip. I heard the slight squealing of steel against steel as the engineer began to apply the brakes. Then the sound grew louder as he increased the pressure. After that came the sound of the following cars taking up the slack in their couplings and whamming into each other. Lew had Davilla waving his arms also though he looked pretty reluctant about it.

The train slowed and slowed and then stopped some ten

yards short of the flares. Instantly Lew began to hustle
Davilla toward the cab of the engine. Lew had his pistol
drawn but out of sight behind his back. Davilla had an
empty police holster. I could see the train clearly because
the smoke from the flares was drifting the other way. There
were six cattle cars and a caboose besides the coal tender.
Through the slats of the cattle cars I could see the beef
animals within. They weren't the skinny cattle raised on
Mexican rancheros. These were Texas cattle. They were
bound for the big cities of Mexico like Mexico City and
Vera Cruz and Tampico to be eaten by the big shots there.
They might talk Mexico, but they ate Texan. I knew because we'd made a good profit over the years shipping our
crossbred steers south of the border.

As I saw Lew push Davilla up the steps to the cab of
the locomotive, I broke from the door of the shack. I yelled
behind me for Ben and for Norris and for the rest of them
to get their jobs done. It was only about ten yards from
the front of the shack to the locomotive, but just as I was
about halfway there I heard two shots and saw Davilla
suddenly come pitching backwards out of the cab. I
stepped over him as I went up the steps. I had seen a
rapidly increasing spot of crimson on his chest. I entered
the cab with drawn pistol. Lew was covering a man with
his arms upraised. Another was laying on the steel floor
of the cab with a mortal wound.

The engine was making the *chuf-chuf* sound a steam
locomotive makes at rest. I said, "What the hell happened?"

Without taking his eyes off the man with upraised arms
Lew said, "Davilla decided to get brave. We got in and
he went to yelling we were gringos escaping from the police. The engineer went for a pistol. I shot him and he
shot Davilla. I think this here is the fireman."

"Can he run the damn train?"

Lew stuck the barrel of his pistol in the frightened man's face and asked him in Spanish the question I'd posed in English. The man babbled something. Lew said, "Yeah, he can run it. But somebody has got to shovel the coal. Make steam."

I put my gun away. I said, "I reckon that's going to be us."

Lew said, "I ain't shoveling no coal."

"Sure you ain't," I said. I turned around and looked out the door of the cab to see how the other business was proceeding. Down at the end of the train I could see Ben herding two men into the caboose, their hands raised. But what was more rewarding was seeing Norris organizing the process of jumping the cattle out of the first car and getting the ramp down and getting our men and horses in it. Elizandro's two men were helping him. Behind came Hays with a load of provisions and water.

I said, "Tell that son of a bitch to throw this thing where it will run backwards and get ready to go."

The fireman gave Lew a blank look and said something in Spanish. Lew answered him back. The fireman said something else. Lew stuck his gun in the man's face again. The fireman shrugged and went to playing with dials and levers and throttles and such.

I looked out the door again. Ben had disappeared into the rear caboose with his charges. The last of the horses were being loaded. As I watched, Hays and another man pulled up the ramp. Hays leaned out the opening and signaled.

I said, "Tell him to get it going. Toward Nuevo Laredo."

I looked out the cab window. Still off in the distance were the rural police, but they seemed to be coming faster. I said, "Tell him to hurry. But I'm going to want to stop in two miles. Ben has got to cut the telegraph line again.''

We moved with agonizing slowness for the first half mile. Then the train started to speed up as the cars caught up on their couplings. I tell you, it was a thrill to watch that barren, killing desert speed by. I only knew I was glad I was on a train and not crossing it horseback. On the trip down I hadn't paid it much attention. It was like a real ugly woman—you had to see it up close to realize how bad it could be.

After what I deemed was a couple of miles I signaled Lew to have the engineer stop. It took longer than I could have expected. It sure as hell wasn't like pulling up a good horse. When we finally drug to a stop I got down and looked toward the caboose. After a moment Ben got out and waved at me. We weren't that far apart, it being a fairly short train. I could see he had his rifle in his hand. After a second he stepped back to take a steady rest against the side of the car. I heard him fire. Then there was a pause as he jacked another shell into the chamber. I couldn't see the wire. He fired again. I waited and then he waved and got back into the caboose. I said to Lew, ''Tell the son of a bitch let's get the hell out of here. The line is cut. Ain't no way they can get word ahead.''

The train agonized its way out of its tracks and then slowly, once again, began to pick up speed. I hung out the window, enjoying the breeze. After a time I turned back into the cab. The fireman was at the controls. Lew was right behind him, pistol drawn. He looked uncomfortable. I said, ''What the hell's the matter?''

He looked away.

''Lew, what the hell is the matter?''

He sighed. ''Something I reckon I ought to have told you.''

''What?''

"They is a train coming out of Nuevo Laredo in about two hours."

"So what?"

"It's on this track. We're backing into it. It's an express."

11

I wasn't sure I'd heard him right. The roar of the steam engine tended to blot out every word. On top of that the cab of the engine was hot as the door of hell. In front of us was the firebox where the coal burned to heat the water to make the steam that drove the engine. Sweat was pouring all off of me. My shirt was soaked and I could feel runlets of sweat working their way down the inside of my thighs.

I yelled, "What? What's that you say?"

Lew yelled in my ear. He said, "I told you they is an express out of Laredo due along in two hours."

I hadn't been able to hear him when he'd first said it because of the unaccustomed engine noise. But now there was no mistaking his words. I drew my head back and stared at him. I said, "What was that you said about a siding?"

He yelled, "I said they wasn't one."

I just stared at him. I said, "You mean to tell me that

a fast train is going to come roaring up the tracks and we are going to back straight into the front end of it?''

He didn't look happy. He said, ''That's about the size of it.''

I commenced to swear. I said, ''Why didn't you tell me this before?''

He said, ''Didn't know. Not for sure.''

''But you told me they had a timetable posted on the wall in that shack. Didn't you take note of that?''

''Well, hell, Justa, you know these Mexican railroads. Besides''—he pointed at this gauge that showed how fast we were going—''I thought we could do better than twenty miles an hour. I figured we'd be in Nuevo Laredo before that other train come along. Some of these trains can make forty mile an hour.''

I stared at him, incredulous. ''Going backwards?''

He looked uncomfortable. ''I never give that no thought,'' he said. Then he flashed back at me. We might have been responsible for getting Lew elected sheriff but he was still his own man. He said, ''What? Would you druther have shot it out with them damn *rurales*? Or tried to make a run on worn-out horses? Goddammit, Justa, don't you git in *my* face!''

He had a point. We hadn't had no whole bunch of selection. I guess I was more disappointed than angry. Once we'd stopped the train and got us and our horses loaded I'd figured we were home free, that a short run would put us near the waters of the Rio Grande and we'd go splashing across and our troubles would be over.

And now here was this new difficulty, and it was one, frankly, that I hadn't had no training about and hadn't the slightest idea how to handle.

About then the fireman, the man that was running the engine, tapped some kind of gauge and said something to

Lew. Lew said, "He says we are running out of steam pressure."

"What does that mean?"

"Means we got to pour on the coal."

"How does that happen?"

Lew said, "Well, it means one of us has got to open that firebox door and then one of us has got to take that scoop shovel laying right there in the mouth of that coal tender and start slinging coal in the firebox."

The fireman tapped another gauge. I could see it was the indicator of how fast we were going. It had dropped down to fifteen miles an hour. I reckon he was just as anxious to beat that express into Nuevo Laredo as we were. After all, we might have the guns but we were still on the same train together.

One thing was bothering me. The engineer that Lew had shot was still laying on the floor of the cab, hanging half in and half out of the cab door. I said, "Would you mind shoving him on out? Then we'll talk about this coal shoveling."

It took only a moment for Lew to use his boot to ease the engineer overboard. I hated to do it but I was so damn sick of all the killing I couldn't stand the sight of the dead body.

Lew said, "I reckon we better get to shoveling. Steam pressure is falling off mighty fast."

"I take it that means you want me to do it."

He shrugged. "Well, I can't hardly shovel with this gun in my hand. And I *am* guarding this man."

It looked like there was a first time for everything. I'd ridden on plenty of trains; now it looked like I was going to pay my passage by making one go. There was a thick mitt laying on a little iron shelf just over the firebox. I put it on and used it to open the firebox. Lordy, talk about hot! The blast of heat nearly knocked me down. But I turned away from it and grabbed up the shovel and began throwing loads of coal in the firebox. Every few shovelfuls I'd look over at the fireman with a questioning look on my face. He'd just flutter his hand and say, *"Más, más."* More, more.

Hell, the damn engine ate coal like it was penny candy. I shoveled until I was covered with sweat and coal dust and choking on the vile stuff. When the fireman finally indicated I'd thrown in enough to carry us a little further I fell back against the cab wall and gasped for breath. Lew looked me over carefully. He said, "Boy, you are a sight. I don't believe you could hold that job steady."

"Shut up," I said. "I can hold that gun on that man just as good as you can. Your turn is coming next."

He looked alarmed. "Now hold on!" he said. "Ain't no point in both of us looking like pickaninnies."

I said, "Gawd, what I wouldn't give for a drink of whiskey right now. Or a cup of coffee. Or even some water."

"They got water," Lew said. He kicked out at an earthen jug. "Take all you want. Might hand me a dipperful also."

When we'd drunk we watched the speed gauge carefully. It crept up from fifteen to twenty and finally come steady at twenty-four. I said, "Ask him if he's got that throttle all the way open."

"Don't have to," Lew said. "I can see he does. We don't have to prompt this boy. I've already explained to him what is at stake if he don't get us to Nuevo Laredo in time."

I took another look at the gauge and my heart suddenly sank. At the bottom it said, in bold letters, KPH. I knew enough about Mexico to know what that meant. It might have been sixty miles to the border by my map, but we were on a train that was running *kilometers* per hour. And a kilometer was only six tenths of a mile. In reality we were only going about eighteen miles an hour. At that rate we'd meet the express a good forty-five minutes to an hour out of Nuevo Laredo. In a kind of low voice I told Lew the news.

He looked at the gauge and then he looked at me. Then he said something to the fireman. The fireman said something in Spanish and nodded. I didn't understand the Spanish but I understood the nod. I said, "Ask him how fast that express will be running in kilometers per hour."

Lew did and then he said to me, with a kind of sick expression on his face, "About twice as fast as we're going. Maybe more. This hombre says it depends on the engineer and how he's feeling that day. But one thing for sure—we ain't going to beat him to Nuevo Laredo, not unless he is mighty late getting out."

So then the question became, How close could we get before we had to abandon the train and take to horse? Would it be fifteen miles? Would it be ten? I didn't know if the horses could even make ten miles in one stretch. And there would be just as many rural police in that last stretch as we'd encountered all the way along the trail. I had to figure some way to get us closer.

I looked at my watch. We had been traveling for about forty minutes. I just leaned back and thought. I got interrupted once to shovel more coal, but that was no longer a hardship, not with this new problem to figure out.

The only thing I could think of was that I had to figure a way to make that express back up. And he wasn't going to do that with the first glimpse of us. By the time he realized he wasn't just overtaking us, that we were actually coming right at him, it would be too late to stop and we'd have one hell of a collision. My only other choice was to keep careful watch for him, stop in time to unload the horses and then try to make it the rest of the way on horseflesh. But that wasn't a good plan at all. I had to figure out a way to warn the express in advance, get him stopped and somehow get him going the other way. I figured if I could get him stopped he'd see us bearing down on him and throw her into back-up gear and stay the hell out of our way.

But how to do it?

After about a half an hour of thinking an idea came to me. There wasn't a hell of a lot of time left. I said to Lew, "Get him to show you how to make this thing go and how to stop it."

"Why?"

"Do what I'm telling you."

It wasn't all that hard. The throttle that made the thing go was just a lever you pushed to the right to make it go faster. When you wanted to stop, you drawed it all the way back to your left and then pulled on two big levers that were mounted on the iron floor, pulled them all the way back. Lew said you was supposed to take it gradual on the brakes until you got her slowed down or the brakes would wear out on you.

I said, "All right. Have you got it straight?"

"Got what straight?"

"How to run this train."

He gave me a look. "Why the hell should I have to know how to run this train?" He tapped the fireman on the back of the head with the barrel of his revolver and said, "That's what we got Pancho here for."

I said, "I'm going to try something and I ain't going to have time for a lot of delays to interpret and all that. It's going to have to go quick. Tell that man to jump."

"Do what?" He squinted at me.

I said, "Tell him to jump. Tell him we don't need him anymore. Tell him to get the hell off the train. That plain enough for you?"

He stared at me a long time and then he shrugged. "I

reckon you know what you're doing. But I don't think he's going to jump, not at this speed. I know I damn sure wouldn't."

Then he holstered his pistol and, with one swift move, jerked the little Mexican up by his armpits and flung him out the door. For a second he leaned out, watching, I figured, how the fireman had fared. I said, "Well?"

Lew turned back into the cab. He said, "Don't seem to be hurt too bad. He bounced a couple of times, but when he come to rest he kind of sat up. I do kind of hate to leave him afoot out in this damn desert, though."

Well, in point of fact, the terrain was beginning to soften up a little. Here and there were patches of green, and trees were starting to make their appearance. I said, "I hated to do it myself, but I didn't have no choice. What I got in mind is going to have to be done and done damn quick."

Lew put his hand on the throttle. It was one of them kind of gadgets you had to hold in place else it would pull back. I figured it had some kind of spring pressure on it. He pushed it forward so we once again began gaining speed. He said, "Hell, I'm running a train."

With as few words as I could I explained what I had in mind. He mulled it over. He said, "I reckon I see your point. It might work."

I picked up the coal shovel and began slinging more coal into the firebox. I said, "If it don't we are in one hell of a storm."

Lew said, "Is the engineer the boss over the fireman?"

"I guess," I said. "I don't really know."

"Well, let's just figure he is. More coal, fireman."

So I shoveled some more coal. But time was running out. Finally I took the big glove and closed the firebox. I said, "Be damn alert from now on. Move when you get the signal."

I looked at my watch, trying to calculate how many

miles, or kilometers, we'd made and just about where that express would be. There wasn't a hell of a lot of time. I started climbing up the coal on the tender. Lew said, "Don't fall off."

I didn't bother to answer him. Climbing across a load of coal ain't my most favorite form of recreation.

I got to the end of the coal tender and then descended a little ladder they had there. There was a slight kind of shelf you could stand on. I stared down at the couplings that held one car to the other. They kind of fitted tongue in groove but there was an iron rod that appeared to hold them together. I got hold of it. It had a kind of handle on it. I give it a slight tug and it appeared willing to slide right on up. I figured they kept it greased as they had to constantly be changing the cars out. Once I was pretty sure what I was doing I stepped across the coupling to the little ledge on the next car and used the little ladder to climb to the top of the car. It was the first cattle car, the one my men and horses were in. I got to the top of the car. There was a kind of broad plank that was laid along its top as a sort of a walkway. Well, that didn't make no difference to me. I wasn't about to get up and try and trod that thing in high-heeled boots. It was amazing to me how much a train swayed and bounced around when you was atop it. I contented myself with going its length on my hands and knees.

I took it one car at a time, leaving one by going down the ladder, stepping across the coupling, then getting on top of the next with the ascending ladder. It was much slower going than I'd thought, and the wind was fierce. I was certain, if I'd stood up, that I'd of been blown off. In such a fashion I made my way back to the caboose. Hanging over the end, I leaned down as far as I could and banged on the woodwork just over the door with the butt of my pistol. There was this little kind of porch at the back and, after a second, the door opened and Ben came out. He was carrying his rifle. He glanced up at me and then back into the caboose. ''What?'' he said.

I yelled at him against the wind. I said, ''You still got them two hombres in that caboose?''

He nodded.

I said, ''Throw them off the train.''

He gave me a look. ''What?''

I yelled, ''Goddammit, is everyone gone hard of hearing? Throw the son of a bitches off the train and then come up here. We got a situation to handle.''

He ran his hand over his jaw and then he shrugged. He disappeared inside. After a moment he came back out with the brakeman and the conductor. He started making motions for them to jump. They looked around at him, walleyed. I didn't blame them. That damn ground was rushing by mighty fast. Finally I seen Ben run out of patience. In quick succession he put a boot in the seat of first one and then the other and sent them tumbling off the train. I watched. Like Lew had said, they bounced a little and then rolled for a spell, but they finally appeared to come up sitting with no harm done. What would have done them a great deal more harm, possibly, was what I was fixing to do. I motioned for Ben to climb the ladder.

When he was beside me, sitting on the roof of the caboose, I said, ''I want you to make your way up to the cab of the locomotive. Well, not really the locomotive. I want you to stand in the middle of the coal tender where I can see you and where you can see me. When I wave at you I want you to count ten and then yell at Lew to cut the power on the train. Slow her down.''

He gave me a blank look. ''Lew?''

''Yeah. He's running the train.''

''Lew?''

I said, ''Look, I ain't got time to explain. Just go and

do what I tell you. I'm going to be at the end of this caboose, on one of them little ladders. I'll be looking back at you. You see me wave, you count ten to give me time to do my business and then you tell Lew to shut down the throttle. He might also put on a little brake. Now go on. And hurry up about it.''

He said, ''What is this all about, Justa?''

I said, ''If I felt like explaining I would have already done it. Now go on and do like you're told. And be careful making your way up to the locomotive. The tops of these cars ain't exactly as steady as a hay wagon.''

He crawled off, on hands and knees, going reluctantly, but going nevertheless. I made my own way back to the end of the caboose and let myself down until I was standing over the coupling. It was the same as the rest. After I'd given it a good study I climbed back up the ladder and took a look down the tracks toward the border. If my figuring had been correct it wasn't going to be no hell of a long time before that express came in sight.

Like I'd said, the terrain had fallen off and it was pretty much downhill toward the Rio Grande. I was counting on that. I was counting on that a good deal.

I ducked my head down to stay out of the wind and lit a cigarillo. I'd had my hat jammed down so hard on my head to keep it from blowing off that I was starting to get a headache. I loosened it, lifting it up to where it generally sat. Then I raised back up to take a peer down the tracks. A gust of wind hit me with sudden force and my hat went sailing off. For a minute I swore some mighty oaths, words I wouldn't have wanted my mother to hear me say. I looked back, thinking it might have caught somewhere on the train, but it was gone. A damn good fifty-dollar hat, gone with the wind. I added it, mentally, to Norris's debt.

Then when I looked again down the tracks I thought I could see a little bit of smoke in the air. I looked back. I could see Ben standing up in the coal tender. It was going to call for a nice bit of timing.

When I came back to the direction we were heading I could see the smoke more distinctly. I reckoned it to be some seven or eight miles away. We were closing at a pretty good clip. It wasn't going to be long. When I judged the distance to be no more than four miles I turned around on the little ladder and gave Ben a wave. Then I climbed down to the coupling. I took a deep breath and took hold of the rod I hoped would sever the tie between the cars. I waited. The instant I felt us slowing I pulled on the rod and the caboose separated from the next car. I could hear the slight squeal as Lew applied the brakes. I looked north. The caboose, aided by the helpful downslope, was leaving us like a redheaded stepchild. I watched it go, just hoping the engineer of the express would see it in time to apply his brakes and begin backing to avoid a collision. I estimated we were about twelve miles outside of Nuevo Laredo.

I watched. I could clearly see the express beyond the caboose that was bearing down on them. I saw the smoke from his exhaust suddenly change from white to black as the engineer reversed power and direction. He'd seen his trouble, all right. I climbed back up the ladder and signaled to Ben for Lew to pour on the power. Then I went up the ladder of the cattle car and went on hands and knees down to the couplings between the next two cars. I had him backing up and I didn't intend to give him any rest.

I waited, watching, to see what he would do. The engineer was retreating from that caboose like it was a wave of scalding water. I figured to give him a little more to think about. I got up on the ladder of the car behind me and waved to Ben. Then I descended and pulled out the connecting rod and sent that express engineer a load of high-priced crossbred Texas cattle. It went careening away, going even faster than the caboose because the slope was even further down. After that I worked my way back to the next car.

Each time I would release a car Lew would slow the train, giving the car momentum to leave us. Then he'd pour back on the steam. That express was backing up as fast as it could. I knew it was a passenger train and I reckoned the engineer didn't want to kill his passengers, much less ruin all that rolling stock of the Mexican railroads. I'd figured jobs weren't that easy to come by in Mexico and that the job of an engineer was too important to risk.

I kept backing him up, releasing cars one at a time, until I could see the houses and buildings of Nuevo Laredo. I let Lew go on a couple of miles further and then I signaled him, through Ben, to stop. I had damn near backed that express all the way back to where he'd come from, but I didn't want him to get into the station where he could put out an alarm for the soldiers or the police.

When Lew finally got the train stopped I figured we were about a mile from the Rio Grande. I jumped down and ran back to the only cattle car that was left, throwed open the door and began urging everyone to hurry. Hays and Norris and Ben and the *vaqueros* of Señor Elizandro got the horses off and got them cinched up and ready to ride.

I said, "We ain't got a minute to spare. We got to move!"

Everyone got mounted and then Miguel's two men helped him into the saddle. I went up beside his horse. I said, "Señor, you have to hold on for a little while. Then you will be all right. Can you do it?"

He was white-faced and sweating, swaying in the saddle. "Yes," he said. "I will do it."

I said, "We will have to go fast to cross the border before they can intercept us."

He said, "Go as fast as you have to. I will be with you."

I looked at his two men. I said, "Hold him in the saddle."

They didn't understand a word I said, but they nodded.

I swung aboard my own tired horse. We started due north at a lope. I was not going to be caught now. Lew caught up with me after a half a mile. He said, "That was one hell of a trick. That one with the railroad cars. Where'd you learn that?"

I said, grimly, "By trying to make a wedding on time."

12

We splashed across the river in good style, all nine of us. Señor Elizandro was wobbling a little in his saddle but, with the help of his two men, he kept up. We hit Texas soil, finally, and I swear there come a sigh of relief out of all of us you could have heard to Oklahoma. We'd made a hard run since we'd left the train so I stopped in the shade of some willow trees along the riverbank to give the horses a bit of a blow. Ben came up and said, "Boy, it is going to be good to get home. Reckon what time that next train is?"

I said, "Hate to disappoint you but we still got a little work left to do."

He gave me a startled look. He said, "What work?"

I said, "You'll find out."

We rode on into Laredo. I badly wanted a bath, a drink and a bed, in no particular order, but I had to get Jack Cole and Miguel Elizandro seen to. We rode straight to the little infirmary they had there. The surgeon that was

on duty took one look at Miguel and had him rushed back
to a bed. He examined Jack but wasn't that concerned. He
said, "Whoever put these drainage rags in here has either
had a hell of a lot of experience or got lucky."

I said, "I just got lucky."

He gave me a thin smile. "Never seen a gunshot wound
before?"

I said, "Not me. I'm just a simple cattleman."

He kept Jack, too. But since Jack lived in Laredo it
wasn't no big deal.

The surgeon was going to operate on Miguel Johnny
Quick so I walked back to bid him adieu. I figured he
didn't have any money, him just coming out of jail, so I
leafed off about a hundred dollars in pesos, that being the
bulk of the money I had, Mexican money, and laid it beside his pillow. He was looking mighty thin and drawn but
he put up a hand to shake mine. He said, "I have plenty
of money. All I have to do is wire Mexico City."

I said, "Well, pay me back when you can. Half-Moon
Ranch, Blessing, Texas. Come on down if you ever get
the chance."

He said, "I owe you a great deal."

I shook my head. "Naw. You paid me back when you
faced Benito down. I helped break you out of jail; you saved
several killings. I figure we're even."

He said, "But you still have my thanks. I will see you
as soon as I can get rid of this business." He nodded his
head toward his left shoulder.

I said, "They got stuff here they can give you that will
kill the pain. Laudanum and such. I'm just sorry I couldn't
have helped you more on the trail. I know it must have
been a hell of a hard time for you."

He said, "Someday you may need a friend in Mexico.
You know who that will be."

"Get well," I said. I wasn't much for them parting kind

of talks. "Come on up to Blessing and we'll cut a water-melon."

We headed for the Hamilton Hotel. The boy outside took our horses around to the stables in the back. I had left Elizandro's two men with him at the infirmary, but just looking at Lew and Hays and Ben and Norris, I had some idea of how I must have looked and none of them had been shoveling coal. We went trooping into the lobby, going past curious stares like they'd never seen a bunch of cattlemen who'd just outrun the Mexican police. The desk clerk on duty didn't recognize me. I told him I wanted two big suites and everyone of us wanted to book a bath and to make it damn fast. I also said we wanted five steak dinners sent up with several bottles of their best whiskey.

He cleared his throat. I'd been staying at that hotel longer than I wanted to remember. The clerk was one of them starched, high-collared individuals I never cared for. Or maybe I was just feeling giddy after all the trouble we'd had. I said, "Ben, put one right between his eyes. He ain't moving fast enough to suit me. Shoot him and maybe the manager will send one out here that will be a little more cooperative."

Ben didn't actually pull his revolver, but the clerk looked like he was near to fainting. About that time the manager, whom I'd known for some time, came out. He said, "Well, Mr. Williams, looks like you've been on the trail for some time. Jenkins taking care of you all right?"

I said, "We were about to shoot him, but I reckon that won't be necessary now."

Well, you never saw a desk clerk get so busy in all your life. It was "Yessir!" every time he opened his mouth. When he'd cleared his throat I'd figured he was going to tell us he didn't have any rooms left or that we would have to pay in advance. But all that suddenly got changed. He didn't even ask me to sign the register.

There was a big clock on the wall behind the desk. It read going on for five o'clock. I asked this Jenkins, this desk clerk, "What's the date? The date of the month?"

He said, "Why, Mr. Williams, it's the ninth. The ninth of June."

I just stood there. There wasn't another damn thing I could say. Finally I turned away from the desk and started up the stairs to my suite on the second floor. The saddlebags I was carrying over my shoulder seemed to weigh a thousand pounds. It was my wedding day. I was supposed to have been married that afternoon at four o'clock. I was fifty minutes late and two hundred miles away.

As we started to head up the stairs I turned around to Ben. I said, "Go buy me some clothes. Shirts and jeans and some socks."

He turned around without a word and went back down the stairs. Ben could buy clothes for me because he was an exact size smaller than me. He didn't say anything because he knew what June 9 was. He knew it was my wedding day and he also knew how Nora was going to feel about me not being there.

Norris passed me without a word. Wasn't much he could say. I said, "Hays, you room in with me. Lew and Ben and Norris will take the other place."

They brought my bath pretty pronto. I peeled off the clothes that I'd seemed to have been wearing since I was born. I gave them to the two boys that were handling the bath and told them to burn them or sell them or give them away. The only thing I kept was my belt. I give them two dollars and they kept bringing up hot water until I was nearly back to normal. I couldn't have sworn to it, but it seemed like my body just sucked up the water out of that tub.

After I felt like I was good and clean I got up and shaved. The boys were right there with hot water. Hays just sat and watched me. He said, "What are you going to do, boss?"

I said, "First I'm going to kill Norris. Then I'm going to try and get Nora to understand and forgive me."

"Reckon she will?"

I washed my razor off in the basin of hot water and gave him a look. "After all the times I've let her down? Would *you* forgive me?"

"Well," he said, "reckon if I knowed all the facts I might."

"But you ain't a woman."

He said, "Yes, that do make a difference."

I said, "Hays, just shut up. You ain't doing me one damn bit of good."

Ben arrived about then carrying my new clothes. I got dressed. I said, "Y'all just sit steady until I get back. I don't want this bunch getting scattered. And pass the word next door."

I left the hotel and walked about three blocks to the telegraph office at the railroad station. It took me quite a while to figure out the wording, but I finally wrote:

HAVE BEEN DELAYED UNAVOIDABLY STOP IN LAREDO
STOP ARRIVE IN BLESSING IN TWO DAYS STOP PLEASE
FORGIVE ME STOP OUT OF MY HANDS STOP HOPE YOU
WILL UNDERSTAND STOP WIRE ME HAMILTON HOTEL
STOP

I sent it and then I walked back to the hotel hoping. She'd have it within the half hour. If she understood and was willing to forgive me I'd have an answer within two or three hours. Of course I knew she'd have to sit down and think about it and discuss it with her mother. I also knew all about those guests, some of whom would have come a hundred miles for the wedding. I reckoned she was angry and I didn't blame her. And I reckoned she was embarrassed in the bargain. June 9 at four o'clock had come and gone and there'd been no bridegroom there. I reckoned she was mad and angry and embarrassed and on the warpath for my scalp.

The steaks came up not long after I got back to the room. There was no dining table but I reckoned by then the desk clerk had figured out who we were and had one sent along. He also sent two waiters to stand behind us and take our orders like we was real gentry. Hays just ate it up like it was pie, but I kept warning him not to get used to such treatment.

Everybody had bathed and put on fresh clothes, some store-bought new, some clean out of their saddlebags. Even Norris had somehow managed to find himself a seersucker suit from some shop in town. It did, however, not quite fit him after the poor feeding he'd got in the Mexican jail and then on our run across the desert. But I was in no mood to josh with him. As far as I was concerned he might have lost me Nora, and if that was the case, he was in more trouble than he'd ever been in in his life.

Ben took a big drink of iced water and said, with some satisfaction, "I was beginning to believe that this was something I'd just dreamed up. I never thought of ever having it again."

I said, "Little brother, them was some fine shots you made at those telegraph lines. I don't know anybody else could have done it."

He said, "Oh, yeah? Why don't you tell that to Buttercup when we get home. And speaking of that, when are we going home?"

I looked directly at Norris. I said, "Why, I reckon when we've got the business tended to we came down here to get tended to."

Norris just looked down at his plate and didn't say anything.

But, naturally, Ray Hays had to pop off. He said, sounding just as innocent as you please, "But hell, boss, I thought the main part of our bid'ness was to get Norris out of jail. Hell, we done done that."

I was looking at Norris, who still wouldn't look back at me, but I said, "Shut up, Ray."

It was kind of a dreary supper, nobody saying much. This wasn't one of them kind of situations where anybody come out the winner. The initial effort had just been one of trying to hold on to something that already belonged to us. And we'd spent a lot of time and money doing that and I couldn't say for sure, even at that point, that I had it in my back pocket.

So there was nobody exactly suggesting we go out dancing. Besides, I had Nora on my mind. I kept waiting for a knock on the door with an answer to my telegram but it didn't seem like it was ever going to happen.

Then Hays decided he would lighten the mood by telling us of one of his boyhood experiences. He done that from time to time whether we wanted him to or not. He started off by saying, "I ever tell y'all about my days on my daddy's ranch up in the panhandle? One we couldn't run but about one head of cattle to the hundred acre the land was so poor?"

Ben said, sourly, "Yeah, you told us."

We were all still pretty dried-up and disgusted from that trip across the desert.

But you couldn't head Hays off once he felt a story coming on. He said, "Y'all knowed that if any of us boys ever let the sun come up and find us not working, ol' Dad would take a strop to our backs."

Ben said, "Goddammit, Hays, we know. You've told us about twenty different versions of how hard you had it."

Hays would not be stopped. "But did I ever tell you that I was so used to goin' to work before the sun got up that the first time I tried to saddle a horse in the daylight I couldn't do it. I had to shut my eyes."

Ben said, "Oh, what a liar."

Hays kept insisting. He said, "Truth be told, it's a fact. I was goin' to my uncle Art's funeral and I was seventeen years old at the time and I'd never saddled a horse where I could see, you know, not after the sun got up."

Ben said, "Hays, you keep this up I'm going to throw you out that window over yonder."

I said, with a little more edge in my voice than I meant, "You both shut up. I got to figure out about tomorrow."

Lew said, "What's tomorrow?"

"Job of work," I said.

I was moody and blue about Nora, but I was also determined to finish the job that had brought me to the border in the first place. I said, making damn sure Norris could hear me, "We got to run them squatters off that big, important five thousand acres that all this bullshit was about."

Well, that fetched him. He got his chin up and said, "You've got the paper now, the title you flaunted in my face. I assume that you'll do something lawful for a change. All you have to do is take it to the sheriff. After that it's his affair."

I said, as sarcastically as I could, "Well, by God, now he knows all about how to handle this business. Reckon why that couldn't have been so ten days ago. Maybe you're a slow learner, huh Norris?"

He started getting red in the face, but Ben said, "C'mon Justa, we all know how you feel, but that ain't going to do a damn bit of good."

Norris suddenly got up without a word, not even bothering to pick up his hat, and walked out of the room. Ben said, "See what I mean? I know he's got plenty coming and he was in the wrong, but he ain't exactly had no easy time of it. Justa, he's family. You got to give him a little breathing room. You don't know you've lost Nora yet. Wait until we get home."

I didn't bother to even answer him. I just finished my steak, had a drink of whiskey and went down to the lobby to inquire at the desk if a telegram had come for me. The now oh-so-eager Mr. Jenkins said it hadn't come but as soon as it did they'd get it to me if they had to look all over town.

Well, I still had hope. Only a couple of hours had passed since she would have gotten mine and I knew there would have to be a certain amount of delay while she decided how much punishment I ought to have.

It was just coming dark as I walked out on the street and set out to find a little diversion. I walked along the boardwalk. The town was full of folks, most of them, naturally, being of Spanish extraction. Now and again I got jostled or bumped and I found my temper rising unreasonably. I am normally a pretty steady fellow, but I felt raw and on edge and it was all I could do to keep from turning around and knocking hell out of some poor little man who'd accidentally brushed up against me.

I walked along, thinking. Hell, if I'd of had any sense I'd of got a train out that very night and hied it back to Blessing and laid siege to Nora. But something told me it was too soon, the wound was too fresh. Better to give it some time. Besides, I was determined to personally see this land business through if for no other reason than to embarrass Norris.

But I also had the sneaking suspicion that the house wasn't even finished. That would be all it would take—me to show up late and the house not to be finished. I was halfway tempted to wire Harley for a report, but by the

time he got my telegram and got me an answer back I'd
be halfway to Blessing.

That was assuming matters went the way they was supposed to the next day—a fact I couldn't be all that sure of.

I walked about three blocks from the hotel and took
notice of a pretty respectable-looking saloon. Gazing
through the window, I could see a couple of poker games
going on and it come across my mind that a game of cards
might be a good way to take my thoughts off my troubles.
Consequently I went on through the swinging doors. The
place was doing a pretty brisk trade, but then I reckoned
all the saloons in Laredo never went wanting for clientele.
You take a place like Laredo, a border town, and you are
going to have more than your average count of bandits and
desperados and just general trash. The border is a good
place to go if you've got to get away from the authorities
on one side or the other. Ain't nothing but a shallow river
standing in your way. So you'll draw more folks that prefer
whiskey to Sunday-school books.

Of course it didn't bother me. I had enough time in
Laredo over the years that I could tell what some yahoo
was going to do even before he thought of it.

Once inside I took a look at the two poker tables and
saw they were full. I went over to the bar and ordered a
beer and a shot of whiskey to give it time for a seat to
come open. One of the tables appeared to be playing pretty
big stakes so I figured it wouldn't be long before one of
the gentlemen players decided it was time he ought to be
home, that his wife was waiting supper on him.

But I just bellied up to the bar and stared at my reflec-
tion in the mirror. Lord, I was a sight. I looked like old
saddle leather from the beating my skin had taken crossing
that desert. But it didn't go with my clothes and my hat,
which were shiny new. About the only two things I still
carried were my belt and my boots, them and my revolver

and holster. As near as I could tell I looked like I'd aged about ten years.

There was an ol' boy standing next to me at the bar. He was bigger than I was but he was soft looking. He was dressed like somebody's idea of what either a big-shot banker who loaned money on cattle or a successful rancher figured they ought to look like. I could see him watching me in the mirror that ran nearly the full distance of the bar. After a minute he said, "You must like what you see. You been starin' at it long enough."

I just gave him a look. I knew the mood I was in and it didn't involve talking to strangers.

But he wouldn't be satisfied. He kind of flicked his hand over at the sleeve of my shirt and said, "Just make a payday, cowboy?"

I could tell he'd had about one too many, but that was fixing to become his problem. I said, "Keep your hands to yourself, fellow."

He said, "Scared I'll mess up them nice new clothes? Say, what does somebody like you mean by coming in here drinking with the quality? You better get yourself down to one of the cantinas down along the river."

Right then I turned and stared at him. I said, "Fellow, you are either drunk or crazy. Either way, you open your mouth to me again and you might not open it again for a long time."

I knew he was going to take a swing at me. But he was so slow and he drew back so far that I didn't think he was ever going to get the punch off. Before it could get halfway to me I hit him a vicious right hand in his soft gut. He went "Ooof!" and wanted to double over, but I wouldn't let him. Just as he started to bend over I hit him with a driving left hook that straightened him up and dropped him like a limp sack of flour.

But it hadn't been him I'd been concerned about. As

he'd gone down I'd seen the man to his right start to react. Rich bullies never go into bars and start fights unless they got somebody behind them that can get them out of the scrapes they get themselves into. So, as the fat-belly dropped, I was already reaching for my revolver. I could see the man behind the fat-belly doing the same thing. I drew, clipping the man under the chin with my heavy revolver as I did. It staggered him. With my hand up in the air I just completed the play by bringing the barrel of my revolver crashing down on his head. He dropped like he'd been poleaxed.

The bar had gone quiet. I cocked my revolver and was about to turn to face any new threat when I suddenly felt a pair of strong arms pinning my arms to my side. For an instant I struggled and then I heard Lew's voice in my ear. He said, "Justa, let's get out of here. I don't like the odds. Just walk backwards, following me. Keep that revolver playing over the house."

We got to the door. The place was quiet, watching us. On the floor, beside the bar, the fat man was starting to move around, groaning and feeling his belly. Lew let go of me and I saw he also had his revolver drawn. He said, "I'd stay indoors if I was y'all. We didn't start this fight and ain't nobody hurt. At least not yet."

Then we were through the door and out onto the street. Didn't take us but a minute to get lost in the crowds moving up and down the sidewalk. We holstered our weapons and strolled toward the river. After about six blocks we come to a little plaza. We could see the lights from the riverfront stores and saloons reflecting off the water. We found a little stone-and-concrete bench and sat down. We didn't say anything and, after a moment, we both lit up cigarillos. We smoked in silence, watching the white smoke float up toward the dark sky. Finally Lew said, "She mean that much to you?"

I studied the glowing end of my cigarillo and said, "I reckon. She must or I wouldn't be feeling this way. What the hell were you doing there?"

"Oh, I seen the way you was looking. I figured you'd go looking for a fight. Thought I'd be there."

"I wasn't looking for no fight. They started it."

He gave a little laugh. "Who you joshing, Justa? You get that look on your face and walk into a saloon you know damn good and well somebody is going to challenge you. You don't reckon I know you that well by now?"

I didn't say anything. Wasn't much I could say. I knew what he was talking about was the truth. If the fat man hadn't started in on me I'd of found a way to get somebody else to cooperate in getting their head knocked off.

Lew said, "Well? What about Nora?"

I shook my head. I said, "I don't know. I don't reckon I'll know for some little time."

Lew cut his hand through the air. "Then what in the hell did you risk it for? You could have sent somebody down to get Norris out of jail. Or let him set there and cool his heels for the while. It wouldn't have killed him. Might have taught him a little lesson."

I looked into the distance. "Lew, some years back I took a job from Dad, from Howard. I don't know no other way than to do it. I reckon that's been the biggest problem between me and Nora, me and that family business. Seems like sometimes she understands better than others. I thought I could make it back in time. Get my family business done and get back for the wedding."

Lew said, softly, "I reckon what you don't understand is that she figures you're her family now. That you owe her as much as yore brothers or yore daddy or that ranch. Women think that way, you know."

I looked over at him and laughed, just a little. "When

did you get to be such an expert on women? I ain't seen you being led to the altar no time lately.''

He had the good grace to smile. He said, ''Well, maybe I ain't no sage at firsthand, but I'm hell on givin' advice to other men.''

I got up. ''Let's wander on back.''

''We ain't stopping in no more saloons?''

''No,'' I said.

As we walked he said, ''What now?''

I shrugged in the dark. ''Reckon I'll go see the local sheriff and get that business tended to about the squatters. Then I reckon we'll all head back. Hell, you been gone too long from your duties as high sheriff as it is.''

''Want me to go with you?''

I shook my head. ''Naw, ought to be nothing to it. I got the Spanish land grant free and clear. Ought to just be a formality. You and the rest go to getting ready to pull out. Check on trains and so on.''

There was no telegram waiting for me back at the hotel. I looked at Lew. He didn't say anything. On the way up the stairs I said, ''Reckon I'll have to plead my case in person.''

''More than likely,'' he said. ''More than likely.''

13

I took Ben with me the next morning to see the sheriff. I done it for no particular reason except Norris gave me a kind of self-satisfied look when I announced where I was going. I guessed by that he meant that since he'd had trouble with the sheriff, so I would also. I didn't much think so.

Ben and I walked over from the hotel and mounted the boardwalk in front of the sheriff's office and county jail. The notice painted on the big plate-glass window announced that somebody named R. E. "Buck" Gadley was the sheriff. But I didn't give a damn what his name was, I just wanted him to do his job. Ben and I clanked across the boardwalk and opened the door. There was a middle-aged man with a droopy mustache hanging around his upper lip and a lined, bewhiskered face that appeared to be running about two days behind his razor sitting behind a small desk in the middle of the room. He had his boots on top of the desk and he was chewing tobacco. He seemed

to time his chews with our steps as we crossed the room.
Just as we got up to his desk he leaned over and spit on
the floor. I could see by the condition of the wooden floor
it wasn't the first time he'd practiced that habit. Looking
left I could see a younger man sitting on a little bench
running a rag over a shotgun that was already plenty shiny.
I said, "Sheriff Gadley?"

He looked up, about as disinterested as if I was a fly.
He said, "Yeah?"

I said, "My name is Justa Williams. I'm from up in
Matagorda County. On the coast. I got some squatters,
some trespassers, nesting on my land. I need them run
off."

He spit again and then regarded me for a long time.
Finally he said, "Whar's this 'yere land of yor'n?"

"On the Rio Grande. About three miles east of here.
It's five thousand acres. My brother has been down to see
you about it once before, but you said we didn't have a
clear title. Said there was some trouble about the Spanish
land grant."

"So?" he said.

I took the paper out of my pocket and held it out. I
said, "So, I got that straightened out. Can't be any question about clear title now. I want those trespassers run off
my family's land."

He looked at me a long time, chewing his cud of tobacco slowly. "What'd you say yore name was?"

"Williams," I told him. "Justa Williams. My brother's
name is Norris Williams. He's the man came in to see you
a little over a week ago. I've had to go down to Monterrey
to get this business cleared up."

Moving his head like it hurt his neck, he looked over at
the young man on the bench. He said, "Soup, was thet
thet smart aleck in that funny suit come in here throwin'
his weight 'round? Actin' like he was some big shot?"

Soup said, "I reckon it was, Shur'ff. Lord, wadn't he a sight! I liked to have died laughin' when you tied a tin can to his tail."

I looked around at Ben. I said, "It appears we ain't going to get much cooperation around here. Looks like we'll have to tend to matters ourselves."

The sheriff took his boots off the desk. They hit the floor with a clump. He said, "Now, as I understand it, ain't none of y'all from around these here parts. That 'bout right?"

I nodded. "That is exactly right."

He said, "Then I reckon we ought to set matters straight. Ain't a vote amongst you so I don't be obliged to do shit for you. You get my drift?"

I said, as calm as I could, "Sheriff, it's going on for nine of the morning. We've got a four o'clock train to catch this afternoon. We intend to be on it. But we also intend to clear our land of people who ain't got no rights being on it before we catch that train. You get *my* drift?"

I had just about had enough, what with first one thing and then another, and I could feel the anger rising in me. Ben said, lowly, "Take it easy, Justa."

The sheriff stuck a finger out at me. He said, "Listen, boy, you go to takin' *my* law in yore hands in this here county an' I'll throw yore ass in jail. You understand me, boy?"

I said, "What did you call me?"

He said, "You heard me, boy."

I said, "Watch my left, Ben." Then I put both hands on the sheriff's desk and leaned toward him. I said, "Now you understand me, *old man*. Don't give me no trouble or I'll put you in the cemetery, *old man*. Understand?"

He started to bluster but we were already backing for the door. I could see the one holding the shotgun looking for some sign from the sheriff. None was forthcoming.

Ben and I just kept backing until we got to the door. I said, "Getting a little cut off what's happening on my land are you, Sheriff?"

He didn't answer, just kept watching us, his jaws working.

I said, "One last word. Don't interfere."

Then we turned out the door and made our way back to the hotel. Ben turned his head once to see if we were being followed, but I didn't even bother. As far as I was concerned the sheriff was just a blowhard. And even if he wasn't it didn't make me much difference.

Back at the hotel I called everybody together and told them what had happened. Norris had a cat-with-cream look on his face but everybody else looked pretty grave. Lew said, "This is pretty serious business, Justa. That man is the sheriff."

Ben said, "Yes, and that is our land."

I said, "I ain't real sure what we're going to be running into. Hays, I might better send you out there to scout around. But you got to make it fast because we ain't got a whole hell of a lot of time."

Norris said, "No need for that. I can tell you. I've been there. And been run off. There are three desperado types and about a half a dozen peons who are building a fence and digging irrigation ditches. They had appeared to also be starting a little adobe house."

I said, "Doesn't matter what you've got to say. You're not going."

He stood up. "The hell I'm not!"

I said, coldly, "No, you're not. You stay here where you can't fuck things up no more."

He went white in the face. He was hurt and it was a pleasure to me because I'd meant to hurt him. Ben said, "Justa, I've got to talk to you."

"So talk."

"Not here, out in the hall."

He got up and went to the door and held it open. After another look at Norris I followed him as he stepped out into the hall and closed the door behind him. He said, with pretty fierce determination, "Dammit, Justa, ease up on him! You don't know nothing about Nora yet. He's your brother, goddammit! Now, you want to lose two brothers? If you do you just keep on at Norris like that."

"You think I'm being unfair?"

"I think you are carrying it a little far. You reckon Norris don't feel bad enough as it is?"

I said, grimly, "You weren't in that jail with Hays and me when he wouldn't come out of his cell."

"All right. So that's Norris. You've always known how he is. But you've got to give him another chance. You've got to let him go out there to that land with us. If you don't you will hurt him mightily. Great Scott! How much you need to embarrass the man? How many times you figure to tell him off?"

I studied on the matter for a half a moment. Finally I said, "All right. He can go. But you will have to be the one to watch out for him. I won't."

He shook his head. He said, "Goddammit, Justa, sometimes I don't understand how you can be so hard."

"Comes easy," I said. "You tell him."

Once back in the room, I canvased the outfit to see how many lariat ropes we had. Turned out we didn't have one. But then that wasn't so surprising since we'd been going to get a man out of jail, not to work cattle. I sent Hays on the dead run to get four. I figured we was going to have to rope some fence and pull it down. You let folks get fence around your property and it belongs to them after about a year. That is if you let it stand. I didn't plan to let any stand.

Waiting for him, we checked our gear, carefully exam-

ined our weapons and our supply of ammunition and then
trooped on downstairs, our saddlebags over our shoulders.
The manager came out to complain about our too-short
stay but I assured him we'd be right on back in the future.
I said, "I've got some real-estate holdings down here and
I'll be coming back from time to time to check on them."

"Aaah," he said, just like he knew what I was talking
about.

I paid us out. I still had to use those peso notes and I
taken a pretty good beating on the exchange rate but there
wasn't anything I could do about that. But it served to
remind me that I'd promised Jack Cole five hundred dollars for his help and I meant to see that he got it. I didn't
have time to go over to the infirmary, at least not right at
that moment, but I did ask the manager if he'd send a boy
to hunt Jack out and have him meet us at the train depot
sometime between three and four. That was if he was able.

We all went on over to the livery stable. The horses
didn't look too bad and they weren't facing a bad day's
work, but I knew that mine, at least, would be glad to see
that green grass of Matagorda County and get in some
serious rest.

We saddled up and rode out. Going past the sheriff's
office, I tried to see if he was still in attendance, but I
couldn't tell a thing through the window. It didn't make
me a damn one way or the other, not the mood I was in.
He wasn't going to stop me from protecting my property
and he and I both knew it.

We got out of town and turned east down the river road.
Ben got up alongside me and inquired if there was any
plan. I said, "Yeah. Shoot the first son of a bitch that ever
looks like he wants to get a gun in his hand. Remember,
they are on our land. They are trespassers. They got no
rights."

He digested that and then he said, "You ask after a telegram before we left the hotel?"

I said, "Nope."

"Why not?"

"Didn't expect one. And I reckon they'd have mentioned it if one was to have come. And you might do me the favor of leaving the damn subject alone. I got other business to tend to right now."

He spit over the side of his horse, away from me. He said, "What'd you have for breakfast, prickly pears?"

I was not exactly sure where the land was, it having been some time since I'd bothered with the place. It pained me but I had no choice except to call Norris forward and ask him to point out where our land was.

He said, in a little drier voice than I thought necessary, "I've already mentioned they are digging an irrigation ditch from the river. It runs right through the middle of the property. When I was here before it was about three-quarters fenced. Not good fencing, just single-strand. Something like they didn't intend to hold cattle very long. It is just up the way."

"Fine," I said. "You stay in the back and keep quiet. And don't even have a gun in hand until I do."

He wheeled away without a word. Ben give me a look but didn't say anything. But hell, I would have said that to Norris on any occasion.

We rode on. About a half a mile further there, sure enough, was the irrigation ditch. It wasn't much—about four feet across and anywhere from a foot to two foot deep. But for land as dry as ours what little water it did bring would be a welcome relief and was liable to make the place green up like the coastal plains. Even from where we sat I could see that the water, little as it was, was having an effect.

It appeared they'd just about finished the fencing. There

was a gate, a gap really, with some wire strung across i
and I could see corner posts and wire running off in
northerly direction. Five thousand acres ain't much, bu
it's a fair amount of ground to go poking around in whe
you don't know who or what you're looking for.

I took down my lariat rope and shook out a loop. I said
"Let's get this gate down and some of this fence."

Ben and Hays and Lew threw about the same time I did
The fence posts were just little crooked cedar shafts, no
even set very deep in the ground. It wasn't any kind o
strain on my horse to pull them out. Hays and I rode on
way and Ben and Lew rode the other, letting the wire pul
the posts up as we went. After we had about a hundre
yards jerked up in either direction I called a halt and lifte
off my loop from the pole I had it secured to, coiled i
and hung it back on my saddle. When the others wer
ready I said, "Let's go and see what we got here. Stay
together but don't bunch up. Stay strung out. I'll take th
middle. Ben, you and Lew each take a flank. Let's mov
slow."

We followed the little irrigation ditch. It went on for
surprisingly long time. The river was low and so ther
wasn't much water in it, but I could see from the way th
land sloped that it would be effective. Here and there, littl
side-ditches had been dug, running off through the stunte
mesquite.

We began to see signs of cattle—manure piles and hoof
prints. I said, "Well, it's pretty plain what we got here.'

Ben said, "Yes, they are holding Mexican cattle here
either stolen ones or cattle they don't want to take throug
Immigration."

Norris said, quietly, "I could already have told you that
If anyone had cared to ask."

I didn't bother to even glance at him. I said, "An
unless I miss my guess the sheriff is in with them."

Norris said, "I could have told you that, too. If anybody had cared to ask."

This time I did turn in the saddle and give him a look. But he just stared serenely ahead, not bothering to even notice.

After about a hundred yards, just ahead, I could see the white clothes of some *campesinos*, peons, working on the ditch. I wasn't worried about them, but I knew there'd be *pistoleros* around somewhere. I drew my handgun and nodded for the others to do the same.

One of the problems with that country was that the low mesquite and briar bushes were so thick. They weren't very high, but it was difficult to see any great distance. We put the horses into a trot, following the cleared land on each side of the ditch. We were on the peons before they knew what was going on. They looked up in some astonishment but didn't seem particularly afraid. They were all armed with pick and shovel and were patiently and laboriously hacking out a trench through the hard caleche clay and dirt. One thing a peon has got is patience. You can put him to digging a hole and, if you don't think to go back and stop him, he'll keep digging all day and all night. Whoever said Mexicans were lazy had never seen a peon work.

We pulled up. They leaned on their tools and stared at us. I said to Lew, "Ask them where their bosses are and how many there are and how many guns they got and anything else you can think of."

Lew picked him out one that looked to be a cut above the rest and let go with a string of Spanish. They volleyed back and forth for a few minutes and then the peon sort of pointed off toward the northeast corner of the pasture. Lew said, "He says the men are over in a little house they have built taking the *comida*, eating. Or drinking. Or sleeping. He ain't sure. He says there are two gringos and

one Mexican. He says sometimes two other men come to
bring cattle but these two stay all the time. He says they
got plenty of guns.''

I said, ''Well, let's just walk that way.''

We started through the brush, going slowly and keeping
a sharp eye out. I didn't particularly care to get ambushed
on my own land. After a bit we began seeing cattle. They
weren't immediately obvious in the heavy brush, but they
were obviously Mexican cattle. I saw a lot of different ear
markings which indicated the cattle hadn't all come from
any one herd. That meant they were more than likely stolen.

After a bit we came to the little shack. It was just an
adobe affair, but it had a nice roof of those red tiles that
Nora had wanted. That give me a pang. But there was no
time for such thinking. There was a little clearing around
the house and three saddled horses tied out front. I could
see several more in a small corral in the back. I said,
lowly, ''Let's get down. Norris, you hold the horses. And
keep them quiet. Lew, you and Hays spread out and stay
down. I don't want them to see you. I ain't exactly sure
how to flush them out of that house, but I don't want them
to think they are outgunned. Ben, I want you right behind
me, but crouched down out of sight.''

He said, ''You ain't just going to walk up there?''

I stood up and stepped into the clearing. I'd already
holstered my gun. I said, ''You know a better way?''

I took a couple of steps forward and halloed the house.
I was only about thirty yards away and I was cold meat
for a rifle shot, but so far as I could see, the little cabin
didn't have any windows, at least not at the front. The
door was open, but I'd be able to see if anyone tried to
sneak a shot around the frame and have plenty of time to
hit the dirt before anyone could fire. I stopped and yelled
at the house again. A man suddenly appeared in the door

opening. He had a rifle in his hand, but he wasn't pointing it at me. He said, "What the hell you want? And what the hell you doing on this land? Git the hell off."

I took a couple of steps more forward. I said, "I got a message for you from Sheriff Gadley. Come out and talk."

He said, "Yeah?" Then he turned his head and said something to someone inside. He said to me, "I kin hear you from here. Speak yore piece."

I said, "My name is Justa Williams. You are trespassing on my land. I'll give you exactly ten minutes for you and your stolen cattle to get off my land."

He stared at me for a second. Then, suddenly, there was another man in the doorway. He too had a rifle but he was having trouble getting a shot at me because the first man was slightly blocking his way. I fell forward, drawing as I did. Thirty yards is a little long for accurate handgun shooting but I fired three times. I saw the first man go down. Behind me I heard a sudden burst of fire as the others let go. The second man fell, staggering backwards into the cabin. I yelled, "Keep firing through that door before somebody can shut it!"

Even though the cabin was adobe, that mud can get pretty hard, and I was counting on ricochets. We put about fifteen rounds through the door opening and then something white fluttered out. I yelled, "Stop! Hold your fire!"

We waited and then a man came staggering out. I could see blood on his shirt. He had a rifle in one hand and a revolver in the other but they were both over his head. "Don't shoot!" he said. "I give."

I eased forward. "Then just drop those weapons and keep walking toward me."

He done as he was told. As he got closer I could see he wasn't much more than a kid, eighteen or nineteen maybe. You could tell he was poor white trash and he'd probably— if somebody didn't kill him first—grow up to be old, poor white trash. I'd seen a hundred of his kind along the border.

He said, in a kind of whiny voice, "I never knowed this was nobody's land, mister. Honest I didn't."

"Keep your mouth shut," I said. I turned around. "Hays, go help him load his two friends on those saddled horses out front. Ben, you and Lew get a rope on those ponies in the back. We got to get moving."

The kid started in to whine again. He said, "I cain't do no work. I'm hurt, hurt bad. Cain't you see that?"

"You are fixing to get dead if you don't do as you're told," I said.

When the two dead men were loaded and Ben and Lew had brought up the two horses from the back, I told the kid to take off his boots.

He said, "What?"

I said, "You get shot in the ear? TAKE OFF YOUR GODDAM BOOTS!"

Well, that fetched his attention. He sat down on the ground and did as he was bid. With some satisfaction I noticed he wasn't wearing socks. I said, "Now start walking."

He stared at me a second. Hays laughed. I cocked my pistol. The boy moved, putting one foot gingerly in front of another on the rocky ground. But he was going toward the river. I said, "No, not that away." I pointed with my pistol. "North. Straight north. And don't even look back over your shoulder. Just keep walking. And I don't reckon I have to tell you not to come back this way."

He gave me a sullen look. "You stealin' my horse?"

"He'll be in town," I said. "Waiting for you. You are just loaning him to me."

He wanted to cuss me but he didn't dare. We watched him making his painful way through the brush until his head had disappeared from sight. I picked up his rifle and revolver and slung them off in the brambles where they'd never be found. Then I said, "Mount up. We got to go to a funeral."

The *campesinos* went to work on the job of burying the two *pistoleros* with the same patient approach they'd taken toward the irrigation ditch. I watched them making the holes for the late departed and thought about the little adobe house with its tile roof. I had no doubt my house wasn't finished. A thought kept coming back to me. It was about that time that we heard the sound of horses approaching. We were all still mounted, watching the peons, kind of ringed around the graves. I looked up and here came Sheriff Gadley with two deputies in attendance. He didn't even bother to say any kind of greeting, just pulled out a pistol and said, "You bunch is under arrest."

I asked him mildly, "What for?"

He nodded at the two bodies. "Plain as a cat's ass. Murder."

Ben said, "How you know it wasn't self-defense?"

He said, "Don't give me none of your damn lip, boy! It's murder 'cause I say it's murder."

I spit on the ground. "Then if that's how you see it they is fixing to be three more. You an' them two hombres you got there."

"What? What the hell you talkin' about, boy?"

I leaned my forearms on the pommel of my saddle and said, "Well, *old man,* I'm talking about a gent who is over in the bushes right behind you with a Winchester carbine pointed right at you and your two grandsons here. And he can fire that thing faster than a Gatling gun. You even look like tightening your finger on that trigger he's going to let fly."

It was a bluff. All I was trying to do was get him to look back and then I was going to pull on him. I hadn't quite decided what I was going to do about the two deputies with the shotguns.

But just then Lew came riding around me. He had his badge on and he showed it. He placed himself between Gadley and me. He said, in that voice he's got, "I'm Lew Vara and I'm the sheriff of Matagorda County. These men are under my jurisdiction and in my custody. Also, this land belongs to them. Have you got a warrant for being on it?"

Sheriff Gadley stared at him, chewing his cud of tobacco. Finally he said, "How the hell I know you're the shur'ff of Matagorda County? Anybody can get a badge."

Lew said, "Well, you can either go back to town and wire Blessing, Texas. Or you can take a chance and find out, to your sorrow, that I am. Now, do one or the other, but get the hell off this land."

He stared for a while longer, but then he slowly put his revolver away. He said, "All right. But you ain't heered the last of this yet."

I said, "Sheriff, let me acquaint you with something you might need to hear. Earlier this morning, in your office, you was telling me and my little brother that since we didn't have any votes around here we didn't count for much. Let me make a point clear. Votes seem to count a great amount to you. My family is worth upwards of three million dollars. You give us anymore trouble, or you let anybody spend more than one night on this piece of ground and I guarantee you I'll come back down here, grab me somebody off the street and spend whatever money it takes to get a crook like you out of office. You follow me, old man?"

He stared at me with hate, but he didn't do much more than spit tobacco juice on the ground. As he was about to wheel his horse around I said, "One more thing. . . ." I gestured at the peons. "We'll be taking these men back to Matagorda County with us. The sheriff here has got paper on them.''

Lew gave me a startled look, but Gadley just turned his horse, saying, "I don't give a damn what you do with them peons."

Then they were turning their horses and loping along beside the irrigation ditch, not even bothering to look back. Ben said, "Wasn't very friendly, was they?"

I said to Lew, "Tell them peons to drop their tools and get on these spare horses. Tell them they're going to take a train ride."

Lew said, "Just what in hell are you going to do with these boys?"

"Put them to work. They look like master builders to me. That is if there is still a reason to build a house."

Lew took out a cigarillo and lit it and looked at me. He shook his head. He said, "You beat all, you know that? Do you ever stop thinking?"

"Let's go. We got a lot of miles to make."

We got to the train depot just about three o'clock. I was glad to see that Jack Cole was there and that he was looking pretty nearly whole. I asked after Señor Elizandro and he said the *caballero* was coming along nicely. I give Jack fifteen hundred pesos, about two hundred dollars, which was nearly all I had after paying for fares and hiring a horse car for our animals and the peons that we would be taking back with us. Jack protested about the money but I told him it wasn't nearly enough for what he'd done and I would send him more.

We all sat around having a drink and then it came time to go. I seen that the horses and the peons were made comfortable, making sure to provide the workers with food and something to drink for the five-hour ride to Blessing. They all looked in wonder at these sudden things that were happening to them and I couldn't blame them. But they'd be all right. They'd do me a job of work and I'd send them back with more money than they'd left with. I just turned the desperados' horses loose.

We all said good-bye to Jack and then climbed aboard the chair cars for the long ride back. I knew I wouldn't get back early enough that night to try to see Nora so I pinned my hopes on the morrow. Then I leaned back in the seat and took a long sighing breath and tried to go to sleep. It had been a long, hard trip and I was plenty tired. But I'd got it all done.

Except for marrying Nora.

14

That night we got off the train stiff and sore from having sat so long. Sitting hadn't been something we'd got very used to in the past week. I immediately sent Ben and Norris and Hays on back to the ranch, having them get a wagon to carry the Mexican workers in. Lew, of course, lived in Blessing so he went on home. I put my horse in the livery and then went to the hotel my family owned. Down the street I could see Nora's house. It was dark. So was her daddy's mercantile. I got a bottle of whiskey and went on up to the room I kept special at the hotel. Lew had offered to keep me company but I'd told him I didn't want any. The next day was going to come soon enough.

There were two things I was beginning to think wouldn't hold up in this world. And that was gunmen who thought they were the fastest and suitors who thought they were the lastest. If you're a gunman there is always somebody faster than you, and if you are in the running for a lady's hand, don't figure on being the last until you got it securely attached to the bedpost of your house with a ring on her finger.

So it was with that thought in mind that I set out the next morning for Lonnie Parker's mercantile store. I thought I'd get the lay of the land from Lonnie before I ventured to go by the house. I'd had a shave and a bath and was looking as good as I could considering by past adventures. With a kind of beating heart I walked into the cool dimness of Lonnie's store. He was standing behind his counter and, when he saw me, one look at his face told me how matters stood. Normally Lonnie's face lit up like a jack-o'-lantern when I come in, mainly because our ranch did so much trade with him. But now he just stared at me glumly. I said, "Hello, Lonnie."

"Howdy, Justa," he said. He put out his hand and we shook.

I leaned one elbow on his counter and looked at him. "She pretty mad?"

He cleared his throat. Then he said, kind of miserably, "Well, you know women."

"No," I said. "I don't. If I did I don't reckon I'd be in this mess. I take it I am in a mess?"

He cleared his throat again. "I couldn't say," he said.

"She at home?"

He said, "I reckon I ought not to say about that."

I give him a hard look. "Lonnie, you wouldn't pull my leg about this, would you? It's passing important to me."

He looked away, looking miserable. He said, "Justa, I'd be much obliged if you wouldn't put me on the spot like this. Whyn't you go down an' talk to Mizz Parker. I'd take it as a favor if you would."

"So it's like that, is it," I said. I pushed away from the counter. I walked toward the door. I said, "Well, I might be seeing you again, Lonnie."

He said, a kind of pleading tone in his voice, "Now, Justa, don't take it like that. Hell, I ain't got the slightest thang to do with it. You know women."

I walked down the road to the Parker's house, not even bothering to get my horse out of the livery stable. For a moment I stood by the front gate and looked up at the white-framed, gabled house. Nora might be in there somewheres. It seemed a long ways, looking at that pleasant setting with the shading oak trees and the swing on the front porch, since that desperate flight across the barren plain from Monterrey to Laredo. I walked up the path, stepped up on that front porch and knocked on the front door. There was a considerable wait, one long enough that I knocked again. I had the feeling of someone drawing back the curtains in the parlor to look out to see who it was but I couldn't be sure. After a moment the front door opened. It was Mrs. Parker. Of course I'd hoped it would be Nora but I knew better. She stood there, looking just as sweet and matronly in her gingham gown and apron as I'd always thought of her. But this time she was wringing her hands in her apron. Without me asking she said, "Justa, Nora's not here."

She hadn't even bothered to open the screen door, just faced me with anguish on her face and her hands in her apron. But I doffed my hat nonetheless and said, "Well, Mizz Parker, where can I find her? Or when can I talk to her?"

That made her look more upset. She said, "Justa, I can't say. I'm not supposed to say."

I said, "Couldn't she have understood? How did she know what was going on? I sent a telegram."

She said, "I know. But if it had just come earlier. But it coming on the day of the wedding . . ." She let her voice trail off.

I said, "Mizz Parker, I sent that wire as soon as I could.

Before that I was to hell and—excuse me—I was in the middle of the Mexican desert. Wasn't nothing I could do. I got word as soon as I could."

True misery was written in her face. She said, "I'm sorry, Justa. There's nothing I can do. And the house wasn't even finished. Or the furniture. And then there were all the guests." She got a look on her face like mothers do. She said, "Oh, it was awful."

I said, "If I could just talk to her."

"You can't."

"Why not?"

"She's gone."

"To where?" Visions of her running off with another man jumped through my head. I felt my temper rising. "Where's she gone?"

The words come out of Mrs. Parker like they'd been drawn out with tongs. She said, "To Galveston."

"Where in Galveston?"

She was giving that apron a good workout. She said, "I can't say. I promised."

I looked at her a moment now. I said, "Is that all you have to tell me? She's run off without waiting for word from me? And you're not allowed to tell me where she's gone so I can go and explain? Is that about the size of it?"

She said, "That seems to be her wish."

I doffed my hat again. "Thank you," I said. Then I turned and walked away.

I stayed in town that afternoon. Lew hung around me, not saying much, just kind of being there. We drunk considerable whiskey and then I got my horse and taken it for the ranch. I'd made sure to eat supper in town so I'd arrive too late for one of Buttercup's treats. That evening me and Dad and Ben and Norris sat in the office, us having a whiskey, Dad having one of his rare, watered-down versions, and, talking more to Dad than anyone else, I told what had happened about Nora. Dad didn't say much, just kind of nodded. But Ben said, "Serves her right. She don't know what she missed."

I turned a cold eye on him. I said, "Shut your mouth, Ben. You're my brother or else that remark would have gotten you something you didn't want."

Nobody else said anything. I didn't even have the heart to make any remarks to Norris. Hell, he'd never meant to cause what he had and maybe someday he'd learn what he could handle and what he couldn't. Until then I'd just have to put up with it.

Next morning I had breakfast and a whiskey and was idling around on the front porch when I saw Norris taking off in a buckboard. I figured he was heading for town to try and erase what mistakes his absence of the last ten days had caused. I wandered back into the office where Dad was sitting. I said, "Howard, did you have this much trouble with our mother?"

"Oh, yes, Justa," he said. "Oh, yes. The path to truth or to a true woman is never smooth. She led me a merry chase. But the one thing you can depend on, son, is that once you catch a good one she'll be worth the effort. I wouldn't give up just now if I was you."

I taken another drink of whiskey and said, "I don't see where I got much choice."

Then about noon a strange thing happened. This contractor I'd hired to build the house for me and Nora come knocking at the front door. I answered it because I wasn't in no rush to get in and eat Buttercup's lunch. But this man up and leveled his fist at me and shook it and said, mad as a wet setting hen, "I know I been behind on this house. But by Gawd, sir, you better not send another one of your brothers down to threaten me! We are near to being through, but I can guarantee you that there will be a charge for a man pointing a pistol between my eyes!"

I was that astonished I didn't know what to say. Finally I kind of fumbled out, "How them new, uh, workers I sent you panning out?"

"They are fine tile men!" he said. "But that in no way excuses your inexcusable behavior! I'm a reputable contractor and I will not be threatened by the likes of you range cowboys. I'll finish this job. Your furniture is on the way. But then, by Gawd, sir, you will answer to me!"

And with that he turned away and stalked off the porch. I watched him, wondering. Then I went into the dining room shaking my head. Ben and Dad were already at table. I said, "Ben, I wish you wouldn't go down there threatening that contractor. That house is no good to me without Nora. I don't reckon I care if they ever get it finished. You go ahead and figure out a way to send them peons back to Laredo. That was just a wild idea of mine. Didn't come to nothing."

Ben looked at me, chewing. He said, "I don't know what you're talking about."

I said, "That contractor that has been building Nora and my house just said my brother came up and stuck a pistol between his eyes this morning and told him he'd better get high-behind and get that house furnished and finished. Don't be doing that sort of thing, Ben. That ain't our style."

Ben looked over at Dad. Dad just raised his eyes. Ben said, shaking his head, "Wasn't me, Justa."

"Man said it was my brother."

"Wasn't me."

"Then who the hell could it have been? Hays wouldn't do something like that, would he?"

Ben shook his head. With his knife he indicated the glass in my hand and said, "Was I you I wouldn't be coming to no quick decisions. You been putting away enough of that pop-skull lately to handle an army. You night ought to wait a bit before you go to deciding things."

For the next couple of days I sort of hung around the house, mostly drinking whiskey. Nobody said much to me. Harley came in to report that they'd got the biggest part of the haying done and were keeping the cattle on fresh grass. He said we'd had some rain and that things had sweetened up considerable. I was glad to hear that, in a sort of hazy way.

Then on the morning of the third day Ben asked if I wouldn't care to go down and see my house. I told him I reckoned not, but he kept insisting so, about midmorning, we went strolling the half mile down to the place.

Well, it wasn't quite finished. They were still cleaning up the outside and laying down some carpets and what not, but the contractor was standing out front looking at his handiwork. He said, giving me a look, "Well, there it is. And you will be getting my bill. Pay up promptly or hear from my lawyers."

I watched him stalk away and then Ben said, "Why don't you go in and look around, Justa?"

I shook my head. It was what Nora had wanted. Now she wouldn't be there to enjoy it. I said, "Naw, I reckon not."

"Go. Just for a minute."

Well, I did. It was everything we'd planned, big and cool and spacious. The furniture was all in place. The workmen, who were still putting on some finishing touches, quickly got out of my way as I came in. I stood a moment in the big parlor and then I walked through the rest of the house. It was what Nora had wanted. Too bad she wouldn't have it. I turned out the front door. The contractor was waiting there for me. He said, "Well?"

I shrugged. I said, "You done your part. You'll get paid."

He was still livid. He said, "Then next time don't send your brother down to threaten me."

I pointed at Ben. "There he is. Ask him if I sent him down."

The contractor looked at Ben. He said, "That's not the one. The other was wearing a sack suit. He was bigger and slightly blond."

I turned and looked at Ben. "Norris?"

He nodded. "I told you to ease up on him."

Norris rode in that evening with Nora beside him in the buckboard. He just pulled up in front, tied off the horses and walked away. I went out to the steps of the porch. Nora came shyly to me. But the words she spoke weren't shy. She said, "Justa Williams, if you ever put me through that again I will kill you. I will marry you just so I can kill you."

I stood looking at her. "What made you change your mind?"

"Norris. He came and talked my mother into telling him where I was in Galveston. Then he came and told me all what had happened." For a second her face softened. Then she said, "But I could still claw your eyes out. Leaving me holding the bag like that." She looked around her, taking a long time to study the ranch. She said, "Maybe when I'm really and truly a part of all this I'll understand better."

I laughed softly. I said, "A man said that not too long ago in Laredo. After we both thought we weren't going to make it."

She finally reached up and kissed me. Then she grabbed me by the hand and, in a brisk fashion, said, "I want to go see my house."

I untied the reins to the buckboard horses, helped her aboard and then drove down to the house. No one else was there. It was just coming on dusk and it was quiet as it could be. As I'd done, she wandered from room to room. I waited on her in a big Spanish chair in front of the fireplace that needed winter and some wood. When she was through she came and knelt down beside me and took my hand in hers. She said, "Justa, I'm sorry. Norris has told me how I hurt you. I'll never do that again. I'll be your wife and not only will I never hurt you, I won't let anyone else hurt you. Do you forgive me?"

"Reckon I have to," I said. "You forgave me. After all the disappointments I gave you."

I heaved myself out of the chair. We walked to this big window that overlooked the back pasture. We didn't say anything for a moment and then Nora suddenly exclaimed, "Did I tell you? About our wedding?"

"No," I said. "Did we have one?"

"The one Norris has arranged."

I looked around at her. "What are you talking about?"

"Norris!" she said. She lifted her hands and her eyes, the movement of her hands making her breasts swell so that I wanted to rush back and try out that marriage bed in advance of its time. She said, "He spent all one day telegraphing from Galveston to our guests. They've all agreed to come back. And, Justa, guess what!" Her eyes were dancing like a schoolgirl's. "He's chartered a paddle-wheel steamer from Galveston day after tomorrow. We're to be married on board with all the wedding party. Then we honeymoon in New Orleans! Honey, I'm so thrilled!"

I said, dryly, "I bet." I turned away. I said, "You stay here and look at the house. I'll be back to fetch you in half an hour."

I found Norris in the barn. He was staring at a stack of newly gotten in hay. I walked up to where I was just behind him. I said, "Taken an interest in cattle ranching, have you, Norris?"

He didn't turn around. He said, "Not so you'd notice."

I said, "Where is this money coming from for this paddle-wheel steamer to New Orleans? And then the honeymoon? You figure out of family funds?"

He turned, stiffly, and then said, "I think you have forgotten that I have some money of my own. Just as you do, just as Ben does. The money that will be spent will be mine. Mine personally. Don't come to me with anymore of your bullying questions, Justa Williams."

I turned and started for the barn door. "Just so we had it straight. I meant it back there in Mexico when I told you you was going to pay for every cent this family business was out because of the way you fouled up that deal."

He said, coldly, "I understand that. And I appreciate your attendance to business. I even appreciate you getting me out of jail. I might not have been able to do it on my own."

"Fine," I said. "Thanks for getting the house ready. And . . . well, thanks for Nora."

I was about to step out the barn door when he called to me. "Justa?"

I turned. "What?"

"Can I come to the wedding?"

I regarded him for a moment. Then I scratched my left ear. Finally I said, "Yeah, I guess so. And if you don't fuck up between now and then you can be my best man."

What the hell, he was my brother.